THE REAL DEVIL

JOURNAL ONE

STACIE SANTORO

EDITING—Ashley Williams at AW Editing

PROOFREADING—Janice Owen; Erica Russikoff at Erica Edits

COVER DESIGN—T.E. Black Designs; www.teblackdesigns.com

COVER PHOTO—Depositphotos; www.depositphotos.com

INTERIOR FORMATTING—T.E. Black Designs; www.teblackdesigns.com

And from a song, she was born. . .

PROLOGUE

Let me introduce myself.

Lucifer . . .

is my baby brother . . .

I'M PRETTY SURE EVERYONE IN the known universe, for pretty much all of time, knows Lucifer—Beast, Satan, Wicked One, Beelzebub, Prince of Darkness. That last one seems to be a favorite. He's always been a prince of one thing or another or the harbinger of doom and debauchery and all the fun things. But no matter how many ages have come and gone, one name has always stuck: the Devil.

People consider him to be the ruler of a fictional place called Hell. The invisible bad man who will come and snatch your soul if you don't behave. The hypothetical measuring stick against which all immoral deeds are measured.

Fictional.

Invisible.

Hypothetical.

The people who believe those three adjectives apply to him are so, so wrong.

Annoying, manipulative, vain, and *war-provoking* would be better.

And for those who don't believe he exists at all? Well, they are wrong too.

He is very real.

Whatever side of those feelings you may have for him—love or hate or somewhere in-between—the one thing everyone gets right is that he isn't "good." He's too lazy to put any real effort into being bad, so at least that's something. I think. I mean . . . the last time I saw him put any real effort into anything was when he opened the P.O. Box for his fan club.

He has. A fucking. Fan club. He gets at least four marriage proposals a day, and I can't even talk about the invitations to club meetings, dinners, and parties he gets. Naked pictures? Bleh. Wishlists? Those are actually kind of funny to read, but it's as if he's Santa for the twisted people of the world.

I get it. It feeds his ego and encourages him to be the devil he is famous for being.

He loves the attention, which is annoying, but he's still my brother.

So, being the sister of the biggest, baddest evil known to man, as well as a true asshole and brat? Well, that shit is exhausting, especially since I am the boss, the CEO of the place everyone calls Hell.

I'm the most powerful one.

I'm the one who keeps the balance on Hell's behalf with all the supernatural and divine powers that be.

I'm the one who cleans up my brother's messes—and he makes a shit-ton of messes, most of which he's blissfully unaware of—before they have a chance to upset the balance we really, really need to keep.

What balance, you ask? Basically, it's the push and pull of influence on humans between Heaven and Hell and its outcome on Earth.

Say there was a war or an unexplained peace agreement, a rash of mass killings or a sharp drop in murders. Those types of things would call attention, and a council of the powers would meet and figure out whose head was going to roll.

Luckily, little bits of tinkering with the humans are pretty much always overlooked. Lucifer is constantly walking a very fine line between being entertained and throwing the balance into the red when using his powerful influence on humans.

Basically, he's disaster without purpose. Personal enjoyment without worrying about consequences.

Like the time he used his influence to inspire that song by The Rolling Stones. Yup. That was Lucifer and his fucking vanity. He was so smug about it, too, because he made it read like his resume and almost ousted our whole operation to the topside. He had no idea that I spent a year—a whole freaking year—topside after the council meeting about that song. Hundreds of angels were dispatched to Earth because of the sharp rise in devil supporters. The council agreed to let them stay to counter with their own creative measure. I just kept thinking, *good luck competing with The Rolling Stones.*

Bright side? His nonsense over an immeasurable amount of time has made it so I can tolerate a surprising amount of bull-shit. It also had me on meds for a short time and painting by numbers as part of my therapy, but that's beside the point.

Even though there is so much I am willing to tolerate, I'm not infallible. There are things that piss me off and send me over the edge and into an irrational meltdown. One of those things is definitely imbalance.

Ha! Look at that—something that the council and I agree on.

Who would have thought it?

I know, I know, you are probably thinking that I'm about to go on this long rant about some epically stupid thing Lucifer did to toss the balance out of whack, right? Nope.

The prize for this goes to Mother. Fucking. Nature.

Yeah, you heard me. Little Miss Rainbows and Sunshine.

I thought my brother was difficult, but shit, this woman is nuts—like a roller coaster ride with twists and turns you didn't see advertised in the brochure. An amusement park that promises no clowns walking around because said clowns are just hanging out in the bathrooms, waiting to stab you as you walk through the door. Or like a day that starts out sunny and ends with the Ferris wheel you're on coming loose and rolling into the ocean.

And that hasn't always been the case with her. She and I had made nice once, and I even went out of my way to be . . . wait for it . . . compassionate to her. Then she went and popped a fuse after fucking my brother, and it all went to shit.

And by "it all went to shit," what I mean is that it has reduced me—a powerful, magical, elusive, brilliant creature—to being forced to write a document to help shed all the piss and vinegar I have in my veins from dealing with an immature, irrational, crazy, supernatural bitch.

I don't think it will help, though. I used to love to write, especially poetry. The freedom of expression, the satisfaction. That was another time and in another life. Past tense. Now I strategize and fight. Long ago I put down the pen and picked up the whip. Until now. In my desperation to release the tension of this situation, I find myself taking pen to paper. Go figure. My best friend, Delayna, says it can be "therapeutic" and "calming." Maybe she has a point. Witches tend to be smart when they're not being smart-asses.

Today is the first day of a new year, after all. Might as well try.

But I digress. Yes, my brother is an idiot, but I love him. Yes, Mother Nature is batshit crazy. So, naturally, I had to clean up their mess. Don't think it makes me a good guy. I'm warning you ahead of time, you shouldn't like me because it doesn't matter what my brother does, I will protect him with everything I have. I will continue to keep the balance so that those think-they-are-better-than-everyone supers and those uppity angels stay off my case. Angels are so annoying.

Wait . . . I am an angel. Was. Am. I don't even know anymore.

I will never have the life I used to. That hit me like a machine gun loaded with bricks instead of bullets, coming at me just as fast.

The only thing I know for certain that I am, is a protector.

My name is Vahla.

I'm not the queen of the damned. I'm way more powerful than that badass bitch, who's actually a vice general in Hell. And she serves me, like all of them do.

I'm the queen. The CEO of Hell. The real devil.

And with that comes responsibility.

If I can't take care of issues quickly and quietly, Hell will pay. That means I will pay, because if the angels or supers come for my brother? They will have to go through me first.

Plus, there's the additional stress of my brother ever making his way back into Heaven to fulfill his promise of killing the angels who remained and take control. Those who wouldn't fight with them. Those who simply didn't agree. I swore I would never allow that to happen. A little tidbit my brother is unaware of.

So many whose paths I've crossed or have gotten to know over all this time have told me to let my brother suffer his own consequences from his actions. But I can't. Not yet, anyway. Because his fall was mine, too.

This is the story of my fight with Mother Nature.

This journal is my art of war.

That sounds pretty badass, right? Because it's more like a chronicle of playing a game of Chutes and Ladders. Each time I thought I was up, someone came along and knocked my ass back down, which made me want to set the board on fire. So, yeah, it was a fight. But it ended up being so much more than just that . . .

CHAPTER ONE

Lucifer had been going topside way more frequently than he ever had since we landed in Hell a very long time ago. I could spy or send out my most stealthy guards. I could have asked my witch friend for a spell to cast on a beautiful woman, or three, so they followed him. They could seduce the information out of him.

A shiver of disgust rolled through me. The last time I'd tried that spell, it backfired, and Lucifer ended up throwing a damn orgy in the living room.

I walked in.

Almost went blind.

It was fucking horrid.

At least with Luce topside, he was out of my way, which was always a good thing. No random mass-killings or disasters whacking me in the face. But he was distracted. He wasn't as regimented with the viles as he should be, and that was his job. Everyone who landed down here was a vile of one rank or another. When a person died and ended up in Hell, we absorbed their energy and they became a vile. When Lucifer slacked off, those viles slacked off. When they slacked off, my inventory got depleted. When my inventory depleted, I lost money.

Being broke wasn't something I was interested in trying out.

It was going to be a problem.

Instead of doing his job, Luce was gone at all hours and then came home, drained energy from a vile, and passed out. Each time I tried to talk to him, he answered in a groan. When I followed him to his home, he would walk in and shut the door in my face.

Not okay. So, I waited for him to return again and stuck my booted foot in the door before it slammed closed.

He didn't even notice.

"Luce? I know you must be exhausted from all the work you didn't do today, but we need to talk. Those assholes get restless and have no ability to train, or think, on their own. You need to get back on task."

"Mm-hmm."

"Get your fucking face out of the pillow and answer me."

He turned and smiled. *Smiled.*

"I swear you are going to make me get the whip out." It was the one item I knew caused him pain, and it was almost always my last resort.

"C'mon, V. It's all good," he slurred.

I slowly moved forward and sat on the edge of his bed. "I don't know that, Luce. You're never quiet. Tell me what happened."

"Fuck, it was amazing."

Oh no. He better not have massacred a town. I will fucking whip him so hard he won't be able to sit for a century.

"Did you . . ." My teeth clenched and my blood pressure rose so fast my ears started to ring.

"No. I didn't cause any damage this time."

"Go on."

He lifted his head from the pillow. "Ugh, fine. There was a huge storm, and I was chasing it. I couldn't find the source. I'm fucking Lucifer, and I couldn't find it."

Vanity. It was gonna kill me. Well, kill him.

"And?"

"And I wanted to know where it came from. It was fucking epic."

"Why do you give a shit about a storm?"

"Because I sat in the middle of the desert during the most powerful storm I've ever felt. Ever, V. And we've been here for a long-ass time. Wind, hail, sand as sharp as knives and faster than bullets. Lightning and fire." His eyes glazed over again. "So many elements. Just so many."

"And that's why you can't work? Because you decided to chase storms?" Was he a five-year-old who just saw his first storm?

Apparently, that was the wrong question to ask because he lowered his head and grumbled.

"Let me sleep, V. I will get back to work if you leave me alone." The bed bounced as he turned over, and I imagined using one of the springs in the mattress to stab him.

A second later, the little shit started snoring. I was tired of prying information from him, and my growing impatience with him would only cause us to fight. So, I left him to dream about sand in his eyes and ears (and asshole for all I cared). Some of us still had work to do. Because, believe it or not? I wasn't a thief. I earned my shit.

HE DID EVENTUALLY GET BACK TO WORK. A LITTLE BIT. LA-DEE-da. It was absolutely not enough effort worthy of any praise. I was actually tempted to push him out of the way and do it myself, but that would teach him nothing good.

But if he didn't get it together, the influx of viles that just dropped on us would go to waste. I frowned, counting as twelve more dropped over to our left.

"Hey, Luce. Is there a war I'm not aware of?"

"Nope. Not that I know of anyway. Why?"

I glanced around as if it should be obvious, but he just stood there and waited for me to answer.

"We just had seventy or so drops in the last twenty minutes. That doesn't seem strange to you?" Our normal was between twenty and thirty a *day*.

When he shrugged, I almost punched him. "How about fun gang turf wars? Maybe some hostile takeover in a third-world county?"

"If you're worried about it, go check the news."

I scowled at him as he walked away. I didn't need the news. Why would I when I could more or less predict global events using the magnificent algorithm I'd built during my second time through MIT? I tweaked it every now and then, but human nature was predictable. Politics, however, always kept it interesting.

But something was off. I could feel it in my bones. It was a pulse that I could feel but not shake or stretch out.

My brother told me I was too sensitive, too caught up in my work. That I needed to relax. My getting a massage or taking in a movie wasn't changing my uncanny ability to know when something was wrong.

Unfortunately, I didn't have the superpower to know *exactly* what was wrong. I always had to figure it out. Waiting for the boom always sucked.

Boom.

I woke up the next day and found out we had missed a huge emerald delivery scheduled for one of our topside buyers. That information was followed almost immediately by a text from my assistant, Abhitha, reminding me of a meeting I had in New York that very afternoon. I tossed my phone onto my desk, only to have it beep more. The new text was Abhitha again. She wanted to know when she should expect the delivery.

Three days ago, that was when.

Livid was a gross understatement of my emotional state.

"LUCIFER!" I yelled, slamming my office door open as I stormed toward the front door. He didn't respond, so I fired off a storm of texts, all of which went unread. My calls (all fourteen of them) went to voicemail. Why have a fucking phone at all? I should cancel it on him.

Fuck this.

I went to the lower level, which was where the head viles were. My heels clicked against the metal planks as I stomped down the spiral staircase.

The lower level always felt humid. My skin immediately became coated with a sheen of sweat, and that resulted in my clothes clinging to my skin. My feet always swelled a bit from the heat and it made my shoes or boots snug. I was used to it, but I was still always aware of the changes.

Digging into the mountainsides released pockets of air that mixed with the oppressive heat and made it muggy. Since this mountain was the only place in existence that produced painite, the rarest gem known to those above on Earth, I dealt with the heat. The last stone we found and sold went for three hundred thousand a carat on the black market.

Human nature and their priorities fascinated me.

Anywho, I was unhappy to be wearing boots with stiletto heels because this level got tricky. Stilettos sucked in this region. The floor to this particular mountainside was so much less porous than the others. It was sleek and shiny but incredibly unforgiving to walk on. I tended to slide on it instead of walk. About halfway in, I saw the viles sitting with their backs against the walls. I was hoping it was my imagination, but as soon as they saw me, they all moved. So, I was not imagining them sitting when they should have been working. At least they all remembered to bow their heads.

Bowing or kneeling to me was innate with them once I'd absorbed their energy. I was grateful because it was one less thing they had to be taught. Just like humans, some learned better, listened better, and behaved better than others.

"Where the fuck is my brother?" They just looked at each other, moving their heads around and looking like gross, greasy bobble heads.

Oh, hell no.

I unfurled my whip with dramatic flair, causing a thunderous crack to the ground below. "I will not ask again!"

"We haven't seen him for two days," one offered. He must have been down here a while, since he had no hair left on his body. A natural evolution for all of them over time.

I'm going to kill my brother.

I stood straighter and eyed them with a look that could have killed them had it been what I really wanted to do. But I decided not to turn that eye-mode on . . . yet. They all knew I could do it, and by not doing it, it allowed them to believe I was showing them a modicum of kindness they didn't deserve. Really, I just didn't give enough of a shit to bother.

I wasn't going to let my brother's shitty work ethic make me react like a madwoman. I needed workers, not invalids, and that was what I would end up with if I smoked all these idiots.

"I didn't ask when the last time you saw him was. I asked where he was."

When none of them offered up an answer, I pointed at the one the others kept glancing at. "You. Get up here."

He looked up quickly, confirming he knew I was speaking to him before bowing again and shuffling forward. He knew better than to stare at any part of my body for too long, touch me, or even take a deep breath near me. I was curvy and embraced the attention for it most of the time. But not here. The last one who had the balls to touch me was beaten immediately and then sentenced to fifty-seven years of being castrated daily. I had a lot of fun with that one. Because, he *had* balls. It was a lesson they all took note of. Free will was a thing we were all blessed and cursed with, whether we were human, angel, or super.

"Where is my brother?"

"My Queen, all I know is that he went topside and hasn't returned."

"How do you know this?"

"I know because he . . . he asked me to keep everyone else in line while he was away."

He shook as I strolled a slow circle around him, letting my whip drag on the ground behind me. The power from my hand determined the type of drag, and in that moment, I had a line of fire following me. "You did a shit job of that." I grabbed the clipboard hanging on the wall as I passed it. "You've done none of the work listed here. None. How do you think Lucifer will react when he sees you've failed him?"

He lowered himself fully to the ground with outstretched arms and palms flat, causing already protruding bones to be more pronounced. "Forgive me, my Queen."

I came to a stop in front of him and pressed the heel of my stiletto into his hand until it went through him and clicked against the ice-smooth stone. His cry of pain should have pleased me. As I ground down harder, I eyed the other viles in the group. They automatically lowered themselves to the ground and bowed their heads.

"I'll be going topside. Pull yourselves together and complete the tasks you were given. I want that order of emeralds completed before I get back."

"Yes, my Queen." Echoed in unison off the walls.

I was so mad I could barely see straight. I needed to exit before I exploded again on one or more of them. I had to remember that the viles were my workers. If too many were hurt or killed, production would slow and profits would suffer. That would not only downright piss me off but also it would make me a damn hypocrite. I'd spent countless hours trying to stop Lucifer from his senseless displays of cruelty and violence that there was no way I would turn around and be like him. It was a difficult task but not impossible.

They all got up, scattered like cockroaches when the lights turned on and got back to work—the males in their linen shorts and the women in their linen dresses. No way I was letting them walk around uncovered. Looking at viles' junk for eternity? No thank you.

I carefully wrapped my whip back around my wrist. I chose to have it lay on my skin as a bracelet this time. Other times it sank into my skin like a beautifully etched tattoo. Then I walked out of the mine.

I headed back to my quarters, washed my hands four times, and changed into my tight black dress. I had to take a few moments to compose myself before I set out for my office in New York City, located in my absolute favorite building, the Scarlet.

I really didn't have the energy to chase after my brother and deal with this meeting with Gabe, but I didn't think I was given a choice on the latter. I was told to show up and that it was about Lucifer. Nothing else.

Maybe I could postpone it. All I would need would be two . . . maybe three hundred more years?

It was stressing me out, hard.

So, I methodically cleaned my whip in strokes of four per

section. Four wipes of each of my heels. I sat on my floor with crossed legs and took some deep breaths that did nothing but make me lightheaded.

Then I ate a full sleeve of Double Stuf Oreos.

When I was satisfied, or really just in cream-filled cookie bliss, I went to the teleport opening and closed my eyes.

"Here we go."

CHAPTER TWO

I STARTED MY REAL-ESTATE VENTURES by purchasing a brownstone in Brooklyn, a city that had a unique force that pulled me in with such an undeniable embrace of energy. The first time I set foot there, my body had hummed and vibrated. My eyes had a sharper focus. Colors were more vivid, and in some instances, I was able to see clear through things. Not people but through cars, buses, or trains to the people inside. It turned out that the force pulling me there was really an accumulation of crystals and magical substances in the land itself.

Current research didn't know even half of the elements that lay below the city's infrastructure, but they swirled and flowed in constant currents. There weren't only solid forms, either. Liquids and gases ebbed and flowed and filled the pockets tucked away in the soil. Like the Aurora Borealis on steroids. It was utter, fantastical harmony.

I wasn't the only one to feel the pull, either. The draw to continuously return there affected most beings that could be classified as paranormal, which worked out in my favor as well.

I had made friends there. Cool, loyal, fun friends. Like the sister ghosts who I met with at least once a year to go ice skating with in Central Park. Their joy for the sport is seriously contagious.

Other paras and I would roam around and loiter in hotels. Little pranks were as far as we would go, like knocking on doors or writing on steamy mirrors. We weren't into the killing or sick shit that pissed or downright evil paras focused on, but they never bothered me or mine. Evil and smart, they would have made decent viles.

The Scarlet was a beautiful, eighty-four-floor skyscraper with the sharpest tip for a roof known to humanity. She was made entirely of muted, mirrored glass and steel. Each corner and seam was outlined in crimson with onyx borders. I rented out some of the floors to keep up appearances. The rest were mine.

Floor eighty-three was where the sex and playing take place, which was a strategic choice on my part. I knew my guests smelled the sex on their way up to the top floor for the council meetings with the supers, even if they pretended they couldn't. Some of them were such prudes they could barely stomach the thought of what went on there, and others were closet sexual deviants who always looked a bit fervent when they showed up to talk shop. I loved making them all squirm.

The very top floor was for business only. That was where I held the council meetings when it was my turn to host. Angels, witches, warlocks, Merz (mermaids), Father Time, Father Winter (different role from Mother Nature's), Mother Nature, vampires, fae, werewolves, and a few other types of beasties made up the band. Grim was a fave of mine. He was all quiet and cloaked. When he got bored and nodded off he would snore like a damn chainsaw. I recorded it once, and he threatened to reap my soul if I didn't delete it. I posted it online and laughed when he realized I didn't have a soul he could take. Idiot. But there was that one time he was eerily quiet and looking around for something. Or someone. I figured it was work related, but as he left he paused at Abhitha's office door. I'd meant to ask about it, but I had a crazy brother who needed tending to.

Only one guest would be at this meeting.

My intercom came on and Abhitha's sweet voice came through. "Vahla?"

She'd been with me for a very long time and I considered her one of my best friends and confidants. A beautiful woman in her own right with incredible intelligence and a sharp tongue. I admired her fierceness and ability to keep our businesses so organized. And she was funny. Especially when she drank tequila.

I shocked her a very long time ago with a piece of my power, and she became eternal. She's been by my side ever since. Her importance to me has grown with time, and I would protect her with an unmatched ferocity if anyone ever tried to harm her.

"Yes, Abhitha."

"Your appointment is here, my Queen."

I had to smile. Today, she would call me the normal title of queen, tomorrow she would call me president or the quarter-back or the closer or the ringmaster. And those were only some of the English titles she used. She made a veritable game out of finding different titles in as many different languages as she could. She, like me, enjoyed college as frequently as possible. And when not in college, the Rosetta Stone was her go-to so she could continue her love of learning each language.

"Send him in," I responded as I straightened my spine.

I grabbed my fourth pen and began to write nonsense on the pad in front of me. My palms had started to sweat, and I wanted to smooth my hair and make sure I didn't have lipstick on my teeth. It was ridiculous to have such nerves taking over. Not like I didn't know the man who was coming.

I knew when he came in the door. I knew when he walked to my desk. I knew that he was staring at me. Knew those footsteps. Definitely knew that smell.

I put my pen down with a steadier hand than I'd picked it up with and looked up. "Hello, Gabriel."

He smiled big and nodded. It was a bright, perfect smile. So distracting and perfect that I had to shake myself from the permanent stare I could have stayed locked in. I mentally slapped myself and stood to shake his hand. "Vahla. Thank you for seeing me on such short notice. I wasn't sure you would. I haven't seen you in a—"

"Yes, well, you made it seem as if it were incredibly important. Critical even, when you spoke with my assistant." The last time he saw me was a nightmare I always hoped I'd forget. No such luck.

I pulled my hand away and took my seat. I didn't want to like the way his hand felt, the rough yet smooth skin that rubbed my palm. The zing from the connection. The sonic boom that launched within my chest. I worked hard to shut that shit off over the years. Worked hard to forget his touch. Took as many men as I could to chase the feeling of this man away, and then took more until I didn't feel the urge to vomit every time skin other than his touched me. All that effort was for nothing because one little handshake and *BAM*. It was like being back to square one. And that pissed me right the fuck off.

I cleared my throat and glanced at him, making sure my words were precise and very business. "Please sit and tell me what's prompted this urgent visit." I nodded to the chair for him to sit, and he took it as he sent me a smirk. It was so hard not to roll my eyes.

Then I tried not to look too closely at him and failed miserably. He really was unnaturally and ridiculously gorgeous with his black, wavy hair that had the shine of the divine. The perfect smattering across his forehead, the wisps that I imagined tickled the tops of his ears. The bits of longer locks in the back that rubbed against the collar of his shirt.

Fuckity fuck!

His eyes were large and an incredibly light shade of blue. It was like trying not to look at an accident as you passed it. Impossible. He wasn't even partially naked, and yet, he still managed to command every single iota of my focus.

My eyes were whores.

"Thank you," he said as he unbuttoned his suit jacket, and when it fell open, my mouth almost did too. The way his shirt clung to the hard planes of his torso was absurd. Just enough buttons at the top of his shirt were undone so I could see the tanned color of his skin and the veins that ran through his neck. "There's been a tremendous amount of activity and it hasn't been prompted through my . . . organization. I was hoping you could help me out." He got right to it. Unfortunately, my mind was stuck somewhere else, so it was all babble to my ears.

How the hell does a shirt mold to someone like that?

"Help you with what?" Shit, I missed some important tidbits while I was ogling him, so I'd have to play it off like I heard it all.

"With finding out why this is happening."

I rolled back from my desk and crossed my legs, which hiked my dress up a few inches on my thighs. I wondered if he would look at me with the same lack of eye control as I did with him.

His eyes shot to my legs and followed the curve of my thigh, which only urged me to move just a little more to see if he would continue to stare. He did, and I smiled inside to see that look of interest and desire. I shouldn't want it, but I did. Temptation was fickle, but it was also a given for all of us. It was proving our character and wanting forgiveness from the thought or act of temptation that separated us. Gabe was pure, no doubt. But he still knew temptation. He couldn't truly be good without it.

He smiled that smile, knowing full well what I was doing. Didn't stop him from looking, and that caused a familiar thrill to run through me. An ache. The itch I needed to scratch.

"You'll need to be more specific, Gabe. I'm running a business, not paying attention to the same mundane things you do. I have jewels to deliver and bridges to fix. And my stocks aren't going to manage themselves." Snark was always good when I dealt with him. Otherwise, too much of our past clouded my judgment, and that empty feeling could make me . . . impulsive.

"If you consider mundane to be a tremendous amount of deaths due to unprecedented natural disasters and strong weather patterns, then mundane it is." He leaned forward and rested his forearms on his legs. "You mean to tell me a business-woman such as yourself hasn't noticed a thing?"

Yeah, I noticed I needed to put a bag over that stupid, gorgeous face of yours.

I brought my chair closer and mirrored his posture as I leaned across my desk, loving the feel of the marble surface under my palms. I hadn't realized how heated my body had gotten until I felt the coolness under me. "Of course, I've noticed."

"So, you did notice but didn't think to look into it?" he asked as he picked a nonexistent piece of lint off his pristine suit. That blasé move got right under my skin. So did the bulge of muscle through his coat as he moved his arm.

"Don't be a prick. You know how fickle the world can be. Plus, I don't control the weather. That should be obvious to a man as smart as you. Why are you here when you should be darkening Mother Nature's doorstep?"

He took a deep breath. "I've heard something that I'd rather not share with others in a group setting. Yet."

I raised an eyebrow. "Yet? Say what you need to say. Don't give me any cryptic shit."

"Fine. Essalene has been spotted with Lucifer. More than once."

"So?" I asked, wondering why he would care that my brother was hanging out with Mother Nature. "Who cares if they hang out?"

Is he jealous?

That may have pissed me off. Essalene was stunning with her flowing clothes and beautiful, long, strawberry-blonde hair and golden eyes. Who the fuck had golden eyes? And fair skin. Such glowing, fair skin. *Bitch.* Yup, I was pissed.

I couldn't stop myself. "Are you jealous, Gabe?"

"Come on, Vahla. You know better than to ask me that."

"No, actually, I don't."

"She isn't my type."

Did he just smirk at me?

"Oh, you have a type? Do tell."

"Yes, V, I do." It always kept me off balance when he stared at me like he was doing right then. Like he had when I was still in Heaven with him and at each encounter since.

I wanted to believe that I was the only one to ever see that expression on him, but I wasn't naïve. Too much time had passed for that to be reasonable. But I still wanted to know if he'd fucked anyone else. Specifically, who they were so I could find out where they lived and see them. See what tempts a man like him. And that thought sure as shit pissed me off.

"Is that so?"

"It is. Unfortunately, my type is hard to find."

"Oh, okay. There are billions to choose from. Humans, supers, angels. Take your pick."

"My pick is sitting right in front of me."

My entire body lit up at his words. "That ship has sailed." I snorted. No sooner had the words left my lips, than the mark behind my ear heated, forcing me to rub it. Then the bastard smiled.

"Keep telling yourself that, Vahla."

Since I left Heaven, we'd kept just enough distance between us that the mark wasn't a problem, but when we were this close? It was impossible to ignore, and we almost always snapped. That snap brought me the closest I had ever been to leaving Hell. It wasn't just sex with him, and I knew it. It may have been incredible, mind-blowing, bone-melting, screaming, clawing, biting sex that left me borderline dead, but it wasn't just sex. And quite frankly, it scared the shit out of me and made me want to run far, far away.

Running from Gabe usually meant me going on a sex spree to try to forget him all over again. I never said I had the best coping mechanisms, even with some counseling intervention. And when I thought maybe his coping skills were the same as mine? Well, let's just say I went from one unhealthy choice to the next.

"Whatever, Gabe."

He laughed. "When there's nothing else for you to say but 'whatever,' I know I won."

"Dick." The old, sweet me would never have called him that, much less said a word so vulgar. Cursing, drinking, sex, and occasional violence had become the awesome-cocktail that made me who I was.

Then he went and laughed again. Not a laugh of dismissal or revulsion, just genuine laughter from the jab at him. It quieted the thoughts rattling through my brain because I could only focus on him. His bright smile and his strong shoulders quaking from laughing. Those eyes of his never looking away from me. My lips rose to smile back at him and a contentment settled over me. Sometimes, I really missed him. Gabe reminded me of when I didn't feel so damn soulless. I wasn't sure if I liked remembering, it made what should be my heart, hurt. "Specifics, Gabe. I need more specifics before we pass blame to my brother."

"Grab your pen and listen carefully." Gabe knew I was a note taker proud to be called a nerd whenever it was said, and always ready with pen and paper so I didn't forget anything. For the next hour, I sat, listened, and wrote while Gabe explained what he knew about this current situation.

"It isn't as if she doesn't know where the rain belongs. She has it raining in the desert more than it has in, well, ever," he said. I kept making my notes.

"Then there are the crops that have caught fire somehow and wind that makes sure they are decimated within seconds. I mean . . . I get that she knows her job better than anyone else, but come on. She's also decimating food supplies almost world-wide. She should know better."

"What else?" I asked.

"Well, the biggest concern is the deaths. There are just so many. Too many, even for her. It's like she doesn't care that she's burning down schools and shopping malls. Two weeks ago, she caused an earthquake in South America that destroyed an entire village. Every single person living there died."

I let a few minutes of silence pass between us as I tapped my pen on the desk.

"Emotions," I said as I finally silenced the *tap*, *tap*, *tap*.

"What?" Gabe asked, looking confused.

Stop scrunching your nose and looking so fucking cute.

"You said she was spotted with Lucifer. You said that hurricanes have been spread worldwide. I'm telling you that those are the effects of her heightened emotions."

"You cannot be serious."

"What? You can't tell me you have forgotten the seventeen-eighties. When she lost the baby? The only child she ever carried? She was so upset that she caused an earthquake that killed *millions* of people, not just a tiny village. Then the volcanic eruptions a few years later?" He shook his head. "Holy shit, Gabe! Her marriage to Aldorex was falling apart. You know

Aldorex. Father Time? Every time those two fought, she lashed out and a damn volcano would erupt. It killed thousands of people and caused a famine that ravaged the area for years afterward. You cannot possibly be so smart and so freaking dumb at the same time."

"I do remember." His words were somber. "We met about the earthquake, but I don't remember a meeting about the volcanic distress."

"You wouldn't. I went and met with her alone because the last thing that woman needed was a man telling her to calm down. She was screwing up my bottom line, and I was over it."

That focused stare narrowed on me. His light blue eyes so intense that I wished I could look into them every day. Cruelly beautiful as they tormented me.

"What?" I snapped.

"You mean to tell me you went to her, without consulting the rest of us, and you did it because she was messing up your inventory? Really? There was no other reason?"

"Stop trying to make me the good guy. She still got her famine, so it isn't as if I bargained with her to reverse it or miraculously save the land." His pushing me was making me uncomfortable.

"You couldn't have made that happen even if you wanted to."

I stood, my heart rate spiking at his dismissal of my power. "Don't tell me what you think I can and can't do. I'll surprise you every time."

He rose quickly from his chair. "Surprise me? No." He shook his head and pointed at me. "You'd surprise yourself. Think what you want, but you stopped it from being worse. You aren't Lucifer."

"Fuck you for comparing me to him. I am worse than he could even contemplate being." I hissed. I *was* worse than him. That famine caused desperation, and that desperation caused people to do bad things. And guess where those bad deeds landed them? With me. Working my mines and adding to my energy reserves. Maybe I could have ended it. But the divines could have, too. I just saw an opportunity and I took it. There was nothing ambivalent about it.

I threw up once I learned of the death toll, but I wasn't telling him that.

He laughed again and did that head shake thing, making his muscles shift and ripple. "Whatever, Vahla."

I forced myself to look away from him. He always made me way too unbalanced for my liking. I cleared my throat. "Back to the emotions."

"Yes, ma'am. Let's get back to them," he said with a wink.

He certainly was tempting when he teased.

Annoying prick . . .

We both settled back into our seats. "You've told me how far back you first spotted Luce with her, but according to when the events started, I'm going to say that you're short a few months," I began. "I'm also going to throw it out there that they probably aren't fighting."

"Agreed." For fuck's sake. He needed to put that freaking smirk away. "How few is a few?"

I grabbed my fourth pen, tapping it on the desk as I thought. "It was probably right around the spring equinox? Luce went up to clear his head about something. When he returned, he was different. I questioned him until he gave in and he told me about this 'epic' storm he was engulfed in when he went into the desert. After that, he started going topside more to search for another storm and see if he could find out what created it."

"Did he tell you anything else?"

"Yeah, during our mani-pedis he totally opened up. No, dumbass." I dramatically rolled my eyes. "I've been cleaning up his shit for"—I glanced at my diamond and platinum wristwatch for a few beats—"oh, thousands of years. I know what distracts him. I can sniff out the kind of trouble he's in a mile away. It's pathetically predictable, actually. It's always women or mayhem."

"How did he not know it was her, though? Hadn't they ever met before?"

"Who says he didn't know? Though, I'll admit that it's unlikely that they had met before since I kept him from going to all the council meetings because . . . well, he hates all the angels. He just worries about himself, you know? And she was married for a long time . . ."

"That makes sense." I didn't miss his slight flinch when I said married. "Have you known the whole time?"

"No, but I had my suspicions about the storms. He would come home, sleep it off, and go back. I was glad to have him out of my way for a while, but then the viles started slacking off and screwing up my inventory, so I was pissed. We were fighting every time we saw each other, and he wasn't listening, so I deviated from my original plan not to have him followed. Instead of using other women, I went myself to find out what was more important than his job."

"Because you can't stand disorder."

"Right you are, winged boy."

"Ha! Look at you being funny and using my childhood nickname," he said as he shot me his pearly whites.

"Don't expect that for at least another century." I smiled back.

It was such a sweet sound to hear us both laughing together. It had been years since I called him that. Closeness made me weak back then, and no one had ever been closer to me than this beautiful angel in front of me. The day I left Heaven was one of the saddest and most desperate I had ever seen him, second only to the time he'd shown up at the end of a council meeting that had just ended with Silas beating the shit out of me. To this day, he still didn't know it was Silas who had done it, and if I had my way, he would never know. The last thing I needed to do was stir up trouble between the angels.

"What are you thinking, Vahla?"

"Nothing." *Shit.* "Where was I? I went topside to check out what the deal was. I walked in on them."

"Kissing?"

"Yes."

"Touching her?" His husky voice pushed out the question.

I swallowed hard. "Yes." I cleared my throat. "Let's just say I walked in on the finale."

"You know we can't let this continue, right?"

Damn it.

"Yes, I know. Just do me a favor and let me deal with it. This is *my* brother. He is under *my* charge. I don't need you swooping in and trying to save the day. He hates you, in case you've forgotten."

His fists tightened at my response. "I know he hates me. He never let me—"

Nope. Not going there.

"How did you even find out about this? Did you see any of the storms?"

"No, Michael stopped me one day and asked if I knew anything about it. I asked him if he wanted me to check it out and he said no, that Silas had already been sent."

A cold chill ran down my spine at that name. "Silas?"

"Yeah."

"Shit!"

"I won't allow anything to happen until I know what's going on."

"How the hell do you plan to stop him? Damn it, Gabriel!"

Silas—Michael's brother, a powerful angel in his own right, and Gabe's best friend—wasn't as pure as he led everyone to believe he was. He also hated Lucifer and me because he blamed us for what happened to his sister Ziza.

"But why come to me about my brother?"

"Because once Silas returned, he told Michael that as he was doing some recon, your brother came across his radar."

"And? That's all he said about Luce?" I found it hard to believe he didn't go after my brother right then and there.

"I wondered why there wasn't more to tell. I was surprised he didn't confront him. My best guess would be that Luce went back to Hell before Silas could get to him."

"But wouldn't Silas just follow him?"

"He can't." His answer was clipped, which had my head tilting just a bit as I considered why.

"How do you know that?"

The warmth behind my ear flared again as those blue eyes gazed with an unrelenting focus on me. His voice lowered. "I know that because I have tried to get to you. Anytime you ran from me, I've tried to run to you, and each time, I've been denied access to the Hell realm."

"Gabriel—"

He shook himself away from wherever his thoughts had taken him. "Anyway, I wanted to come to you because I knew how concerned you would be. I wanted to give you the chance to step in before Michael did. If anything ever happened to you —" The desperation in his voice was clear.

"Why him, Gabriel? Why not just go after her? Threaten her? It's her weather. Her disasters."

He pulled at his suit jacket and put his hands in his pockets. "Essalene will always be given more leniency because of the specificity of her job. Your brother is considered expendable because there is someone else who is capable of doing what he does."

He was talking about me. I was that someone.

"Fuck."

"Exactly. I bought you a month by coming to Earth to deal with this."

My body shook. He used "that" tone. The one that told me I better figure this mess out because I wouldn't be given one minute more than that one month.

"I'm going to pretend as if you didn't just call my brother trash and then give me an ultimatum. Just back the fuck off unless I reach out to you." I needed to regain my business demeanor even as I found myself staring at his mouth. Those full lips were like a red flag to a bull. I wanted to scream at him to put those damn things away.

I continued. "I will speak with him and see what's going on. Anyone else will come off as accusatory. Plus, he can't lie to me. Then I'm going to see her."

"Maybe I should see her instead? Divide and conquer," he suggested.

My body immediately warmed. I catapulted into territorial shit with Gabe's offer. I didn't want to, but it was damn near impossible not to. He wasn't mine to defend, protect, or give a shit about. I lowered one hand to my thigh and squeezed, digging my nails into the skin in an attempt to scrape up some focus.

"Absolutely not! I will see her. I know how she can get when she's in a relationship, and I know what it can turn into. How crazy she can get. Men. You fuck things up all the time."

And stop looking at me like that!

"Huh, yeah. Like yours is the innocent gender. You have no idea the pain and torment you all can cause."

"Sounds like you know, Gabe. Been keeping busy all these centuries, then?" Oh, shit, it was coming out. I couldn't rein it back in if I tried.

"Maybe I have," he responded smugly with a shrug.

My vision blinked to red.

"Maybe we both have," I said with my best sexy sneer, thankful my voice didn't shake.

"I know you have, Vahla."

What the fuck is that supposed to mean?

"You don't know shit, Gabriel." Lava-level heat soaked me from the inside out.

I didn't know when we had both stood or when he'd come to stand right in front of me behind my desk. I hadn't realized I'd slapped him across his face until his powerful hand wrapped around my wrist and my palm hummed with the sting of the strike. "Let go of me."

"Sure thing, Vahla. Is this where you start to do that running away from me thing you've gotten so good at?"

I went to slap him again with my free hand, and he grabbed that one too. I literally had no control over my body's reactions at that moment. I was not firing on all cylinders as I tried unsuccessfully to tug free. "You're a dick."

He growled as he pressed our bodies together, making sure I felt his dick.

It was kind of my kryptonite. The bastard knew it too.

Our eyes were piercing through each other. He was taller, stronger, and more dominant than I was. He had always been and would always be. Didn't mean I would ever yield to him— or anyone for that matter. That was what I told myself anyway. When he pressed his chest against mine, my resolve failed a bit more with every inhale.

"You're so beautiful" slipped through his lips right before he smashed his mouth to mine.

I kissed him back with such force that I felt dizzy. His tongue completely took control, licking and demanding mine in return. On a ragged exhale, I bit his bottom lip, and he released a groan I felt rumble through my body, stopping to linger at my core. The rumble became a powerful earthquake as his erection pulsated with each nip and lick from me.

My hands slipped from his and sank into his hair, pulling tightly as he leaned over just enough to swipe his arm across my desk and send everything flying to the floor. That same arm cradled my back and his other hand tangled into my hair as he laid me on the desk. He lifted my leg, pulling it around his back and rocking his hardness against me.

"You make me crazy," I mumbled through our kiss.

"I've been crazy since the day you left me," he said, thrusting his hips against me.

"Gabriel." I hadn't sounded so needy in, well, since him. My hands moved his suit jacket aside as my knees widened. My body broke out in tingles and sweat from the anticipation of what was to come. My panties were soaked through, and the throb between my legs begged for him to enter me. Soothe the ache and need and create the delicious torture only his body could give. I could barely breathe imagining the friction our bodies would revel in.

He never broke the kiss, but his eyes widened with my body's movements. So much heat poured from me, mixing with his and sending small rivulets of perspiration down his temples. His fingers trailed down the length of my arms, the sides of my breasts, and my hips.

Then, without warning, he backed away, shifted my legs, and pulled my dress down. The coolness hit my skin like an ice avalanche.

He rubbed at the spot behind his ear as he took a few steps backward before fixing his shirt cuffs from under his suit coat as if the last few minutes never happened.

"You have work to do, Vahla. You have one month to sort this out, but if you don't stop this, I will have to report it, and I'm pretty sure God would rather lose a fallen who tried to take over Heaven with force and contributes nothing, than the woman who maintains seasonal balance for his favorite planet."

I climbed off my desk as gracefully as possible, which was

not graceful at all. I patted and smoothed my dress and shook myself out of the lusty haze he put me in.

Bastard.

He gave me a slight bow and smiled before turning and leaving my office.

I told myself him being here changed nothing.

But him leaving me like a lust-filled nympho in my office? Not wanting to finish the job?

That meant one thing. I needed to go get fucked.

CHAPTER THREE

T HANKS TO GABE'S LITTLE VISIT, I practically ran out of the Scarlet, but the second my stilettos hit the sidewalk and I saw who was standing outside, I came to an abrupt halt.

Mother Nature. Essalene.

If I could simply summon people by having conversations about them, I would have caused an absolute riot with a few particular actors and Father Winter. Oh, Father Winter. He had a specific job that differed from Essalene. He was too cool to come to most of the council meetings, but when he did? To watch his fine ass pull up on his Harley, his more salt than pepper hair, bulging muscles, faded ass-hugging jeans, facial scruff, leather jacket, and arctic blue eyes? Shit. I took a video a few years back and kept that shit as a favorite on my phone. He was deadly sexy. Obviously, I could go on and on about him, but I could very possibly orgasm if I did. I was way, way, way too worked up thanks to the other blue eyed-guy who just left.

Fuck. What was I doing daydreaming about that shit?

I straightened my shoulders and did my best, most confident

CEO walk toward her. I preferred to meet her on the outside of the building, so I moved my ass pretty quickly.

"Essalene?" Her strawberry-blonde hair glowed against the sun, which seemed to have its rays totally focused on her.

"Hi, Vahla." She glanced over my shoulder, fidgeted, and then glanced back at her phone. The silence was sort of awkward.

"So . . . can I help you with something?"

"Oh, yeah. Um, I was just looking for your brother. I haven't heard from him and I got worried. That's why I came to see you." Her pale but perfectly freckled skin pinkened up, clearly indicating her feelings for him.

I figured it was as good a time as any to start Operation Break Up. "He didn't tell you?"

Her face scrunched in confusion. "Tell me what?"

I stepped a little closer. "I'm not sure I should say anything. My brother lets people know things, but only when and if he wants them to."

"But he's my boyfriend, so I'm sure it's okay to tell me."

"Well . . ." I let that hang in the air, and she looked like she was ready to crawl out of her skin before I finished. "I guess."

We walked closer to the building to get out of the way of the crowd rushing by. "He doesn't usually come to my building unless, well, unless he's meeting someone." I leveled a stare at her and lowered my head just a bit. "If you know what I mean."

Her face fell faster than a hooker to her knees at the sight of a twenty. So, I continued. "He didn't invite you here, did he?" I already knew the answer to that.

"No." Her voice was low and sad. "He hasn't returned my calls or texts. I was just worried and thought—"

"That maybe he would be here since I was?"

She offered a tiny nod.

"I'm sorry that he isn't." I wasn't sorry at all. "Hey, listen, can I ask you something since you're here?"

"Sure." The waver in her voice told me she wasn't really sure.

"Has anyone talked to you about the weather lately? It's been very, um, chaotic and strong."

Her eyes got all dreamy and distant. Then she sighed. I was waiting for little hearts to start floating out of her eyes like a damn cartoon character. "It *has* been exceptional."

Ah, no, it hadn't been. "I'm not sure that's what I'd call it."

So much for the lovey-face she had going on. Her dagger eyes turned my way. "My weather is full of beautiful expressions."

"I'm not sure self-expression should be the reason to create such manic weather."

"Well, when you're crowned Mother Nature, feel free to choose your own style."

That was awfully bitchy. "All I'm saying is I think you should take a look at what you're doing. It isn't natural. I think you may start getting the wrong kind of attention."

"You know what, Vahla? Mind your own business. My weather and I are getting all the *right* kinds of attention."

Calm down.

Count to four.

Nope.

"Are you off your meds? The negative attention is already here. Knock it off. This kind of weather isn't your job."

"It'll be a cold day in Hell when you tell me what to do." She sneered.

I rolled my eyes. "Wow. I've never heard that one before." I stepped closer to her. I was pissed and wanted to be perfectly clear. "You can both get into trouble. I'm sure you don't want that."

"Please. Lucifer is powerful and so am I. We aren't worried." She hiked her unfashionable, ugly-ass hobo bag over her shoulder, flipped her hair, and started to walk away.

"You should be," I called out to her.

She smiled and kept walking.

Without a doubt, I was sure I had a problem on my hands.

My driver had been holding the car door open for me during my exchange with Strawberry Fruitcake. Once I was in the backseat, I used a touch of my mojo to make sure every light we hit was green. I was more frustrated than I was after Gabe left.

I made it to Exalt, the club that reminded me of where I had learned to use my whip so long ago. Both humans and supers frequented it, and what happened inside these walls stayed inside these walls.

"Mistress V." Brutus the bouncer greeted me at the door with a bow. I extended my hand and allowed him to kiss it.

"Nice to see you, Brutus. Where is Kaspar?"

"He's helping prep a room."

"Thank you," I said as I walked past him and into the depths of Exalt. The hallway was dark, painted with blood-red walls and thick black velvet valances with gold tassels hanging from them. A few large sconces glowed with orange flames that cast shadows all around and lit the way just enough. Serene and sexy.

Tabitha, the woman who ran the club, was waiting for me when I reached the large foyer. I extended my hand to shake hers.

"Mistress V. So nice to see you."

"Hello, Tabitha. You look well."

She nodded her gratitude. I could smell the sex in the air, making me anxious to get what I came for and leave. "I need to take Kaspar with me."

She looked to the door on her left. "Let me call for him."

She went back behind her sleek, tall black podium and made a call. Almost immediately, the door opened and Kaspar came out. Tall, blond, and muscular with black leather pants and a tight black T-shirt that made his muscles look like they were screaming for release.

Perfect.

He tried to hide his smile, but a small one crept up anyway. Those green eyes of his sparkled as he came to stop in front of me. Then he lowered his head. I lifted his chin. "Look at me, Kaspar. Would you like to come home with me?"

When his neck tilted back and I looked at his gorgeousness, excitement lit up his face at my invitation. "Yes, Mistress. Very much."

"Wonderful. Follow me." I rubbed his face from his chin to his cheek before turning to leave.

As he took his first step, another man came crashing through the same door Kaspar had just come out of. "What do you think you're doing?"

Vaughn. Such a prick. Last time I saw him was during one of my visits to the club a few months back. I had an insanely long wait list for those who wanted to experience my whipping skills, and I would come in as often as I could.

Vaughn wanted to jump the line, completely disregarding the rules. His goal was to become a master with the whip, trying to use shortcuts to reach his goal. He didn't take my rejection very well that night. He took it so poorly, I was actually a bit shocked to see him still allowed inside the club.

My respect for Tabitha waned a bit.

I walked toward him and stopped Kaspar from following me. "Vaughn, a situation has come up and Kaspar will be leaving with me. Don't plan on his return tonight."

Vaughn stood straighter and growled before he spoke. Looking right at me, he said, "Tabitha, this is unacceptable."

"How unfortunate that you feel my decisions are lacking. If

you really feel that way, perhaps you should reconsider your membership. However, Mistress V's request will be honored tonight."

I grinned at him, and he huffed out an annoyed breath through his nose.

"Is that so?"

I answered for her. "Yes. That's so."

"One day, you will learn that you are not the most powerful. You will not always get your way."

I wanted to tell him to fuck off. Instead, I simply responded with a sweet-as-sin smile, "Good night," and then walked out with Kaspar right behind me.

"Mistress," Kaspar said as he held the back door to my limo open and extended his arm for me to enter first.

I let my finger slide across his cheek before I climbed in. When he settled in the backseat, I closed the window partition. "Take your shirt off, Kaspar, and lie on your back on the floor."

He did as I asked. His shirt came off, and I watched each muscle shift and strain as he pulled it over his head. His abs were perfectly defined, and I could see the clear, large outline of his cock through his pants. Chiseled, carved, and hard. Everywhere.

I lifted my dress and removed my panties as he watched in awe and anticipation, opening and closing his hands as he waited for me. "I want you to eat me like I am your last meal. Your favorite delicacy." I straddled his face, taking a bit of satisfaction in his ability to wait for me to tell him he could touch me. "Make me come. Hard."

His smile was filled with pleasure and power as he grabbed my hips and pulled me down onto him, sending his tongue directly into me. Spearing me in one swift push. I moaned from the feel. His tongue was bigger than some of the cocks I'd come across. He licked and sucked, pulling me up and down as I rode his face. My orgasm was gaining ground, but once I looked down and watched as he feasted on me, the sharp tingles edging up my spine began to crash through me like a tidal wave. "Yes, oh. Yes—"

He flicked his tongue fiercely at my clit as my climax hit. Kaspar began nibbling on my lips, scraping his teeth lightly on my flesh as he changed his rhythm. His big, strong hands gripping my waist and then squeezing my ass. I bucked hard, and he went back to licking with that monster tongue of his. The vibration of his humming and the fingers he plunged into me, made another climax roll in.

Oh, fuuuck.

"Fuck! Yes. Yes!" Then his tongue began long, softer strokes, and his finger slowly but deeply continued to pump inside me. He worked me down from the incredible pleasure coursing through me, stringing out every last ounce of it.

When my breathing was semi-normal, I sat back on his thighs, those fucking solid, strong thighs, and leaned forward, whispering, "Well done, dear. Now let's go inside. We have so much more to get to."

A moment later, his shirt was back on and we were on the elevator, headed to the eighty-third floor. I had Kaspar's back to the wall and my back pressed hard on his chest. I swirled my hips and crashed my ass into him. His body trembled and his fingers flexed with the need to touch me. Exactly how I wanted him.

We exited the elevator right into the room, and I instructed him to stand in front of the large bed in the center of the space and wait for me. He watched my every move.

I walked into a separate changing room off to the side to remove my clothes and build Kaspar's anticipation of my return.

As I removed my bra, my mind flashed to Gabe. To his blue eyes and the outline of his muscles in that damn suit he wore to come see me. To the way his tongue looked as it swept over his lips with a slow lick while our bodies were smashed together.

My hands cupped my breasts of their own volition. I kept seeing him watching me, touching me. I imagined him tearing my clothes off and fucking me on my desk instead of the hot, too brief tease he gave me. I pictured him over me and under me and his fingers in me everywhere. I was so wet that, when I dropped my hand between my thighs, my fingers slid over my clit and around my lips. Each touch of my fingers had my body jolting, like I kept touching a live wire. My breathing escalated, and I was so close to my orgasm that it was hitting me before I could stop it.

"Gabriel." I breathed out. "Fuck." I imagined his hands on me instead of my own. I remembered his lips on my neck, my mouth, and my ear. "Ah! Yes, yes, Gabriel." I mumbled the strained words as I came and leaned forward on the chair in front of me to stay upright. My body ached to have more of him. The real him.

When my body settled down, and my breathing leveled out, I reentered the room. With a deep breath, I turned my eyes to Kaspar, who stood soldier still in the spot where I left him.

"Look at me." So, he did. I closed the distance between us and brought my hands to his pants, roughly taking them off him. His strong body only budging slightly at my roughness. Then I ripped his shirt from his body. That chest was a fucking work of art.

His breathing was frantic at that point. "Thank you for your help tonight." I wanted to make sure he heard that. Kaspar was one I never wanted to take for granted.

"Anything you wish, Mistress."

I smiled at his response and then tilted my head to the bed draped in white silk sheets. "Good. Lay on the bed. Back against the headboard." I needed . . . something else.

Once he was settled, I climbed up between his legs and

lowered my voice. "Grab my hair and pull it hard. Fuck my face, Kaspar." He growled at my command. "And hold on. Don't come until I say to."

I gave him credit for holding on as long as he did.

After a joint shower, I fucked him twice.

It had always worked in the past. Not this time.

The next morning, I had my driver bring him home. I never wiped his memory because I enjoyed our history and our time together. It was . . . comfortable and he was a beast in bed. But it still didn't scratch my itch.

CHAPTER FOUR

I HUFFED AND PUFFED AROUND the office the next day like a temperamental child. Like Lucifer. Except I didn't go on some stupid, selfish rampage that accomplished nothing. No, I just missed a trade today. A huge trade. And I just lost fifteen million dollars because of it.

I'd also broken my laptop, which wasn't anything a rampaging child would do. Nope. Not at all.

Abhitha had been eyeballing me since then, walking in and out of my office as needed, glancing at me as she passed outside my door. She didn't question me or make any wiseass comments until she heard my Mac smash into the window. I just looked at her and crossed my arms in front of my chest.

Totally not childlike.

She laughed. "Like that scares me."

"Why do you think I was trying to scare you?"

Confusion and aggravation battered me, and my concentration today was shit. "Don't psychobabble bullshit me right now. I'm not in the mood."

As graceful as always, she sashayed her way over with her tablet. "What do you need, Vahla?"

"Ugh. I wish I knew." I flung my head back and stared at the ceiling. "Maybe your whip? A razor blade?"

I didn't need to look at her to know that she was pursing her lips in disapproval. "No, darling. You haven't needed that in a long time. And you haven't cut yourself in centuries. Your focus has been pristine. Until now. What gives?"

She settled into the chair in front of me just as a frustrated breath pushed from my lungs. "I know."

"I can't help you if you don't talk to me."

"I don't even know which fucked-up part to start with."

"Lucifer missed another delivery. Why don't we start there?"

That was probably the safest place. "He's been distracted."

"Obviously." She gave me her special, snot-eating grin back. *Fine.*

"He's fucking Mother Nature."

"Ah . . . um . . . you'll have to explain that."

"He got all obsessed with some crazy storms. Now, he's fucking her and her emotions, and I mean *all* of them, are tied to the weather. Her anger, fear, joy, lust. All of them."

"Okaaaaayyyyy."

I blew out a frustrated grunt. "She is creating unbalance with the weather. It isn't natural, which sounds idiotic."

"Why does it matter who he's sleeping with or what she's doing to the weather? I mean, besides him not doing his job, where is the harm in him having fun?"

"Because the divines and supers notice these things. It isn't good for us to have the spotlight on us."

"And the spotlight is bad?"

"Very, very bad." I nodded, and she settled back against the chair.

"But you are both powerful, though. Can they really do anything?"

"Yeah, they can."

"They haven't yet, and your brother has caused some serious wars and destruction over the years. He's lucky the witches didn't fry his brain with their spell."

Ah, yes. The time my brother messed with the witches and they cursed his ass. Not something I wanted to wade into at the moment.

"That's the thing, though. None of the other stuff he's done has been that bad." She raised her eyebrow in disbelief, so I clarified. "We all have free will, so even though Luce was topside stirring up shit and causing wars to break out, he was doing it through his influence on humans. He was never the direct cause of it. It was always someone else making the choice."

"Okay, I get that. So, you're worried for him this time because he's directly involved?"

"Exactly."

"This might sound dumb, but can't you talk to your dad?"

"I can't anymore. It doesn't work like that." I sighed. "And please don't ask me to explain."

"I won't, but can I ask you something else?"

"Might as well."

That little snarky comment earned me a sharp look, but it didn't stop her from talking. "Why do you do it? Why stick up for him when he's the one in the wrong?"

"Because he's my brother. Seriously, how can you even ask me that?"

"Yeah, but him being your brother doesn't give him a free pass, does it?" It did. He was the devil. He got a free pass on, like, everything. "It's okay to love someone and have to let them go for your own good."

Tears pricked the backs of my eyes. I had left someone because it was for their own good, and it was the hardest deci-sion I'd ever made. "I did leave someone."

"Ah, the man from the meeting. Gabriel."

The hives and jitters that would normally bombard me each time this conversation drew near, didn't come. I waited. I waited some more. The only thing that crept through me was a warm, soothing current of relief.

"Yes, Gabriel. Yes, he's an angel. And yes, he is the man I left behind to take care of Luce."

"The man you love."

Fuck. She liked being direct.

The pinching at the corners of my eyes should have made me feel weak, vulnerable. Tears were a betrayal of my body that I could never afford. It meant all types of feelings would follow. The kinds of feelings I could never survive. The kinds that ate away at a life force from the inside out.

"You've never talked to me about your past, and I've never pushed. I've heard you cry some nights. Maybe it was long ago, but I heard your pain. I will always support you. But, Vahla? I think it's time, my sweet."

I swiveled in my chair, head back and eyes up to the ceiling. My leg shook as I thought. It was my reaction to the nerves or fear. It was my body humming with the anticipation of letting this go. I never allowed myself to picture this moment. Really picture it. Because when I did, the panic that hit was fast and furious. The pounding at my temples and darkness that seeped into the corners of my vision making it so that the only thing I wanted to do was scream until it stopped.

Walking away from my brother would mean that the sacrifice I'd made meant nothing. That I gave everything away for *nothing*.

"Lucifer wasn't always like this. He was sweet and kind. Fierce yet gentle. One of the most powerful angels ever created, with a brilliant, creative mind. What he is now was more of an evolution, you know? And then some shitty circumstances."

Abhitha nodded. "All the other stuff around him just propelled him to become who he was sooner."

"What stuff?"

"Like when he was told no in situations where he felt his way was the right way. The time when his version of training other angels became too violent, and Michael, the highest-ranking angel and general, turned him away and took his training classes from him. Stuff like that took a toll on him."

"I get all of that, I do. But why do you stay with him? Not that I want to give you up for anything. I love who you are. Who you fought and worked to become."

I snorted.

"What the hell was that for, Vahla?"

"I'm just so different from how I was when we met."

"When you don't know who you are anymore? You start searching. When you leave the love you loved the most? You start trying to forget. Fill the void." *Tell yourself you're pretty. Tell yourself you're fine. Tell yourself you're a ninja for fuck's sake. Make a few million. Then make more. Fuck someone else until you don't puke after fucking someone else. Eat ice cream. Read. Drink. Drink. Drink. Create a new vibrator because none of them were good enough. Learn how to use your whip. Then master it. Then be the master of all masters. Because when I mastered it? I stopped needing it on my own flesh.*

"You made a choice. I get that, and I also respect it. I've never seen you blatantly do what your brother does. Have you been a perfect model of what a good, upstanding citizen is? No. But you've always been fair. You aren't an asshole for the sake of being one. You've taken enough shit over the years and main-tained that balance you say you know is needed. You could let that balance slide at any time and let your brother take his licks, but you don't. You save him each and every time."

"It's nothing compared to what he did for me. Even from a young age, he always stuck up for me. We were very close. The best of friends. His sweetness was just so pure. It might not seem like much, but everything added up. He would hand-make my birthday gifts every year. Sometimes it was a picture, other times it would be something for my hair. One year he took parchment paper and bound it to make a journal for me. For my poetry." I closed my eyes and thought back to that beautiful boy. "Then he began to create flowers. He learned to plant and started a garden. He gave me the first bouquet of flowers he grew." Warm tears slid down my face. "And no one was allowed to pick on me. He made sure of it."

"You left your home and your love, Vahla. Tell me how that doesn't compare."

I opened my eyes and stood slowly, taking my time to straighten out my wobbly knees. Wrapping my arms around my stomach, I walked to the windows. So high up, a place where no one could touch me. Yet, I was more exposed than ever. My reflection showed an impeccably dressed businesswoman who was a stark contrast to the mess of a woman inside.

"He saved me from being raped when I fell."

Her sharp intake of air told me that wasn't what she expected to hear.

"There were men in the town where I landed." I let out a humorless laugh. "They just came out of nowhere. I was watching children play one minute and being dragged into the woods the next. Shit, Abhitha. I was so scared." I thought that, after all this time, my own reaction to what happened would be different. Less. But the same visceral reaction hit me like a battering ram to my chest.

"Did you use your powers to fight them off?"

"No. I didn't know what to do. I begged and screamed, but I never once thought to use my powers. They were so rough." I remembered how they tore at my linen dress, my wings to fly away nowhere to be found. "They had been drinking and their breath . . ." I closed my eyes and saw the yellow teeth of the man who climbed on top of me. I could feel his fingernails cutting the skin of my inner thighs as he pried them open. "Finally, I had nothing left. No fight, no voice. I knew what was going to happen next."

"Oh, Vahla."

I turned to see the woman who had been with me for so long. The beautiful person who hadn't feared me wore a mix of horror and pity on her face.

"Luce stopped them. I had never seen rage like that in him before—or in anyone, for that matter. His light blond hair glowed white and his normally deep blue eyes changed color. The black that engulfed them was alarming. Then he broke their necks. It was so vicious and quick that he tore the spine clear out of one of them. I was in and out of consciousness by that point, and then we just . . . fell. The Earth opened and swallowed us."

"That's how you ended up in Hell?"

"Yes. I still don't know how it happened. I only remember waking to Luce pounding on my chest. Four compressions and four breaths. That's what I remember until I heard and felt my bones crack under his pressure as he screamed for me to wake up." The memory alone had my chest pulsing to that very same rhythm Luce had kept up to save me.

"But you're . . . you're you." I heard the struggle in her voice. I watched as the pain etched in her face mixed with confusion. She viewed me as powerful. Unbreakable.

"But it happened anyway. Lucifer continued to take care of me. The terrain of Hell was so foreign, so rough. The air was thick and wet. Everything about it was offensive to the senses. He offered to carry me, and then tore off the rest of his wings to make a bed for me."

"Your wings came back?" The awe in her voice was unmistakable.

"His did as we fell. Mine didn't." I crossed my arms over my chest. My back thumping with that familiar, empty ache. The phantom feeling that broke me a little each time I thought of not having them anymore. Jealousy and turmoil over why my brother could have his and I couldn't. "Are you seeing it? The picture becoming clear?"

"But wouldn't the fact that he got his wings back and took care of you make him stronger?"

I shook my head, my own disbelief making the information fuzzy on my tongue. "One would think. It just didn't happen that way. Once we started roaming around, we stumbled on the two mortal men who almost raped me, and I lost it. Like, kicked and screamed and lunged at them lost it. They looked lifeless as they lay sprawled on the ground, but it didn't stop the reaction I had. I shook with rage and just let loose. When the skin of my hand touched one, it was the first time I had experienced that transfer of energy. My body lit up."

"That didn't happen for your brother?"

"Oh, it did. But when the one he touched moved, I got scared and protected him. I grabbed the man with one hand and Luce with the other, trying to shove them apart, but it was like I'd completed some circuit. The power that moved from the guy to me and then into my brother was incredible. When I dropped the guy, he looked between Luce and me, and then dropped to his knees at my feet."

"Oh. Wow."

"Yeah."

"But, honey, is that all really enough to continue to give up your life?"

I squeezed my arms tighter to my body. "He hates humankind. He hates the angels. Lucifer has made it clear that he will hurt them, kill them if given the chance. I have to protect them. He's started wars. You've seen them. He's incited violence and influenced humans. But it's the angels he is biding his time for."

"Why hasn't he done anything about that yet?"

I breathed deeply. "I suppose it's because he is still having fun. He plays with the humans. The viles are workers, but I know he still trains a good amount of them for war. A separate faction from the soldiers we keep sharp, just in case. A special breed for when he's ready."

"You expect yourself to be able to stop him?"

I stared into her eyes, sure of my next statement. "Of course I do. I'm more powerful than him."

"And if the time comes, you think you'll be able to use your power to fight him?"

I wasn't in that position, yet I could feel myself torn in two. My brain tried to rectify what she was asking and what my answer would have to be. "I try not to think about that. I know my brother loves me. He shows me the side of him that no one else sees. We take care of each other." That sounded like I had my head thoroughly stuck in the sand.

"It isn't enough, Vahla."

I pressed the heels of my hands against my eyes so hard that I thought they'd come out the back of my head. "I made promises, Ab."

"To whom?"

I remembered the day. The private conversation between a father and his daughter.

"To whom, Vahla?"

I clenched my teeth to stay quiet. Pushed my hands in harder. Tried to shut out the words that were said back then.

"Vahla!"

"My father, okay! My dad! The big man himself." I flailed my arms and started to pace. "Shit."

"I can understand your loyalty, but it's been so long."

I turned to face her, and my breathing was as unsteady as my knees. "I'm waiting for the other shoe to drop. I'm hoping it won't. But I'm not deviating from my job, Abhitha. I won't do it."

She nodded thoughtfully. I was sure she was trying to process everything. I knew the story intimately, and I still had a hard time processing it.

She uncrossed and re-crossed her legs while shaking her head. "But what about Gabriel? Why has he waited so long to come back?"

"He's here for the issue with Mother Nature, but I doubt he'll stick around once I get it all sorted out."

"I think he's given you your time and space and he's done waiting. A man in love can only take so much."

Instinctively, I rubbed at the script behind my ear. "I don't know about that."

"I guess we will just have to see."

That shot a wave of nerves through me. I had a hard time trusting anyone's intentions. I had an extremely small circle of people I trusted but never truly let my guard down. "I can't deal with all of this right now."

"If not now, when?"

"Fuck. Never? I don't know."

"I don't know why you aren't with him. If anyone can pull it off, you can."

I flopped onto the couch that sat along the windows and let out a grunt. "This shit was supposed to get easier."

"How's that working out?"

I had to laugh. It was so not working out at all.

"That was what I thought." She laughed. "Maybe it's time to reconnect with your family upstairs."

"No!" I sat up in a whirlwind, and a wave of panic hit me. Abhitha flinched. "No. Not everyone is good. Please promise me you'll remember that."

"What? How is that even possible?"

"Free will. Everyone has it. Angels, humans, supers, viles." I stood and pulled her from her chair. I took her shoulders and squeezed. "Please, promise me you'll tell me if you see any angels around. Any at all, even if it's only because you passed one on the street, okay?"

She placed her hands over mine. "I promise, Vahla." Her words were soft, meant to comfort. I didn't want to scare her, but I would if I had to. When she hugged me, I knew I had rattled her. "You'll need to tell me who to worry about or I won't be able to protect you."

"I do the protecting. You just let me know when your spidey-senses act up, okay?"

"Can I at least get the name or names? Any type of heads-up would be good. I can't be guarded enough if you don't share something."

She wouldn't know any names. I never had her in the building when I hosted the council meetings because not a single one of them was to be trusted.

But she was right and only one name came to mind. "Silas."

She leaned back and took me in with her eyes, assessing. Not sure what she was looking for, but looking all the same. "Okay." She nodded, and I knew she had committed that name to memory. "You've come so far. You deserve so much. No one gets to you. They'd have to go through me first."

I had come far.

"What are you going to do now? We really didn't come up with a plan. I meant to be a little more helpful."

"You were very helpful. I didn't know I needed to talk. It felt good."

"You know I'm here if you need me. But I know you, Vahla. You've always risen to every challenge thrown your way."

I may have risen to those challenges and won. Didn't mean at some point I wasn't going to fail.

Time to go have another chat with my brother.

CHAPTER FIVE

I TRACKED WHERE LUCIFER WAS through my cell phone app, which was something I'd installed after the last time he went MIA. A minute later, I teleported from the Scarlet and landed in Canada—more specifically, the Yukon.

Since it was such a vast expanse of forestry and nature, I didn't have to worry about running into people. Just animals. I had way more of a tolerance for animals.

The first thing I noticed was the waves of dampness. It was a warmth that was not familiar in this region for this time of year. It saturated the air and stuck to my skin and clothes. Foreign and unnatural always belonged to Lucifer, so I figured I would find him somewhere close to the center of the anomaly.

The ground had begun a slow rumble, a vibration that started off ever so slightly but gained strength with every passing second. The wind whistled a low howl. That was when I knew I was fucked. Well, someone else was fucked. *Ugh*.

I continued my journey, making sure to always be moving toward the storm and never away. I came to the opening in the forest and found Essalene and Luce. Each one of her wrists was secured to a different tree so she couldn't lower her arms. My brother, in all his naked grossness, was taking her from behind. Her moans were the low howls, which grew into screams, which then shifted into the fury of the wind. I swallowed back the bile at the thought of what exactly was causing all the moisture in the air. When her orgasm hit, so did the hurricane gusts. I looked up, smug and pissed all at once, and whispered, "I told you, Gabriel." Then I had to dig my heels firmly into the ground so I didn't end up flying into a tree.

I figured I'd let her ride it out and give them their privacy this time. I had to be non-threatening. But, honestly, I could have puked from my brother's grunts, which carried on for far too long. I consider myself a pretty sexual person, but this was so not working for me.

Once the calm settled around me, I ran from the tree line, ready for the lie to spill from my lips to pull him away from her. I needed to have this conversation with him in private. In Hell where there were no other ears or eyes to intrude. Without a reason that stroked his ego (ewww on that choice of words), he wouldn't leave with me. I had to do a believable damsel-in-distress.

Pretending to be out of breath, I began my plea, "Luce! Holy Shit! I was so worried, where have you been?"

My charge obviously took him off guard. "V? Shit. What are you doing? Worried?" He started jogging toward me, literally leaving Essalene hanging.

Ha.

Oh, I was going full-on Academy Award shit for this, and I was pretty sure she was going to cry.

When we were mere steps away, I wobbled, almost falling to one knee, and then worked to right myself. I couldn't go overboard.

Lucifer grabbed my shoulders and lifted me the rest of the way. "Hey! What the fuck is wrong?"

Um, first would be that he was still naked and I was trying not to dry heave.

"Your fucking vile is what's wrong! He surprised me and . . . and . . . well, you haven't been around, and I think he assumed he could take advantage of that. I've been distracted with making sure your shit is all done. So, I put a hole in the fucker's hand to get away." Not entirely a lie.

Luce was looking back and forth between Essalene and me. She was absolutely livid and embarrassed to still be naked and caught up in the ties binding her to the tree, and the red tint on her face and neck grew by the second. So, I looked to her. "Essalene? It's me. Vahla."

I guessed playing nice had its advantages. Losing some of the distortion on her face, she responded, "Vahla? Are you all right?"

I looked up at Lucifer and wiped some nonexistent shit from my cheek. "Yes, yes. I'm okay. I'm sorry to interrupt."

She softened a bit.

"It's okay. You can take care of her first," I said.

"Give me a minute," he responded. He jogged back over to her, untied her, and whispered in her ear. Then he was back at my side, and we were leaving.

Our feet had barely made first contact with the ground in Hell when he demanded, "Tell me which one."

I told Luce which of his viles took the liberty of getting too handsy with me. He bought it, of course. Good thing I didn't have a huge conscience about necessary lies.

"For fuck's sake, V! No one gets one over on you. Where was your whip? I can't even wrap my head around this!"

Here we go . . .

"Gabe called a check-in, so I guess I was off."

At his name, Luce stopped walking and narrowed his navy-blue eyes at me. "What did that fucking douchebag want?"

I sighed and grabbed his arm, dragging him down the corridor. "It was just business stuff. I was thinking about strategy, and the fucker grabbed my thigh. It just pissed me off. They know better. But they are viles for a reason. Such assholes! You know we sporadically see ones who think they are mister big swinging dick, and then do something like that." I sighed for effect. "I want you to make a point to them." I looked into Luce's eyes and saw the fierce protector that he was, come to life.

Since I was speaking directly to the one who thought he was the biggest of the swinging dicks, this made him more determined to prove his point for all the viles to see.

We looked down to the pits from the balcony off my office. Although the jagged rocks of the landscape were incredibly unique and much smoother, beautiful stone was my jam. I had white swirled marble for my desktop and a beautiful creation of black-and-light-gray stone for the floor and balcony. I put my hands on the iron railing and leaned forward. "I see him."

Lucifer followed my gesture and scanned the faces of the viles below. "Which one?"

"The one not working as hard as the rest even though he tells me that you put him in charge while you were gone."

He narrowed his eyes to focus on the viles below. I rolled my eyes. "The one with a fucking hole through his hand, Luce."

He turned from me and stormed down the iron spiral staircase that led to the pit below. I smiled and twirled like a dancer before following his lead. He could be such a condescending, mean asshole and I didn't want to miss it. Plus, if blackout rage hit, he could potentially kill a huge amount of them. That I wouldn't allow.

When we reached the main pit area, the head viles all lined up and bowed. I was behind Lucifer, which never happened, and

I looked to the group of them. They knew the order of power, so they looked to me as well. I grinned and put one finger to my lips. They all listened. No one would question what my brother said anyway, but I had just made sure of it. The "offending" vile took it like the vile beast he was. Then he was sentenced. Fifty-seven years of whatever Lucifer judged as punishment.

THREE HOURS LATER, I SOUGHT MY BROTHER OUT AGAIN. THIS time, he wasn't hard to find, though. He'd promised me he wouldn't leave me alone in Hell and had then disappeared into his room. When I leaned against his threshold, he looked at me, giving me a chin nod of acknowledgment.

"Hey, sis, you all right?"

"Yup. Right as rain," I said.

He laughed. "I always hated that stupid phrase. Plus, now I have firsthand knowledge that rain is not right. Or straight. It comes at all angles and speeds. It can be harder and softer."

I held up my hand. "Eww. My ears are going to bleed."

"You get where I'm going with that proof, then?" He winked and kept laughing.

"Oh, I got it. And I'm trying to pretend I don't."

"Such a prude all of a sudden, V."

I took a deep breath. "We need to talk, Lucifer."

He sat up, and I walked in and shook my head. Clothes were everywhere. His iPad was on the floor. I picked it up, noted the cracked screen, and set it on a shelf. A flash of anger ran through me at how little he regarded what he had. I worked hard for all of it.

"Oh, no. Using my full name with that somber face. What did I do now?"

I picked up a few items of clothing and put them in his

hamper, then went into his bathroom to wash my hands. He was such a slob.

"Hilarious. So powerful and still a germaphobe."

I gave him a smile and the middle finger before I sat in his desk chair. This area was relatively clean because he never did any work at it, so I considered it safe.

"Listen, Luce, I know you've been *enjoying* your time with Essalene, but I need you to stop seeing her."

"What? Why?"

"She's creating too many storms with you. The weather is tied to her emotions, and she is choosing not to temper it at all. She's killing a lot of people. It's why Gabriel came to meet with me."

Malice ran hot across his features. "You know I don't give a shit about those humans. Let them die for all I care. Fuck that asshole angel."

One . . . two . . . three . . . four . . . breathe.

"I know you don't care about them. But do you care about me? Can you have some patience with Gabe for coming to me with a heads-up to let me know the angels have noticed and are watching."

This got his attention and he straightened. "You know I care about you. Them, not so much."

"Then, please, just trust me on this."

"Are you in trouble, Vahla? Because of me?"

"No." I lied. "No one is in trouble . . . yet."

You could be, though. Very, very soon.

"You'd tell me, wouldn't you?"

I moved over to his bed after hearing the concern in his voice. I sat next to him and took his hand in mine. "I would, which is why I'm here talking to you about it in the first place. I need you to stop seeing her. It's caused issues, and it's only a matter of time before all eyes are on us."

He put his hand over mine. "Okay."

"That's it? No fighting me on this?"

Keeping my hand in his, he turned his body toward me and sighed. "She's kind of crazy, anyway. I mean, she's a great lay, and I like the storms, but . . ."

"But?"

"But it's all the time. Even when I don't want the storms. And she's all like, 'Let's have a baby,' and, 'Let's get married.'"

"What?" I screeched.

He laughed. "Yeah, I know. So, I'm good not being with her anymore. Got a few hotties in the wings, anyway." He looked to the side and then back at me. "Should I go and break up with her in person?"

"No. I think you should just let it cool down between you. Don't take her calls or answer her texts for a while. Maybe she'll just . . . I don't know . . . move on?"

He looked skeptical, but he still nodded. "I will."

I was so happy to hear this, that I decided not to let the nagging suspicion that it was too easy bother me.

"I'm sure it is." I laughed and then moved to hug him. "Thanks, Luce."

"It's the least I can do."

"Yeah, that and clean up this pigsty." I let my arms fan out to encompass his whole room.

"Woah. Let's not get crazy."

I shook my head and laughed. "Okay. Just do a little something. I'll keep my expectations low."

I continued to pick up his mess because old habits die hard. He was texting someone as if he didn't give a shit about what I'd just asked him to do, and it made me wonder how this man could have ever turned out the way he did. Nostalgia could be a sneaky bitch. Memories of our childhood flooded me. Running, playing, picking flowers for the girl he crushed on.

I reached into the space between the desk and the wall and scooped up some garbage. I hesitated as something heavy rested in my hand. Clearing away the paper and a single black sock, I sucked in a startled breath. "Luce?" I turned to him with the object in my palm.

"Yeah?" He finished whatever he was typing before he looked up. When he finally saw what I was holding, he got up and grabbed it from me, angrily throwing it into the garbage pail.

I turned on my heels and bent to get it out. "Why did you do that?"

He huffed and stalked back to his bed, completely ignoring my questions.

"This is beautiful. Why would you throw it away?"

He still ignored me.

"Luce?"

He typed more furiously, and each click of his thumbs pissed me off even more. If my brother knew anything, he should know that when I wanted to talk, I wanted to talk. One more time, and if he didn't answer me, I would break his fucking fingers. And his phone.

"Lucifer!" I yelled and smashed my palm into his wall. I was done playing this game with him. The force of my hit shook the walls of his room and rattled every light fixture.

"What?" he yelled back.

"Why would you have this and then want to throw it away? The chocolate cosmos is your favorite. Creating that flower consumed you and—"

"Shut up, Vahla."

"It's okay to talk about it. It isn't your—"

"I said shut up!" The floor shook with the force of his scream.

"No! I won't. Your pride may have gotten the better of you, but this?" I picked up the glass paperweight that held that beautiful flower. "This is something to be proud of."

He grumbled. "Yeah, it did me a lot of good."

"Just because it wasn't the way you wanted it to go, it doesn't mean it wasn't amazing."

"Guess that didn't matter. He decided. But *I* was right. *He* was wrong."

The chocolate cosmos flower was part of a huge variety of creations and the last straw for my brother. Who would have ever thought that flowers would be what broke him? He should have had control over sending those flowers and plants to Earth since he had been the one who created them, but sometimes there was a bigger plan. That plan included letting his plants go to Earth without his consent because some had medicinal properties that would save human lives.

"I'm sorry, Lucifer."

"Yeah, me, too."

I placed the weighted glass gently on his desk and turned to exit his room. Before the door closed, I heard him mutter, "Not as sorry as they will eventually be."

Even after all this time, the hate and vengeance were still deep in his bones.

"*You expect yourself to be able to stop him?*"

I had to. I gave everything up so I could.

CHAPTER
SIX

"D? Hey, it's me."

"Hey, Vahla. How's my favorite she-devil?"

"You're so ridiculous." I snorted. "But I better be your only she-devil."

"Ha! I only have room for so much crazy. And you're it, girl."

Comfortable silence sat between us as I cradled my phone on my shoulder. Never one to push, I knew I'd have to go first. For so long, I'd hated needing people. Felt too exposed and thought that opening up meant they could use all of my information or weaknesses against me.

"He's back, D."

A whooshing sound and a loud *thump* had me pulling the phone away from my ear. The phone must have fallen from her grip as I continued to hear a frenzied rustle. Her mumbled voice sounded like she was in a wind tunnel as she called out, "I'll be right back," to someone who wasn't me. Then a door slammed shut. "What do you mean he's back? How the hell did that happen?"

"I mean he's back. He came to my office."

"In New York? What the fuck! He shouldn't be able to *ever* enter New York, never mind your building! How the fuck did he break my spell?"

"Oh. Shit, Delayna. No. No, no, no. Shit. I'm sorry. Not *him*. Gabriel."

"Can you please lead with that next time? I almost had a fucking heart attack. If I dropped dead in all my naked glory I would come back and haunt your ass until the end of days."

"Why are you naked?"

"Damn it!" I knew the phone had tumbled from her hand again as her words grew farther away. The *tap, tap, tap,* must be her trying to catch it. Too late. She couldn't catch for shit. So, I did what any good friend would do. I laughed at her. "Ugh. You are such a bitch, Vahla."

"So I've heard."

"It's less dangerous for me and this phone if I sit. Okay. Tell me, tell me, tell me. Did he swipe everything off your desk and strip your clothes off and fuck you unconscious?"

My coffee quickly and without warning shot out my mouth and nose. "What is wrong with you?" I swiped my sleeves across my mouth and nose. Shit, that burned.

"Dude, I had a sex fest for a week following my swim around that head of yours back in the day. You and that man are hawwwwt."

Yeah, we certainly were.

"I know you're smiling." She sighed. "But why so glum, my sweet?"

"He's here because of Mother Nature."

"You mean because of the crazy weather?"

"Yup."

"What does that have to do with you?"

"Guess who's helping with those wind gusts?"

"Ewww. Can your brother ever keep his dick in his pants?"

"Nope. And Gabriel said that if the angels have to come fix it, they won't blame her because she's too valuable."

"Shit. Did you talk to Luce?"

"I did. But I can't trust it will last."

"Tell me what you need."

"Huh, where do I begin?"

"Anywhere. I got your back."

She certainly did. "I need a spell to keep Luce occupied. Something that will keep him very *active* with someone else. I don't trust him to not jump the fence and go back to screwing Essalene. Her type of power is addicting to my brother."

"Done. Pick it up tomorrow. And, V?"

"Yes?"

"If you fuck Gabriel, get that shit on tape for me."

"I'll see what I can do."

We were both laughing as we disconnected.

CHAPTER
SEVEN

THE FIRST THING I DID when I got home was a power absorption. I needed the biggest pool of candidates to find the right choice for the spell to keep my brother occupied. It wasn't like I absorbed their power individually anymore, anyway. Nope. I absorbed hundreds, sometimes thousands, at a time. All their crimes mixed and smashed together in a black, shithole cesspool movie in my head. Good times it was not.

I designed areas where the new viles were herded and had a little magic help from my friend. The new viles were gathered by other viles I considered my bounty hunters. Newbies were placed on miles of onyx slabs, the best stone for me to absorb energy from all of them at once. Onyx ran throughout my entire empire, at least the empire I've discovered to date. Miles of onyx road led a path to my home. It was the only place I could comfortably absorb that much energy. I always passed out, but not until the power-flowing pain crushed my body, nauseating me and creating a light show coming out of each of my pores. Hurt like a motherfucker doesn't do it justice.

Oh, and did I mention I can't move too much while I take it all in? Yeah, I had to lay down on my back with outstretched arms. One hand had to be on the onyx that ran into my room and made a path to the middle of my floor. The other hand had to be resting on the amethyst stone slab that led to the energy vats we used to store the energy, feed all the viles, and power everything else. Like electricity does for the humans. I could only do this once a month because I always felt close to death each time.

So, once that was done, I crashed for a few hours before heading out to check out the work going on in my empire.

I wanted to feel powerful and one of the best ways I knew how to do that was with my wardrobe. Black leather and metal. Yup, that was what I needed. The tank-style top I chose was thick, tight leather with bold, shiny metal toggles holding it together down the front. Nothing muted or simple today would do.

The leather skirt landed under my ass and fit like a second-skin. The black leather boots boasted five inches of deliciously sharp stilettos, slightly rounded toes, and one-and-a-half-inch platforms. But the backs of these babies were fucking hot. The zippers ran three-quarters of the width of them and were polished to look the metal clasping my top together. My long hair went up into a high, sleek ponytail. Bold black swipes of eyeliner around my eyes, deep-plum matte lipstick joined the party, and I was done. I grabbed my whip and flinched at the zap of energy it passed to my hand before settling it in a coil around my wrist. Cracking my neck and sighing at the gratifying pops, I left my suite and headed for the first pit. I wanted to visit the diamond mine.

Abhitha needed stock for the private collections commissioned by some of our top buyers. I wasn't ready to trust Luce to make the deadline, so I decided to check the progress myself. And I needed to find a vile suitable for Delayna's spell.

One of my higher-ranking viles was examining his list, and he glanced up and checked something off on the page. The fucker had on his spectacles because, yeah, he had blurry vision. If I weren't so pissy, I might have laughed or at least smiled because there was absolutely no rhyme or reason to these assholes I housed down here in this underworld. They're dead-ish, so why did some of them still have their defects from their human life? I had no clue. It was a detriment sometimes when I had to figure out their punishments. Wanting them to suffer for fifty-seven years could be creative, but if you had to create around an ailment they still carried with them, it was a pain in the ass. The last sentence I gave was to a female vile who thought she could "borrow" the lip gloss I had in my back pocket. I didn't have to worry about working around any human ailments with her sentence. She still had thirty years left of her daily and very intense menstrual cramp punishment. I take few things as seriously as my lip gloss.

I walked for miles, breathing in the fire and brimstone that made me feel at home. Elements that I inhaled and swallowed into my body that made me feel powerful. Amazing that what used to make me feel ill, made me feel strong. The more viles that landed in my underworld, the more workers I had and the larger the profits I could turn, which made me just that much stronger. It also made me smile to watch the viles scattering like ants within the caves and stretches of rock, all very focused on their tasks.

I had to give my brother credit. Ever since my little lie about the vile who overstepped with me, he had been keeping them in line, running his drills to make sure they stayed as sharp as an army should, just in case, and making sure they worked hard every day in the pits. I never pushed him to tell me about the other army he was training. Those seemed to be specialized. I had a feeling that, one day, we would need to have a conversation about them, but that time hadn't come just yet.

"What the fuck?" I mumbled as I looked toward the next mine.

In the distance, I saw Isla, my Vice General and the disher-of-torture. She was bending down and peering into a small hole on the side of the mountain. She and the vile in charge were looking at something and speaking amongst themselves. He, like the other viles in charge at other mines, looked to his clipboard and then back up at the hole. He took his loupe that was attached to his clipboard and stepped in closer, placing it to his eye. I could tell he was speaking to Isla, reporting on what he was looking at. She was shaking her head and speaking back to him, not noticing the vile behind her. But I did.

He was standing behind her pretending to thrust into her in the classic "air fucking" move. That coil of tension in me that had just started to relax? Yeah, that fucker popped, and I flashed in a quick teleport so I was right behind him. He was so lost to his movements that he didn't realize I was there until it was too late. All the viles around us knelt at my arrival, but because mister nasty-swinging-air-cock had his eyes closed, he just kept right on doing what he was doing. When he turned, he fell hard to the ground on his knees.

"Queen Vahla," Isla said when she turned to see what the viles knelt at and bowed her head before lifting it and continuing. "How nice of you to stop by." She smiled. "And good timing, too."

"Yes, good timing." I smiled in return.

Her eyebrows came together at the tone in which I used to speak. "Is there something wrong?"

"The vile at my feet was quite disrespectful while you were hard at work." The head vile began to shake, knowing that I held them responsible for those they oversaw. "Relax, vile. I could see you were obeying your vice general as she was looking at something." His body lessened a fraction in its quaking, but he could have shaken enough to break his body for all the shits I gave.

Isla's eyes narrowed, and she clenched her teeth together. "He was, was he?" Oh, this girl was a fireball.

"He was pretending to fuck you from behind while you worked."

Her eyes flared with anger, and her steel-toed work boot came up and pressed against the vile's back. "Is that so?" she snarled.

I sighed, loving this exchange between us as the guilty vile began to violently shake with fear. "It is."

Isla reached into the thick belt of her cargo pants and pulled out a switchblade. I didn't want to smile because I was so pissed off and so ready to beat the shit out of him, but I couldn't help myself. Her eyes met mine, and I saw the barely restrained fury. "May I?"

I nodded. She stepped closer to the vile and the crunching of the stone below her boots pierced the air. Isla came up nice and close, standing right in front of him. She placed her palm on his head and let her fingers rest on top of it.

Her grimace was immediate, her face pinched and her breathing came fast and shallow. I worried about her reaction, but I allowed her to continue. She couldn't effectively do her job if I didn't give her the power to read the minds of those around her.

The one she was reading was younger than most in this pit and still had some chunks of long hair left. Which Isla took advantage of when she grabbed a section and pulled back. "So you wanted to display your desire to fuck me by mocking me?" Her knife kissed the skin on his chest. Bubbles of crimson coated the opening and balanced on a fine line of staying put or dripping a path down his body. It was mesmerizing to watch.

"You are wise to keep your mouth shut, vile." She hummed. "I wonder which hole you were imagining fucking." Another kiss of her knife. Another trickle of blood. "It would seem you didn't have a preference while you were alive. Nothing more than a rapist. A taker, a beater, and a predator. Girls and boys."

Her neck visibly pulsed while her hands flicked and twisted the blade in her hand. This type of vile always hit her hard. Hit way too close to home. I never denied her the punishments she gave them. Instead, I saw her grow stronger every day. It was as though her actions gave her solace. Gave her power back. Power that hadn't existed when I'd found her.

No, back then, Isla had been broken. Cast down to me because she killed every last man who had touched her without her permission, and she'd done it with unrestrained violence. Then she tortured and killed her mother for allowing it to happen and making money from her suffering and abuse.

I squeezed the handle of my whip tighter and rubbed along its sleekness with my thumb. Isla looked at my hand and approached me. In a hushed voice, she said, "I'm fine, my Queen."

"I'm sure you are. I'm not questioning your strength."

Her smile reminded me of the first real one she gave me when she finally realized that she would be safe with me.

My smile back to her was immediate. You see, this whip, my powerful weapon and my crutch when I needed, was the long, raven-colored hair that used to sit on her head. In trying to save her from a fall from the mountain when I found her, I had grabbed on to her hair and literally ripped it from her scalp. She bled and screamed and those screams turned into laughter. Laughter and gratitude. Not too long after, she informed me that her nightmares no longer plagued her dreams.

When her hair had grown back, it had been the lightest blonde instead of the darkest black, and her nightmares, the ones I'd ripped from her, had become my favorite weapon.

"May I continue?"

"As you wish." I wound my whip back around my wrist and turned to leave. "You've become strongest with the blade?"

Without missing a beat, she pulled hard on the vile's head and pushed her boot between his shoulder blades. It reminded me of someone riding a horse and pulling back on the reins. Isla flipped the blade in the air and caught it flawlessly as her hands and arm descended upon his chest once again, making another cut. She released him and his body slumped forward. The impact of him hitting the ground made a rather satisfying sound.

Isla looked at me with a slight grin. "No, my Queen."

I cocked my head, urging her to explain and relieve my curiosity.

"I am better with two blades."

The air-fucking vile suffered a full-body tremor at her words.

"Forgive me," the vile mumbled as he lifted his head to look at me. The blood trickled down his chest and began to outline his legs. His body shook, releasing even more of his bodily fluids to the hard ground below, staining it and turning those areas a darker gray.

"Not a chance in hell." She laughed at her own joke as she reached into another pocket and drew a second blade. My chest burst with pride as she winked at me before I turned and walked away. I had to find Luce a new sex toy, and I needed to do it sooner rather than later. Didn't want him wandering back to the Wacko of the Woods.

I LEFT ISLA TO DO HER THING AND CONTINUED TO OTHER MINES. Each one of the three mines I passed was bustling with work. I enjoyed the sound of the jewels clinking together as they were poured into large containers. Even with muted light this far down, the gems reflected on any inch of light they could grab. A kaleidoscope of color burst all around, bouncing off the mountainsides and filtering through the smoky clouds that billowed above them.

The utmost respect and discipline were shown to me from each vile, making this end to the check-in much better than the start.

And then it got even better as I walked away from the emerald mine. Because walking ever-so-slowly toward his favorite place, was Vile Four. I never referred to him as just a vile. He was always my Vile Four.

He had to look down as he walked in order to navigate the path with his walker. His limp was severe and his right foot dragged instead of lifted. He had the same hunchback all the viles ended up with after spending time in Hell. I figured out with him how to use my power to stop the gross changes from happening, or to at least slow them down. So, he never ended up with the greasy, slimy, wet look of all the others.

I couldn't help but smile each time I saw him. Waves of pride and protection ran through me when it came to him. He hadn't had an easy human life. He wasn't born with the same abilities or intellect as most down here, or at a time where there was more tolerance and understanding of his needs.

Everything about him was much slower, and tasks were so much more difficult and confusing for him. It was a recipe for disaster topside, so he ended up down here with me. He just hadn't been given to humans capable of realizing that different wasn't bad. Slower wasn't defective. The beatings he took from his parents and uncles were the only way he knew how to deal with his emotions. It was what he was taught by example. By suffering. They enjoyed beating down a boy who was taller and wider than all of them. They reveled in his pain and their triumph, even though he never fought back. So, when he saw them physically harm the pets in the house that he loved, Four dealt with it the only way he knew how. The result was him beating his family to death.

"Hey, Four." I made sure my voice was loud enough for him to hear me but sweet enough that it wouldn't scare him.

He stopped his walker and managed a lopsided smile as he struggled to straighten his body as much as it would allow. He was the first case that I wished I could heal the frailties that viles came down with. I did everything I could think of, short of praying, which I wouldn't do because I couldn't bring myself to blaspheme like that. Not even the spells I'd requested from supernatural friends could interfere. At least I halted the full vile transformation.

"My Queen, hello." I saw the strain on his arms as they began to shake from trying to hold his body higher.

"How is your day?"

"Green stones. Like summer g-g-grass."

"You going to make sure the green stones are taken care of?"

He shook his head. "F-f-f-for you, my Queen. F-f-f-for you."

I walked forward and touched his hands, and that lopsided smile grew bigger. I so wished my touch could heal him even just a little bit.

"You're the best at taking care of our green stones. I'll let you get to them, okay?" He nodded slightly. "Have a good day, Four!"

"G-g-good day. Green stones."

I moved to the side to let him pass. If he knew about manners and understood better, I knew he would have let me pass first.

I watched as he made his way back to his walker and slowly got going again, wholly focused on finding the green stones.

Back in the early days, I was the one who trained the viles to recognize the stones and gems. Each time I named one, the viles would take off in search of it. Not Four. He stood and stared at me for days, never once wavering in his attention and always being fourth in line—hence the name.

On the third day of the training, I explained the green stones, describing the color as *green like the summer grass*. It was the first time the vacant look in Four's eyes cleared. There was a change to his expression that made me think he recognized something, so I continued. *Green like leaves in spring. Broccoli. Pears.* I called out as many green things as I could think of while I assumed I had his attention. The look he had lasted for a full minute before he turned and limped deeper into the cave system.

I had forgotten all about him until he showed back up, five days later. All he kept saying was, "F-f-for you, my Queen. F-f-for you." Settled in the middle of his dirty, blood-crusted palm was an emerald the size of an egg. My smile was huge and genuine. I admired the stone and touched his hand. He may not have been very expressive, but I knew what I saw. Pride. And acceptance.

To this day, it was my favorite stone, locked away in a safe place in my suite.

To this day, no one was allowed to fuck with Four.

I TURNED RIGHT AND TOOK THE PATH THAT I HADN'T BEEN DOWN more than a handful of times. It was much darker than the rest of Hell, and the air hung heavier with sulfur and stagnation. The damned stench clung to my hair and clothing. I didn't like it, but something pulled me down the rock- and dust-covered path anyway.

"What in the hell?" I yelled as I flew forward and braced for the fall of my body and imminent crash to the ground with my hands. "Ouch! Shit." I twisted my body around and sat on my ass as I surveyed the damage to my hands. My wrists took the brunt of my weight and my palms stung like a motherfucker. I brushed my hands together to dislodge the pebbles that had embedded themselves in my skin.

I stood to brush off the dirt and stones that stuck to my bare legs, pissed that my leather skirt had some scratches on it. "Damn it." I spun to brush at the back of my skirt when I saw him. The vile, who must have been a recent drop, splayed across the path. How the fuck did I miss him? Not only was he a full-grown human but also, he was an exceptionally big one. He was lying on his side, and I looked from his head to his toes, taking in the hard ropes of muscle that moved with each one of his breaths.

One side of his back held a black-and-white skull and the other white wings with the tiniest pink heart nestled in the middle. I had to snort at the absurdity of it. But those thighs? Damn. My favorite part of a man. Besides his cock, of course.

I walked closer and let my gaze linger on his thighs a little longer. They were so muscular, so powerful-looking, that I just couldn't help myself. Even his damn calves were glorious slabs of muscle.

"Holy shit," I whispered because he was that stunning from the front. His face was as chiseled as his body. Strong, high cheekbones. Full lips that were parted just enough for breath to enter and escape. A sharp, masculine nose askew just enough to know that he had it broken a few times. His eyelashes? They were jealousy-inducing.

I walked closer and knelt, sitting back on my calves. I put my palms out and laid them on him—one on his head, the other on his chest. A powerful energy surge hit me, stronger than I remember any vile's energy blast, and his eyes flashed open to display the most amazing pair of green-dominated hazel eyes. He began to lift his arm and extend his hand toward me. I couldn't release my own hands to smack his away because I was fused to his body. This had never happened to me before, and I started to panic. Frantically, I pulled back, trying to break myself free, but I was well and truly stuck.

My heart raced and the ever-at-the-surface anxiety and panic started to wrap itself around me like a million tentacles. I shook from the energy and shook more from his hand getting closer. He was staring at me as his fingers came up, trembling but firm. His thumb swiped right under my nose and across the very top of my upper lip. His eyes flashed to the red that all viles possessed when I took their energy, only to bleed back to the hazel before he rolled to his knees and bowed before me. Another quick tug, and my hand separated from his body. I crawled as fast as I could away from him, noticing the blood on the hand he touched me with. With the back of my own hand, I swiped my nose and saw the bright red streak across it.

What the fuck?

I stood slowly, confused at my body's reaction and its sudden lack of strength. Fury at the situation took hold of me, and I straightened and stomped back toward him, my ankle buckling from stepping on the larger stones on the ground. Without any regard for what may happen, I placed both of my hands on the vile's head. Impulse control was not my strong suit. My eyes rolled back and flashes of white light stung every nerve in my head. I always knew the reason viles landed down here, I saw in quick pictures what they did. This one was different. This one was the whole story . . .

"Xavier, I'm pregnant. Shit! I don't want a baby! I'm too young still, and . . . and I'm not ready."

Shit. "Pregnant? You sure?"

"What the fuck, Xavier! Yes, I'm sure!"

I didn't know what to say. All I knew was that was my baby and I wanted it.

"And before you go assumin' I've been sleeping around, I haven't. I was home visiting my folks and then . . . and then I thought I just had a stomach virus!" Jenna sobbed.

I walked over and sat on the couch next to her. "It'll be okay. I'm not going anywhere." I didn't love her, and we had only slept together once, but I wasn't the type of man to leave her alone like this.

She turned to me and sniffled. "No, you don't understand. I don't want to be a mom."

The hair on my arms rose. "But I want this baby."

"Didn't you hear me? I'm not ready for this!" she yelled and cried, and I could barely think.

"What will it take for you to have this baby? I want him or her. I will take full responsibility." That made Jenna perk up.

"Anything?"

"Just tell me what you want, Jenna."

"Well, I . . . I don't want to work while I'm pregnant, but I won't be able to pay my bills."

"Okay. Done. I'll support you. You can come and stay with me." I would have done that anyway, so it wasn't a big deal.

"No. No way. I want my own place."

I scrubbed my hand down my face. "Fine. But you can't be with other guys while you are carrying this baby. Gotta make sure it has the best chance to be healthy."

She rolled her eyes. "Like, no oral from anyone either?"

Seriously? "Just, let's just say nothing for right now, okay?"

She nodded and then started twirling her fingers. "What else? C'mon, I can tell you want to say something."

"I want to go back to school. I don't want to be stuck in a shit job, and I want to move." Well, damn, that was a tall order with a lotta dollar signs.

I rubbed the back of my neck. "Done."

I knew without checking that my nosebleed returned. The hot blood seeped past my lips to my chin and dripped to the ground. It was the only feeling I had until I was thrown back into this vile's memories.

"Everything looks good, Jenna. You're doing real good with this baby. Real good." When she looked at me, it was one of the times in the last few

months that I saw how young she looked. She had gone out on a few dates, and we had become friends. She hadn't changed her mind about the baby and neither had I.

"So, um, here. You take this. I'll take a picture of it with my phone and decide if I'm gonna keep it or not."

She handed me the most recent ultrasound picture. It was the one showing us the baby girl she was carrying. I was grateful she did. I went home and stared at it. It was the first time I had cried in years.

Fuck! The blood . . . so much blood coming out of me. I was getting lightheaded. My body swayed so I grabbed his head tighter. And it burned. My hands burned.

"Hey, Jenna! It's just me. Door was unlocked. I got you some Chinese and that pecan ice cream you like." I placed the bags on the counter, froze, and then bolted toward the living room.

What I saw made me dizzy. Two masked men. One standing next to Jenna and the other holding her from behind and covering her mouth with his black glove. I went for my gun.

"Uh, uh, uh, Sergeant. None of that."

Fuck! How did they know me? I looked to Jenna, whose eyes were as wide and wild as they could be. Tears streaked down her face and fear shown on her features.

"Okay. All right. Let's all just relax. What do you want?" I held my hands out in front of me.

The laughter from the one not holding her was nothing less than sinister. "Well, you should have thought about that when you received a certain message about your investigation."

I broke out in a cold sweat. I'd been working on the investigation into that drug ring for months. Military people were involved, and a special unit had been put together to bring it down. "It's got nothin' to do with the girl. Let her go and take me. She can't hurt you."

I nodded toward Jenna and prayed they would let her go. The guy spoke again, placing his hands on his hips. "You're right, she can't hurt us."

Jenna took a breath, and I was hoping I could get her out of here without any violence or harm. And then my heart stopped.

"But she and that bundle of joy can definitely hurt you." He reared back and stuck his knife right in her swollen belly. She looked at me and opened her mouth in a silent cry. Tears flooded her face, and a second later, so much blood pooled from the belly where my daughter laid that I lurched forward and vomited. I went to draw my gun, but before I could, two more men I hadn't known were there grabbed me from behind. I screamed and fought, but there was nothing I could do to get out of their hold.

The man stabbed her again and again. All the strikes were to non-lethal spots. He didn't want this to be quick. Jenna was being held upright by the man behind her as the other man worked. A cut down her cheek, more slices to her stomach, her arms, her thighs, her chest . . .

She tried desperately to protect our daughter, but the damage was done with the first blow. I knew it had been.

The fire in my chest was overwhelming. I was watching my daughter and her mother die. Right in front of me. I wouldn't have felt the needle in my neck if they hadn't twisted it to make sure I felt the pain. My muscles were weak, the bright colors Jenna decorated with becoming grays and whites. Fuzzy and distant.

Her eyes met mine, and my name fell from her mouth in a low tone as the blood bubbled and distorted the word. No more sounds came out as her struggle ended. Cold, empty, lifeless eyes looked at me. I couldn't save them, but I knew I would make all these fuckers pay.

I saw how each one of the men involved paid for that heinous crime. Xavier had tracked them down and killed them all while carrying around the ultrasound picture of his daughter. He never let a drop of blood touch it, no matter how brutal the beating or murder was.

My body shot backward and hit the stone wall behind me so hard that it knocked the breath right out of me. Ash and black dirt came up in a cloud and surrounded me, filling my nostrils and sticking to the blood. I fell forward as my lungs burned and struggled to take in air as my eyes found Xavier, who was still on his hands and knees. His breathing was labored, kicking up small plumes of dirt with each exhale.

He was crying, which I added to my list of Crazy Town events surrounding this new vile. They didn't typically relive their memories with me, and by "didn't typically," I meant they never did. Ever.

Yet, he relived that whole experience.

I forced myself back to standing and made my way back over to him. He had suffered enough. "Rise, Xavier. It's time to go get some rest." When he rose, I looked him over and nodded. Why? I didn't know, but my head was bobbing slowly as I stood and wiped the blood from my face. Not much I could do about hiding the emotional state I was in from that entire experience.

I brought him to Isla's mountain and set him up in one of the smaller suites, tucked away and a bit higher in her home on the mountain so he was separated from the other viles. I sent her a message that he was there and she was to watch out for him, making it clear that he was not to be touched. Even by her.

I returned my phone to my back pocket and turned around. Xavier stood at ease, as I had seen military men and women do over the years.

"First thing's first," I announced as I went into the bathroom.

I came out with one of her oversized bath towels and handed it him, and he took it and then secured it around his waist. A damn shame, if you asked me, but fucking viles was my brother's MO, not mine. It didn't matter how hung or ripped the vile was.

"I know that is your version of at ease, but please sit. I'm sure you're confused, and I mean you no harm."

I mean him no harm?

What the fuck had gotten into me? They all needed to know I meant them harm. Yet, I couldn't force myself to say it to him any other way. Instead, I pulled out the quilted, comfortable bench from the vanity and motioned for him to sit. He complied.

I went and sat on the end of the bed facing him. "You must have a ton of questions. I'm giving you the opportunity now to ask."

Hazel eyes looked thoughtfully at me. Assessing. Making a plan. Strategizing.

I saw his decision as soon as he made it and right before he spoke. "Where am I?"

"You're in Hell."

His thoughtful nod was more a confirmation of what he already knew.

"Okay, then."

"That's it?"

"I know what I did, and I'd do it again."

Resolve and acceptance of punishment were not typical in my empire. If I gave other viles the chance to speak I bet almost all of them would beg for their lives and deny any wrongdoing. I couldn't give a rat's ass. I wasn't a therapist. They were here, period.

"I would have done the same."

"Will you torture me for it? Punish me for eternity?"

I placed my hands on my thighs and leaned forward just a bit. "Right now, I mean you no harm. None, Xavier. And none will come to you at anyone else's hands."

His jaw tightened, and he stared at me. There was that resolve rolling out of hazel eyes that I swore looked right through me.

He stood, and I flinched, but I stayed seated, wondering what this man was doing. If he tried to kill me, I'd turn him into the disgusting cretin the rest of the viles became over time. I'd speed up the process and make it hurt.

When he was close enough, he reached out his hand, his

thumb poking out of the soft fist. And he wiped at my nose. The blood streaked across the towel as he wiped it off his finger.

"Are you okay?"

What the what?

He wanted to know if I was okay? Did he realize who I was? I sat there. Stunned. The devil herself sat there like I was the shy, not-so-pretty girl who just got asked to dance by the hottest guy in school. I mentally slapped my own face.

"I'm . . . I'm fine. Thank you."

Thank you?

"I felt it, you know?"

Oh, for the love of chicken fried rice . . . did I grab his junk by accident? Shit.

Fake it 'til you make it. "You did?"

"Yes. Just now. Your turmoil. You don't know what to do next."

Uhhhhh. "Explain."

He went back to his chair. "You have a problem. It needs a solution. A nonviolent one if you can help it." He paused. "I'm not asking you to tell me. But do what you gotta do."

I must look like I sucked on a lemon as he continued.

"I'm sorry. Not my biz."

I relaxed my face, which was no small feat. "No, it isn't, but I'll allow you to continue." *Please continue!*

"Once you have your sitrep, sorry, the details or report on your current situation, that's when you need to get strategic. Seek out someone who hasn't crossed your radar yet. Someone close, or someone who used to be close. Someone with information and influence. Try to nip it in the bud if you don't want the attention that engaging with the hostile will bring you."

Right. Right. *Right!* Fucking brilliant. I was pretty confident I could keep Luce from Essalene, but I wasn't so sure I could keep her from trying to get to him. She was certainly my number one hostile. He got me thinking, though. I had other resources. Other people that could help in getting her to back off.

I stood, ready to go solve this problem. It wasn't herpes-level. I could totally get rid of it.

"Give me your hand, Xavier. Palm up."

He did, and with the very tip of my finger, I drew a circle. He hissed at the sting it produced on his cut-up skin. "If you need me. If anyone bothers you. If you are unsure. If a blond man with a bad attitude, control issues, and a penchant for violence gets on your shit? Touch this circle. It will alert me, and I will come to you. Let no one know you have this. Do you understand?"

Once I was sure he would be reasonably protected, I cleaned the blood from my face, found him actual men's clothes (I didn't know why Isla had them), and made sure to zap his gorgeous ass with a bit of my power before I headed home. There was no way I wanted him turning like the other viles. Not even a little bit.

He didn't belong here, that much was clear, but I didn't think I was allowed to return them once they came to me. That left me trying to decide what the hell I was going to do with him. What I knew was that my promise was solid. No harm was coming to him. I was protective of very few people. I felt a connection with Isla and Four, and my relationship with them was certainly different from the other viles. But what happened with Xavier had never, *ever* happened before with a vile.

There's a reason for everything.

CHAPTER EIGHT

I GOTTA SAY, XAVIER RATTLED me. Like, a canary sitting on its teeny tiny wire in a cage when some little shit comes up and thinks it'd be funny to shake the whole damn thing.

"Seek out someone who hasn't crossed your radar yet."

Xavier's words of wisdom twisted me up and centered me all at the same time.

There was a time I had sought someone out. The last time I'd done it, though, was when I went to plead to save my brother. I went to the big-man himself.

I clearly remember how hesitant I was as I entered the room, one glance around told me I was alone. Well, as alone as one could be when meeting with God himself. I sensed him the moment he arrived. The air stilled and a peaceful quiet blanketed the room. "Thank you for coming." He didn't respond. "Are you mad at me?"

"No, my dear. I thought we needed to talk. Your feelings have always affected me deeply. Sadness isn't the only one you have right now."

I sighed. "No, it isn't the only one."

I clasped my hands in front of me, twisting and twirling them. I took large, deliberate inhales of breath while hoping my heart rate would slow down. My head dropped, and my chin almost hit my chest as I shifted my feet, focusing on the way the movement created swirling wisps in the beautiful, cloudy floor. My nerves began to settle, and my pulse finally began to slow.

"Are you sure you're not mad at me?" I asked.

The soft rumble of laughter rolled through the warm, blue-sky-filled space around me. "I am not mad, my daughter. But I feel your anger at me."

"Is that why I'm not allowed to see you right now?"

His own deep breath swept across my body, lifting my hair from my shoulders. "Not seeing me is for you. I need you to speak freely. I need you to say your truth without the temptation to run into my arms for comfort, only to have the hug stop you from telling me what you need to."

Father and I had a special relationship. He loved everyone, but I was the one he held above all others, the one to whom he denied nothing. Our bond was amazingly unique. He created each family separately. Each archangel had their own family bloodline, and mine was quite strong—my brother, sister, and I were almost unmatched.

"Yes, I am mad."

"At me?"

I lowered my head farther in shame. It hung heavier than it ever had before. It wasn't as if I had never been upset with him, but this time it was more. It was real, and it weighed on me like a secret that was physically painful to bear.

The wind kicked up again and became stronger than before. A whisper of its strength swam through the air. A gust settled under my chin, forcing it up. My tears fell swiftly as the smile crept onto my lips. My dad was showing me love. Telling me in his small command of the wind not to be overcome by shame.

So, I straightened my shoulders and lifted my head. I would unload my burden because he asked me to.

"Yes, at you." Telling the truth usually felt great, but I was finding it hard to swallow, and the tears kept streaming down my face. "You didn't allow Lucifer the control he earned with his creations." I began to twist my fingers as my anger at the way my brother was dismissed came slithering into my mind. It may have seemed small to most, but my brother was truly hurt. "He deserved to make the decision, and that was taken away from him. You hurt him."

"Therefore, you hurt as well."

"Deeply." It was as if every ounce of pain my brother suffered hit me too.

"He's rebelling, Vahla."

"He's hurting."

"It's more than that."

"He needs you. Help him."

"My dear, I have tried."

I could hear the change in his voice. The somber tone. The lower pitch.

"Try harder, Father."

"Vahla—"

"No. No!" My feet moved quickly as my panic set in. I stomped around in circles, trying to get closer to him. My sobs pushed at my chest and back as the breaths I took became heavy. I heaved to get more air, but no matter what I did, it was not nearly enough to fill my lungs. "You can't give up on him! He's my brother!" I cried. "Please, Father. Please." I crashed to my knees and clasped my hands to my chest. He was breaking my heart. "Please. For me, Father."

I knew after I spoke those words, even though he was unseen, he had moved to me.

"He rebels with more than just his tantrums. He has burned all of the plants and flowers he created. He has fought the other angels and has threatened their families if they don't side with him against me. He has some who follow him because of decisions I have made. Lucifer has created his own army out of vengeance from his unhappiness with me."

I sat back on my heels. Even though my brother thought he was clever, I knew he was sneaking around with some of the others who didn't have the best reputations. I had hoped and prayed it was just a phase.

"I can talk to him. Make him see reason. I . . . I can bring him to speak to you and be with him to help. I . . ."

"My dear, sweet, loving daughter. I would do anything for you, but your brother has chosen. I can no longer interfere. He has been quite clear that any meeting with me will result in his trying to kill me. Michael is aware of this, and as the leading general of the archangels, Michael has a job to do. Lucifer will no longer be allowed to see me privately."

"But . . . but Lucifer is going to leave!" I screamed.

"Yes, he is."

My body shook uncontrollably as the fear and reality of it all set in. Then a warmth settled on my shoulders, offering me a modicum of comfort.

The kind of comfort only a father could give.

I wanted to embrace and reject his affection in equal measure.

"I've felt him shifting, Father. He has so much anger and hate. Lucifer no longer wants to belong here." There. I'd said it, and my heart shredded more with every word that fell from my lips.

A light squeeze to my shoulder told me he understood. Told me to continue and free myself of my worried thoughts. I inhaled as much air as my lungs would allow and blew it out slowly as I continued. "He can't be left alone. He hates the humans. He hates the angels. He may hate Heaven, but he hates Earth more. He talks and dreams of violence and killing. Even as he sleeps, he yells out his hatred."

"You want to go with him." His response was more comment than question. He never barged in on our thoughts— although, he easily could. With me, barging would never be necessary. He knew me too well.

"Yes and no," I said.

"Gabriel?"

My best friend. My soulmate. "Yes."

"All will be as it is meant to be."

"Does that mean it will be okay?"

His soft laughter wasn't meant to be humorous or dismissive of my question. Rather, it was that of a father knowing his daughter was trying to finagle the future out of him. "You know I cannot reveal those things, not even if I wanted to."

"Have faith?"

I sensed his smile at my words, and the warmth wrapped me in a hug that spoke of love and acceptance.

"I will miss you, but I know your heart will never be settled if you stay," he said.

I was silent for a long moment because he was right. My heart and head would never truly be settled, no matter where I decided to stay. It was the thought of Lucifer torturing the humans and having to watch from Heaven as he spread pain and death that I could have stopped.

"Do you truly believe in love, Vahla?"

"I do, Father."

"Then you and Gabriel will figure it out."

My Gabriel. I pictured him in my mind as I closed my eyes. My wet lashes tickling my cheeks. His black hair and beautiful, light blue eyes. The sparkle they held. His smile so straight and white and genuine. The sly grins only aimed at me. How that smile would slide from his mouth as he came closer to me and then place his soft full lips on mine. My body tensed, and my hands formed fists at the thought of leaving him.

"It won't be easy for me to leave," I whispered.

"It wouldn't be easy for you to stay."

"Tell me what to do, Father. Please." My eyes remained closed, but the tears poured from them anyway.

"I cannot."

"I know." I sighed, trying to contain my emotions. I pressed my lips together to hold the whimpers back as my mind and body started to unravel. "Will Lucifer and I change? Where will we go? Will we still have powers?"

"Both of you will always have what I gave you. But you, my dear, you will be granted more. Once you have those, I will never take them away."

"More what?"

"More powers, of course."

I drew a deep breath and forced myself to think. If I didn't make the decision then, I was afraid I never would. "I will protect him. I will protect all of them. Everyone I can." A knot formed in my stomach. Fear. I was making a promise I had no idea how to keep.

"I know you will." There was a short pause before he said, "Vahla?"

"Yes, Father?"

A deep breath swept over me in the form of a breeze. It carried Father's sadness and concern. It carried disappointment and pride. It carried the mixture of emotions for my brother and me. But it also carried resolve. "There will be changes in you. I cannot control them all, but I will have an angel in charge of watching out for you just in case."

So many questions crashed into my head. Who? Why? What will they do? Why can't it be him? Instead, I could only get out, "Will I see you again?"

"Not in the way you have always known, and I cannot promise you will return, but you will always be special to me."

"Oh."

"You are strong, Vahla."

"Strong enough?"

"Time will tell."

"I'm scared—terrified, really. But I am going with him. For him and for everyone else."

"It is decided then."

I raised my head slightly. "Yes."

"I will miss you every day, my daughter."

My head lowered as my sadness crashed over me. "I'll miss you, too." Sobs tore from my lips, and his arms came around me. Father couldn't deny me this, even when he thought he had to for my own good. He couldn't deny me my last hug in Heaven. My last hug from him.

He tightened his squeeze.

"I love you, Daddy."

His tears fell and crashed down, making the ground below us rumble and shake.

SINCE I'M ON A FUCKING MEMORY-LANE ROLLER COASTER, HERE you go! I'm in my one-piece footie pajamas with some strong black coffee and I'm baring my secrets to white-lined paper. So, why not just keep the tragedy-train rolling?

Wait. I'll be back as soon as I dump some Frangelico in my coffee . . .

Okay, I'm good.

I have tried for years to separate these two conversations, and I refuse to give Crazy Pants Mother Nature any credit for my finally being able to do it. Nope. Nope. Nope.

I can't just write about the conversation I had with God,

and since I promised myself I wouldn't rip any of these pages out, I'm going to have to write about what happened next.

Do I want to?

Fuck no.

What happened next is little more than a giant fuck you to the emotional pieces I want to salvage, to the last time I had the comfort of my father to myself. Alas, where there is good, there is bad and everything is about the balance, right?

"Vahla!" My name was being yelled on repeat. I closed my eyes and wiped at them furiously with my hands. I had just left my meeting with Father. My final goodbye still too fresh and raw for me to be able to hide my emotions. He called my name again, and I tried to pretend I didn't hear him.

I would know Gabriel's footsteps anywhere, even without hearing his voice. There wasn't an ounce of him I didn't know. "Vahla! Stop!"

I turned, trying to act as if nothing was wrong. Because, yeah, I was going to be the coward who snuck out one day. I knew it was only a matter of time until Luce left. I'd be ready to follow after him when he did. I couldn't bear a goodbye with Gabe. I feared I would cave if he begged me to stay. I couldn't stay. My brother would find a way to kill humans and wouldn't stop until he found a way to also kill the angels. "Oh, hey."

"Oh, hey? Didn't you hear me calling for you? Where have you been all day?"

"I'm sorry, I just zoned out."

He looked at me skeptically and rightly so. We knew each other. He knew I was off. He cupped my face in his hands. "My love, tell me what's wrong."

I melted against his hands, my eyes closing at the warmth and comfort of his touch. "I'm worried about Lucifer." Which was true.

I opened my eyes when he released a long, slow breath. "I know you are. I am, too." He laid his forehead against mine, and we stayed in our silence until the scraping of metal caused us to jump.

"What is that, Gabriel?"

The shouting and scraping became louder and longer in its piercing of the air. Thunderous roars and earthquake-force shaking under our feet made us both lose our balance.

"Stay here. I'm going to check that out."

I frantically grabbed at his arm. "No! Please don't leave me here. I'm scared to be alone."

He looked into my eyes and then off to the distance, his brain warring with what to do. Then he grabbed my hand tightly and started to move forward quickly. Glancing back at me, he said, "You hold on to me tightly, Vahla. If I tell you to do something, you do it. You understand me? I don't know what we are walking in to, and I need you to be safe."

I nodded.

He stopped moving and looked harder into my eyes. "Promise me. Say you promise."

"I . . . I promise."

His lips captured mine in a quick, hard kiss, and then we started to run, hand in hand.

Neither of us were prepared for what we saw.

Swords and screams and blood. So much blood. I covered my mouth to muffle my scream. Gabriel choked out, "No . . ." And then I spotted my brother in full battle armor, and he was fighting Michael.

They screamed at each other as they swung their swords and lifted their shields.

"I will get to him, Michael."

Michael's tears were so contradictory to the situation. He fought his lifelong friend, knowing that he may have to kill him. But Lucifer's eyes told a different story. His bloodthirsty look said he wanted to kill Michael and wouldn't hesitate to strike the final blow. I couldn't believe the horror unfolding in front of me.

"You will never get close, Lucifer. Stop this now so we don't kill you all!"

The band of friends my brother had considered family had become the army fighting against him. I needed him to stop. To see the light and come back to us. I dropped Gabriel's hand and started sprinting toward my brother. "Lucifer! Stop!" I screamed. Both Michael and my brother glanced my way. Then a strong arm came around my waist and carried me back. I kicked and flailed and screamed and punched. "Let. Go. Of. Me!"

Gabriel pinned me to the first tree we reached. His body pressed hard against mine as I fought to get free. "Please . . . I have to stop them . . . stop them!"

"Look at me, Vahla. Look. At. Me!" He grabbed my chin rougher than he ever had before, and I met his eyes. His sadness tore me apart. His fear mirrored my own. His determination to keep me away pissed me off. "I can't let you go over there."

I shook my head back and forth, and my hair glued itself to the sweat that had formed on my face. Gabe focused me again with a stern grasp of my chin.

"Stay. Here. I will go to them."

I calmed momentarily, until he said, "I'm sorry, Vahla."

Sorry? Sorry for which part? Then he was pressing me back against the far side of the tree so I couldn't see the fight and using his power to hold me in place before he took off running.

It took some time, more time than I would ever admit, but I managed to get free. As soon as I made it to the field, I became physically ill at the sight of the death and destruction around me. I clutched my stomach with both hands, unable to keep the vomit down. My heaving tore at my throat and burned me from the inside out. The blood rushing through me made every sound echo and magnify. I covered my ears with my hands, but it still gave me no relief.

Then I froze. Fear and shock too overwhelming. Michael had my brother pinned on his back with his boot laying on his chest. Gabriel stood with his shoulders hunched next to Michael. All three sets of eyes looked at me as my body stood petrified in its spot. I dropped to my knees, no longer being able to stand the crippling pain.

Lucifer's eyes met mine and he released the sword that he gripped in his hand. He lifted it slightly and reached it toward me. "It's okay, Vahla," he said resolutely with a forced, slight smile on his face.

Michael raised his sword, and then I was running. "No!" The thunder and lightning that crashed knocked us all down. Heaven's floor opened and swallowed my brother whole. I ran to the spot where he had been, and for the briefest moment, he was there, looking up at me and smiling. A true smile. He wasn't dead, but he was gone. The ground below me shook again and those who had followed on the side of my brother into this battle began to plummet as well. I watched them go, one by one. As each one disappeared, my vision started to blur. Darkness crept in at the sides of my eyes. Then everything went black.

I woke to the familiar scent of our sheets and the warmth of Gabriel's body next to mine. I took a deep inhale and sighed as I stretched, foggy for almost a full heartbeat before I was sitting up wide-eyed. "My brother!"

Gabe's arms came around me, trying to hold me back from getting up, but I was already halfway to the door. When I reached it, I yanked it open, and ran without looking back.

"Stop, Vahla! Stop!" he yelled behind me. He was getting closer.

I made it to the field where the fight had taken place and stopped short. There were no bodies, but there was a faint sheen of the blood that hadn't been fully washed away. My tears burned as they rolled down my face. I turned and saw Gabe. He had stopped running and stood there, just watching me. Both of us struggling for breath.

"How could you let this happen?"

"There was nothing I could do to stop it."

I continued to cry and swallowed past the lump in my throat. "I can't do this."

He took one step closer, still a good distance away from me. "Do what?"

I outstretched my arms, making sure the gesture encompassed everything. "This!"

Gabe took in the landscape. "Then let's leave here. Go live farther away from this spot."

He didn't understand, so I shook my head. Deep, brutal sadness sliced through me. "No, Gabriel."

"Don't say that, Vahla." I heard the desperation creep into his voice.

"I can't be here."

He started to move forward. "Then I'll go with you. Together. That's us. How we do things."

I stepped backward, retreating in time with his advance. "Not this time, Gabriel," I whispered, just barely enough for him to hear.

His roar at my response shook the ground, and he started to run toward me. Out of nowhere, Silas grabbed him and slowed his progress. Gabriel was much stronger, so he was dragging Silas forward with him.

"Don't do this, Vahla!" Gabe screamed to me, getting more traction and the upper hand on Silas. Then Michael appeared and held on to Gabe from behind. He was strong enough to hold Gabe back, and Gabe knew it. "You can't do this to me! To us!"

I kept retreating, kept shaking my head in denial, torturing myself with the face of my love filled with anguish and desperation. I already knew where my fate would take me. I just didn't plan on it being this way, this soon. I thought I would have more time. I wrapped my arms around my stomach, feeling the sickness of this moment engulfing me. "I'm sorry, Gabriel," I said and then I turned and ran.

"You said we were forever! That you'd love me forever! You said you'd never leave me! You promised in our vows!" They were the last words I heard as I ran and ran.

I couldn't think straight, and I could barely see where I was going. When a hand grabbed my arm and stopped me cold, for a second, I thought Gabe had broken free, but when I spun, it wasn't Gabriel. "Silas?"

He dragged me closer to him by both arms.

"You can't make me go back there! I won't! Let me go." I tried to pull myself free of his hold, but he was steadfast.

"Stop! Vahla, stop! I'm not here to take you back."

His words halted my movements. "You aren't?"

"I'm not," he said.

"Oh."

I expected him to let me go, to step back, but he didn't. He leaned closer with an unsettling smile on his lips. A glint in his green and blue mismatched eyes. "Why are you here, then?"

"For this." He growled the words a second before he crashed his lips onto mine. Momentarily stunned, I didn't move. Once I registered what was happening, I tore myself from his grip and, in doing so, ended up ripping one sleeve of my dress, making it fall on one side almost low enough to expose my breast, which was exactly where his eyes landed.

I put my hands up to cover myself and backed away. "Leave me alone, Silas."

He stalked forward with a sly grin. "Or what?"

"Or . . . or I will tell Gabriel," I said with a shaky voice.

He laughed. "Nice try." Then he was lunging at me, trying

to take another kiss and squeezing my body to the point of pain. "I've wanted you for far too long, Vahla. Without Gabe, you will be mine."

He was mad. Without Gabe? I was *bonded* to Gabe, which made that statement an implausibility. Even if the angel who held my very heart were not at my side, that fact wouldn't change. Then I lifted my knee between his legs, and he grunted and fell forward. He stumbled after me, reaching for me but finding nothing but air. I was already gone, running away from him. Already gathering the words on my tongue. Gathering the courage to say them.

"Now, Father!" Then I fell through the sky on my way to my brother.

It was one of the last days I remember being the sweet, loving, naïve angel I was born as. The smart, brave girl who was worthy of love. Fuck, was she worth loving. I wonder even while writing this if a girl like her would be friends with a girl like me.

Probably not.

CHAPTER NINE

Xavier's advice to find someone who was outside the usual suspects was all fine and dandy, but who?

Well, there was only one obvious answer.

I walked slowly up the paved driveway. It was rather long and gave me enough time to take a good look at the property, which was surprisingly impressive, almost as impressive as the house. The house was a sizeable colonial with a white exterior trimmed in black and had an arched window above the door. Through the window, I could see the sunlight glinting off a massive chandelier.

The door was a stunning oversized piece of mahogany wood with ornate black iron hinges that should have been gaudy, but fit somehow. The natural color of the large stones around the door was earthy and gave a warm, homey feeling. I was wholly impressed.

As I approached and lifted my hand to press the doorbell, voices and commotion rang out from the back. So, I headed back down the walkway and around to the backyard.

What I found was a man with his back to me, yelling at a small child, who was on the ground crying uncontrollably.

I would never wish anything bad on children, but adults were fair game. If Father Time had done something to make the child cry, there was no telling what kind of retribution I would inflict on him. Sure, sure, parents disciplining their children was fine, but—

He turned, glaring at me and stopping my thoughts cold. "What the fuck are you doing here?"

Wow, he looks old.

I smiled big and brightly in return. "I came to check on you."

His eyes narrowed. Suspicion and curiosity mixed with a little . . . hope? "You just came on your own? Or did Jizzy send you?"

Deer. In. Headlights.

I had that look on my face, and I knew it.

Did he just say Jizzy?

"Uh, who?"

His eyes narrowed, and his tone grew sharp. "My wife."

I had to force myself to breathe. I finally blinked. Did he say his wife's name was Jizzy? *Jizzy?*

I went to speak while trying to hold my laugh at the same time and ended up letting loose some type of snort. Spit flew out of my mouth and more liquid sprayed out of my nostrils. Her name was some form of the word jizz.

I just couldn't . . .

"Don't sneeze on my kids, Vahla. I don't need them getting sick so I can stay up all night. I don't sleep much as it is."

I looked around, counting the kids who were running around the backyard screaming their heads off. Seven.

Did the guy not have cable? Had he not heard of condoms? For crying out loud, no wonder he looked like shit.

"Like I said, why are you here?"

I looked away from the two older children who were busy building with sticks and met Aldorex's eyes. "I need to talk to you." He rolled his eyes. "Essalene needs help."

The eye roll transformed into a look of complete disgust. I did some deep breathing and tapped the tips of my fingers, in sets of four, on my outer leg. I wanted to be calm because his help could go a long way. Essalene was spiraling, which was something the man in front of me had experience with handling.

"Go away." Then this fucker turned his back on me. So naturally, I walked toward him.

"I'll go away as soon as we are done talking."

He mumbled some shit under his breath before he placed the baby from his arms into a seat that was surrounded by toys, balls, and things with wheels. I smiled as the baby's toes hit the ground, and he started to take off while swatting at his toys. The barking from Father *I'm-On-My-Period* Time, pulled me from enjoying watching that little guy.

"What the fuck, Vahla? I don't give a shit what's going on with that crazy bitch."

"Woah! You were married to her. You loved her once. Almost had a baby with her. Suffered a huge loss with her. Show some fucking respect."

The grumble and head-cocking dismissal of what I said lit my pissy, internal fire even more. I was trying hard to keep it under control, but it was only a matter of time before it was unleashed. Pun definitely intended.

"Used to. Get it? All you bitches are so thick in the head."

Do not smack him in front of the children. Do. Not.

"All us bitches? If we were all bitches, why did you get married to one?"

His jaw tightened, and his nostrils flared.

Fuck. Him.

"Where is the baby-mama anyway?" I asked glibly.

"Momma shoppin' 'gan!" I turned to the little squeaky voice to my right. A beautiful little girl with bright green eyes and silky, long black hair was smiling up at me. She was pinching the material on each side of her dress and twisting from side to side.

I crouched so we could be eye to eye, and her smile grew bigger. "Ooooh, shopping is fun!" I smiled back.

"Yup! Momma yuvs it!"

"Most girls do."

"She pwomise me a new, pitty dwess wif sprarkles!"

Oh my goodness. When this little girl clapped and jumped up and down, my smile could have cracked my face in two. "You are going to look beautiful in your new dress. I just know it."

She clasped her hands to her chest as she spoke. "Oh, fank you, miss!"

"You are very welcome." I straightened and patted her head. She ran off to play with her siblings. With a choice of six, it seemed like there were endless possibilities. I turned back to the Time Twat. "She's beautiful, Al. They all are."

Another repulsed grunt came out of him. "Yeah, until you have to live with them."

That was when I knew he was a lost cause. A dead end. And I knew without a shadow of a doubt, he would be nothing but toxic to an already mentally fragile Essalene. I shouldn't care. I really shouldn't. But this guy was shit personified, and I suddenly understood a bit of how Essalene ended up how she did. No one would stay sane having to deal with a guy like him.

I stepped closer so the children wouldn't hear us. "You know what, Aldorex? You are a miserable man. You have all this." I gestured widely to the entire area around us. "You've been blessed. Look around you." He rolled his eyes, not bothering to try to see what I saw. "Never mind." He was absolutely unworthy of all of this.

"Yeah, Vahla. Never mind. You done?"

I moved closer again and our noses were almost touching. His breath puffed out of his nose, and it gave tiny, warm punches to my face. I smiled. Not a happy one, a sinister one, but one I knew the kids would mistake for fun if they happened to look over at us. "You are so fucking ungrateful."

The fire stung my eyes, and I knew that special red glow had appeared in full force when his eyes opened unnaturally wide. My hands were like living torches, ready to burn and destroy at their touch.

He regained his composure enough to take a step back. "Look, I'm not sure what kind of trouble Essalene is in or why you thought I could help, but I can't and I won't. Coming here and losing your shit in front of my kids is low, even for you. You should leave. Now."

I let the fire die out and glared at him. "You're a dick. I have no idea what Essalene or your new wife"—I could not say her name because I would screw up how serious I was trying to be —"ever saw in you that made them decide to marry you." My eyes went back to normal and I took a small step back. His face pissed me off, so I kept going. "And with a name like Jizzy, I'm sure she'd have no problem getting plenty of male attention."

He stared at me and grunted, but that was it.

Our standoff was abruptly cut short by the cry of the baby in the seat with the wheels.

"Fuck!" He groaned.

"Watch your mouth. What's wrong with you?"

"You got kids, Vahla? Because if you don't, you should shut the fuck up."

I flinched but tried to hide it. No, I didn't have children, but it didn't mean I didn't have respect for them. "You chose to have them. And then have more of them. Do your fucking job. I highly suggest you take it more seriously because nothing is promised, Aldorex. You have no idea how much time you'll have with them."

"Is that a threat?"

"No. Just a reality check."

"Here's your reality check. Essalene is nuts. Full-on psycho. She lost a baby. So what? We never even met it! How she could be so attached was beyond me. No one cries that much. It was stupid. It was time to move on and she was all, 'you should understand me, we are the only two who know how this feels.' Blah, blah, blah. All I felt was relief."

I wanted to kill him.

"So, you see, Vahla, she and I were never going to work. The baby meant more than me. The loss was probably her fault, anyway."

For fuck's sake, I really was going to kill him. I have been bombarded by the most vicious crash of waves in the ocean and laughed in its face. This? Ten times worse. The complete and utterly horrifying shriek of that same child running around in that little seat on wheels, broke me from my murderous thoughts.

Aldorex rolled his eyes (shocker) and went to the baby. When he lifted him, I saw the massive weight to his diaper and the clear indication that what exploded in it was beginning to escape. Aldorex let out some noise and looked at his hand. When he tried to wipe it on his pant leg, one of the other children was too close and got it on their face, which caused that child to throw up, which caused the child next to that child to also throw up.

I smiled at him and turned to leave. Before I made my way clear of the house, that beautiful little black-haired green-eyed girl came up and hugged my leg.

"Will you come ova 'gan and pway wif me?"

I crouched to reply. "I will certainly try." She smiled. Oh, what a sweet smile she graced me with. "May I see your hand?"

"Kay!" Such enthusiasm she had for a stranger.

I moved her hand so her palm faced up. "Can you keep a secret?"

Her eyes opened wide, and her smile left. "Oh, yes. Momma says I'm good at that!"

"I knew you would be good at it. But this is just for us. You can't tell your momma or your dad, okay?"

"It's a secwet for just us?" she asked in an enthusiastic whisper.

"Yup. Can you do that?"

Her head nodded so emphatically that I thought it would pop right off her neck.

"I'm gonna draw this pretty circle. You're the only one who can see it because you have special eyes." Her nodding continued as she glanced so seriously between my eyes and her palm. "If you ever need me, not just to come over and play, but if you're scared or hurt or don't know what to do, all you have to do is press this circle and close your eyes. It will tell me that you need me. Like if you need help or if you're really, really sad or scared. Do you know what I mean?"

"Oh, yes, miss, I do. Like calling the police." She paused. "Or Batman!"

I laughed. This girl was too precious. "Yes, sweetie, just like that. But only if you need me, okay? I will try to get back to you one day so we can just play, but that circle is for emergencies."

She held her hand to her heart, and I smiled. And melted a bit.

"My name is Valencia."

"My name is Vahla."

"That's so pwetty. Just like yawr face!"

Yeah, I was a goner for this kid.

I leaned in and gave her a real hug before I left, and it was the purest hug I had given or received in a very long time.

She lifted her head from my shoulder with a squeal, kissed my cheek, and then ran like a bullet down the driveway. I stood and watched as her tiny legs ate up the space between her and the woman waiting with open arms. The smile on the woman's petite face was big and bright. Like, really, really bright. Her white hair hung straight to her shoulders, and everything about her had a glow to it.

When she went down on one knee to embrace the little girl, I saw the golden embers release from her fingertips. She was fae.

"G-ma! Come meet my new fwend!"

"Okay, sweet girl." She laughed as Valencia dragged her toward me. "Slow down, lovey." Her giggles carried through the air like a song.

Valencia was breathing hard and screeching with delight. "G-ma! This is Vahla. My fwend!" She hopped up and down.

I was smiling like a loon as I extended my hand, and the woman did the same. "Hello. I'm Alazia. Valencia's grandmother."

"Vahla, which I guess you already know."

When we shook, the very instant we connected, my hand lit up. Sparks of tiny flames shot through me and everything between my ears popped. She had the power to read me. I tried to pull my hand back, but Alazia grasped it quickly with both of hers.

"Any friend of Valencia's is a friend of mine." She gave me a serious look. "I don't like leaving the children alone when my daughter is out."

I was confused. "But their father is here."

She sighed. "Indeed." With her grip still strong, much stronger than one would think she could hold on with, she pressed our hands to her forehead. Finally releasing me, she took Valencia's hand and walked toward the house.

I stood still. A little stunned. A little awed. As crystal-clear thoughts and feelings she passed to me flooded my mind. Unease. Unhappiness. Fear. And it all revolved around Aldorex.

When this situation with Mother Nature was over, I'd be revisiting this family.

CHAPTER TEN

O NWARD AND UPWARD. WELL, DOWNWARD.
Aldorex was, and always would be, a selfish prick.
Useless.

So, I went back to Hell and monitored the feeds from the office in my home, scanning the vile pits and new arrivals. I had to find the right candidate to keep Luce sexually occupied, and that was surprisingly harder than I thought it would be.

A week went by, and I was halfway through the month I was given to get Luce away from Mother Nature. The urgency of stopping the storms kept me up at night because, if they continued, my brother would be blamed, whether he was there or not. So, not only was she throwing off the balance of life and causing chaos but she was also ignoring the complete injustice that would happen if she continued. And still, no one was ready to blame her. Well, except me, of course.

Then I had the issue of Lucifer going headfirst back into his role of general. You would think that would be a positive thing to ease some of my stress. That would be a big, fat negative. He barked out every order. Everything frustrated him, and everyone bothered him. I knew where his shit attitude was coming from, and his sexual frustration was enough to drive us both insane. Now his voice had become like nails on a chalkboard. Everything about him bothered me. His footsteps. His face. Him breathing. It made me want to stab myself in the ear.

Repeatedly.

If I didn't intervene, he was going topside and I knew it. The likelihood that Essalene would be the person he went looking for was way too high for my liking. My anxiety hummed at a constant level in my body. I didn't like it.

My head still throbbed from the energy absorption the day before, and I found it hard to focus on the screens. My forehead clunking on my desk startled me. I hadn't realized I dozed off.

Clearing the fuzz from my eyes, I saw a flash of red cross the upper right-hand monitor. "There she is."

I ran to my closet to dress and then grabbed the attraction potion Delayna made for me. She wove the spell into a small patch, no bigger than a tiny, square bandage. All I had to do was place it on the vile's body and it would activate. Delayna promised me that no one else but Luce would be attracted to it. The last thing I needed was a vile war over one female. I'd be tempted to kill them all.

I called Isla and had her line up the new female viles. My direction came under the guise of determining who would be allowed to work on my bridge or do projects in my home. I found the vile I dubbed "Red" and inconspicuously placed the patch on the middle of her back between her shoulder blades. Then I went to seek out my brother.

"Hey, V, what's up?" he asked as I came to a stop next to where he was overseeing construction. This bridge he was working on was my second favorite. I rarely let him near the one that was my baby. Only a select group of viles were allowed to work on mine, and they took their orders directly from me. In their previous lives, they had been architects, engineers, construction workers, and artists, but they all served a purpose for my bridge.

"How's the bridge coming along?" He crossed his arms over his chest and gave me a concerned look. "I'm fine, Luce. Really." I scanned the area. "Wow, they are working hard. That's a lot of progress in the last few days."

That seemed to pacify him, but only a bit. "Yeah, they are working hard. They really are assholes when you let them relax."

I laughed. "No shit. Listen, I'm going topside again for a few days. I need to do some check-ins at the Scarlet." I also needed to go to plan B. Or maybe I was on C?

"Everything okay?"

"Yeah, it's just office bullshit." I knew he was going stir-crazy, and my guess was that he was going to talk to me about going back up soon. "How about you? You doing okay?"

He looked to his feet.

"Yeah, I'm good." *Liar.* "I can always go up when you get back. I don't want to leave these fucks unattended."

"That's probably best. I'll be back soon." I hesitated just long enough to make my next words clear. "Oh, hey. I've been watching the feeds from the new vile training pits. I think we have three good prospects. In my opinion, they might have potential to move up and work under you."

To work under Luce, a vile would have to prove that they were smart, efficient, and could control a small group of other viles enough to reach the work goals of each week. They went through a specific training program to qualify. Lucifer was not a patient, give-you-another-chance kind of guy. Prospects were also comprised of a variety of trades. I wasn't beyond arm wrestling my brother to win a vile. It took him far too long to realize that I was stronger than him. He hated that fact and kept coming back for more. Dumbass.

"Three, huh? We aren't normally that lucky. The idiots nowadays are mostly useless," he said as he raised his eyebrows. He was right. Society had gone soft and, even though they didn't remember their time on Earth for very long after they got here, they usually lacked certain characteristics we prized. Work ethic being a big one.

"Don't you remember the good old days when the viles were actually soldiers? The training? The power? The wars?" His eyes went all distant as he reminisced. Such a longing shown in them. I should have told him I knew he was still training the viles as soldiers and that I knew the angels he took with him when he fell were his captains, but I pinched my lips closed. I still loathed some of them from our days in Heaven. Their bad influence and asshole attitudes had never changed. I just wasn't ready to have that conversation. One thing at a time.

"I'm serious, and I'm psyched because one of them is a woman." I looked at my tablet and pretended to review something. I knew he was staring, waiting for me to say more. I let him stew for a little longer.

He put himself directly in my line of sight and stepped closer.

"A woman? You already have a bunch of them as head viles. And you have Isla. Your badass little minion." He loved to mock Isla's power and my closeness to her.

I shrugged and continued to walk, not allowing myself to engage in his childish bullshit about her. "You have a problem with women in power positions?

"Not unless she's powerfully sucking my dick."

"Yeah, well I can tell you the one I spotted won't. Maybe that's why you shy away. Always having the fear of rejection looming over you." *Oh, I'm good.* "And we are stronger in many respects."

Poke the bear . . .

His face turned red with anger as he huffed. "Yeah, super strong. Because vaginas take a pounding? Gonna jump on that bandwagon?"

I froze. Counted to four . . . four times. I even stepped away to take a few cleansing breaths.

Nope. I had enough of him.

Thwak!

"Fuck! What the fuck?" he yelled.

Yeah, fuck was right. My freaking tablet lay shattered on the ground. I had hurled it straight at his head. Sure, he'd ducked, but not in time to avoid the full blow. My fingers itched to grab my whip, which was wrapped around my arm in a beautiful coil. Even resting in its state as a tattoo, it was calling to me to use it and strike my brother. It warmed and glowed, doing its best to tempt me, but I clenched my hands into tight fists and resisted. My brother knew as well as I did, that she was the only weapon that could cause him unbearable pain. It was not for everyday use.

"So easy to demean things when baby Lucifer feels threatened, huh? Mocking the power of the pussy? Well, well, well. Look who's doubting his abilities to train the opposite sex." I paused and then faked shock. "Huh!" I gasped. "Someone with a dick!" I laughed. "Never mind. I'll do a better job anyway."

He fisted his hands until they turned an angry shade of red and his knuckles looked painted white. Then he walked with hard steps to stand in front of me. "Challenge accepted, Vahla. I'll show you how dicks get it done." He breathed so hard through his nose that I thought a booger would fly out any second. "Where are they now?"

"Go see Isla. She will tell you."

Dicks get it done.

So cliché. What the fuck ever. I had to work so hard not to grin or bust out laughing. He was such an easy target to rile up. He took the bait and would soon be consumed by Red and the spell.

He stormed away muttering "bitch" before he slammed the door shut. Not sure if he meant me or the unknown female vile I'd just tossed into his lap, but after a second, I decided it didn't matter. I couldn't wait to unleash the sexy, flaming redhead with a past that would make the most popular and job-loving prostitute blush on him.

She had already been zapped with a bit of my power when I placed the magic patch on her, so she wouldn't turn into the disgusting thing the others did. At least, she wouldn't so long as she had my brother's attention. I'd also given her little scraps of leather masquerading as clothing and insinuated that bad things happened to viles who didn't win Luce's favor. If she did her job, it would put him in the clear of any connection to weather events. Then the cloud hoppers would never be able to make him responsible. I could put up legitimate arguments to keep them away from punishing him if they decided to throw blame around because of one of Essalene's emotional outbursts. They usually knew when we were topside. In some instances, it took them longer than others to know Luce or I were up there. I could forbid him to ever go topside again since the angels couldn't get down here, but my brother would never stay put. The challenge to get to the fight if the angels wanted one was too strong for him. And I had no way to stop him from going up. If it were only that easy, it would be case closed.

I continued with my work and headed back to my office. I sat at my desk, ready to go through invoices and orders when the slight burning hit me. I slapped at my ear, trying to relieve the prickly sizzle.

"Oh, no." I closed my eyes while I allowed my fingers to slowly tiptoe to the back of my ear. The singe was instant, although not painful. My pen dropped to the marble top of my desk, and my fingers continued to caress my mark. The more I rubbed, the more soothing the feeling became. I closed my eyes.

"Do you remember what they told us, Vahla?" His voice was nothing more than a whisper.

It was both simple and complicated to let him in.

"I do."

"They said we were foolish."

"Maybe they were right."

"I don't regret it."

I saw the day as clearly as I did when I lived it back then. Gabriel brought me into our house with a silk blindfold around my eyes. One of his strong arms wrapped around my waist, guiding me. When he slipped the soft material from my eyes, we were standing in front of the stone fireplace Gabe had built himself. Zephyr, a fellow seraphim, stood in his dress robes and tied the silken scarf around Gabriel's wrist before securing it around mine. Once all the words of love and promise had been said, he etched each of our names behind our ears.

The name Gabriel blazed to life as he became a part of my mind.

"Do you regret it, Vahla?"

Releasing the death-grip I had on my desk with my other hand, I let the answer fall from my lips with a sigh, *"No."*

I still had the warmth caressing my ear as silence settled in.

"How is everything going?" The question of the hour.

"Luce has agreed to stay away from her. But her storms continue."

"I know."

"What aren't you telling me?"

"She has to stop, Vahla. Michael is close to bringing a handful of his soldiers with him to resolve it."

I shuddered at the thought. *"But it's not him! She's doing it!"*

"You and I know that, but they don't want to hear it."

"He's been in Hell. He's had no contact with her. How it is that they don't see that?"

"He doesn't have to be with her to influence her. Your brother is well-known for his ability to whisper and influence thoughts well after he is out of someone's presence. And she is very. . . fragile."

"Do I still have time?"

"Yes. But not more than what I told you."

"Is there anything else you can do from your end? I have to go see her. What more can I do?"

"Trust me."

Immediately, the warmth was gone and so was Gabriel. I wondered what he meant by trust him. In a surprising way, which wasn't all that surprising, I knew I still did.

It was all the other fuckers in play who I didn't trust.

Time to take my issue up with the woman who's been sitting too safely in the eye of her own storms.

CHAPTER ELEVEN

A S I STOOD IN SALMON-CHALLIS National Forest, I could
still see and appreciate its beauty. So few knew the work,
love, and energy put into a place like this. Even the greatest
human appreciation of it couldn't comprehend what it took to
create it. The placement of each tree. Every blade of grass. The
River of No Return, which was the forest's pride and joy. The
celebration in Heaven after its creation was amazing.

It was the celebration of this very forest that unraveled
Lucifer, snapping the already thin rubber band that was holding
his anger and self-proclaimed dominance in check. He had
created several plants and flowers specific for each forest—one
of his many talents—and had been under the impression that
he would control which creations went to Earth and which ones
didn't. This forest signified the time that his control was taken
away. That humans were chosen over him because his plants
could heal them.

Luce and Ziza had worked for years together on making the
plants perfect. Ziza, the most beautiful angel I had ever seen,

was the love of my brother's life. Their connection was undeniable. Always near each other, they could not contain their vibrant smiles and the sweet gestures I caught glimpses of. The woman brought out a side of my brother that died the moment he was cast out of Heaven.

The last memory I have of them seeing each other was on the day he fought the angels, and she watched him fall out of the sky. I'd never seen another person or super as broken as Ziza looked when she saw Michael and Luce fighting.

How she would think about what my brother had become was heartbreaking to consider, and just the passing thought had a migraine blooming.

I tried to massage my temples to thwart its progress, but that task was about as guaranteed as, well, controlling the weather.

I pushed those thoughts aside and continued my trek through the woods, using a locator spell Delayna had given me, much like I'd done the last time I'd been in Idaho looking for Essalene.

When Essalene lost her baby, she had only been a month shy of her due date. That hit me far harder than I wanted or expected it to. Her marriage to Aldorex, whom everyone knew as Father Time, had ended, and between the two emotional blows, Essalene had spread disasters and famine. Her pain when I arrived hit me like a freight train at top speed. We talked, we walked, we went to a beautiful vineyard and she cried and cried until she couldn't cry anymore. But she did it. She found strength enough to stop killing when she realized she may also be hurting children. And I believed that was one of the big turning points for her healing to begin.

Although I hadn't developed a friendship past that time with her and we had been adversaries on different situations in many of the council meetings, I still thought I would be able to reason with her. That this meeting with me today would open her eyes to how wrong her relationship with my brother was. She was killing innocent people with her unnecessary storms. That knowledge was enough to work last time, and I hoped it worked this time.

Bratty? Yes. But totally effective if I had been able to say it. I would have loved to have seen her pretty little face become all scared and twisty at that threat. She needed to know without a shadow of a doubt that Luce was not her hope.

She greeted me at the door when I arrived, looking around to see if anyone else was with me.

That would be a *hell no.*

"Hello, Vahla. This is rather . . . unexpected."

"I would have called, but I've been so busy. And this is important, so I didn't want to wait."

"Oh, okay. Would you like some tea?" Her manners were good, but her tone was skeptical.

"Sure, that would be great. Thanks."

Essalene obviously loved floral patterns and lace. It was everywhere. A lace factory exploded in here, and she was definitely a floral pattern hoarder.

"See this lace?"

How could I miss it? It's larger than the woolly mammoths that used to walk Earth.

"Yes." I didn't mean to exaggerate the word.

"It's the only kind of it in the world. It took years for me to collect every sample and hours to sew it all together." She sighed as she looked to the lace that took up an entire wall. "Isn't it just divine?"

You know that whistle you do when you know the person speaking is looney? Yeah, I was doing that on a loop in my head. "It sure is. You must miss it when you're traveling."

"Oh, no. My house floats and lands where I tell the wind to take it."

"Oh. Well, that's very, ah, convenient."

She brought me to a large deck right outside of her back

door. The yard beyond us was clear, peaceful, and private. Trees lined the property, and the leaves rustled in the light breeze that kissed my skin. As they swayed, various amounts of sun would come through the openings it created and cast bright beams to the ground. Small animals walked throughout the yard and birds circled high above us.

She motioned to the table and chairs to our left. The long, wide planks of the outdoor table varied with the darker knotted sections of natural oak wood, and each chair had a different, uniquely carved design. I chose the chair etched with fish jumping from the water.

Then I cleared my throat. "How have you been?"

Be nice, be nice, be nice.

"I've hit a bit of a bump in the road, but all will be back to normal soon, I'm sure." Her gaze went out to the yard for a beat before she spoke again. "Oh! Let me go get the tea."

When she returned a short time later from the lace explosion, she set the tray with a delicate tea set on the table and took the seat with a large sun carved into it. "So, what brings you to my home, Vahla? Will your brother be joining us?"

I didn't think there was an easy way to bring this up. "Essalene, we need to talk. Just us."

"Hmm?" She mumbled as she took a sip of her tea.

"I need you to stop creating storms to get my brother's attention."

Her delicate china cup crashed to the table. "Why?"

"Well, the storms you're creating are hurting people. Killing them, in fact. I told you there could be negative consequences, and I'm here to ask you to please stop."

"No."

"No?"

"Absolutely not!"

Instead of getting any kind of decent response, like, oh, I

don't know, maybe some well-deserved fucking guilt from her, she went batshit crazy.

"You don't understand our love, Vahla!"

"Wait a second. Didn't you hear me?"

"Just because you are unloved, doesn't mean we all should be!"

Woah. "What the fuck? Did I say anything about love?"

"You don't understand our love!" she screamed.

"Um, what I *understand* is that people are dying. You are causing too many disasters."

"You don't care about death and dying. Don't you try to take some high road with me, you . . . you devil."

"Is that supposed to offend me?" Because, *hellooooo?*

She stood so fast she knocked her chair over and then pointed her long-ass fingernail at me. "You! You don't understand our love!"

And I'd had enough of her on repeat. One more time, and I would have happily poked my ears with a stick until I ruptured both eardrums. But then, to add to this pain, the sobbing started. The fucking sobbing! It was loud and obnoxious. There was blubbering and sniffing and hiccups of her trying to take in air. Crazy.

Crazy got crazier as birds started flying to her with tissues in their beaks. I was pretty sure those birds gave me the side-eye. That right there? That shit was creepy, but it wasn't as creepy as when more water added itself to the teapot and started to boil again even though it wasn't over any heat source. Like, water going to its death because she sang to it to get in the metal and burn? I mean . . . I know how it goes when you make tea. I love tea. I love mint tea, especially. But, shit, this was like watching someone burn their family with a smile on their face.

I was almost stunned stupid at the rate in which she went from politely serving tea to acting like a rabid animal to crying like an unhinged mess. My hell was normal compared to her life.

She needed meds. *Badly*.

"Essalene," I repeated her name a few times before I just started yelling. "Essalene! Calm the fuck down."

"No! You can't tell me that Lucifer and I can't love each other. Love is what makes everything beautiful. My love for him makes me tingle from my—"

"Shut up! Eww! I don't give a shit about your tingles. You are *killing* people, Essalene. Killing. Them. They are innocent. Since when do I care more about humans than you do?"

She turned her head around like the freaking exorcist. Her eyes literally had become outlined in ice that glimmered around her eyes like eyeliner. Crazy withstanding, I was going to head to Sephora as soon as I could to see if I could make that look happen for myself. Without the psycho part, of course.

"You pretend you care about these things. You hate them! My baby needs my strength," she responded.

Um, what?

"What baby?" If my brother knocked her up, I was going to . . .

She rolled her ice-lined eyes. "Lucifer, you stupid woman."

"That's so fucking gross on so many levels." I should have recorded this conversation. Maybe when she calmed down, listening to it would have made her see my point.

"Our love is beautiful," she declared as she flung that long, strawberry-blonde hair over her shoulder.

Okay, maybe she wouldn't see it no matter what I did. I went to grab my teacup and then paused before dropping my hand. There was no way I could trust she didn't drug it.

"I've even denied the gorgeous, elusive Gabriel for your brother." Her eyes went all spacey at Gabriel's name, and she started twisting her hair.

What the what?

One . . . two . . . three . . . four . . . breathe.

"I'm sorry? I don't follow what Gabriel has to do with this." I shook with the sudden burst of anger that made me tremble from head to toe.

She sighed and hummed. "Well, he came to see me not too long ago. Long story short, he told me I deserved a great man. He told me I was beautiful."

Holy shit.

My stomach clenched at her words, and my mouth watered from the bile starting to rise. Had that been Gabriel's plan all along? Was it total bullshit that the angels would be coming for my brother if he didn't break things off with Mother Nature? Was it that he was interested in her and wanted my brother out of his way?

I was going to be sick.

Then red flashed across my eyes.

I'll be sick later.

"So, you fucked him when he came to see you?" I asked. Teeth clenched so hard I was shocked they didn't shatter into pieces.

"Oh." She sounded surprised and clutched at her neck, completely oblivious to the threat I posed to her. "I'm not that easy, Vahla. He would have to work to get me. But my heart is with someone else right now."

Okay. So, was she saying Gabe *wanted* to fuck her but she had turned him down?

I know I should've been concentrating on getting her away from my brother, but I lost all semblance of reason once she brought up Gabe. The constant loop had become "Gabe wants to fuck Essalene."

The heat in my body grew every second with the anger and betrayal I felt. My skin was literally burning.

He said trust him. I never had a reason in the past not to, so this leap of faith was gonna hurt. It was something I had to relearn and nothing in life promised to be easy.

I stood to give her my final warning before I tried to kill her. "You will stay away from Lucifer and you will knock off this nonsense with trying to get his attention with the storms. That's the way it's going to be, Essalene. If you don't, you and I will have a very, very big problem."

She started to laugh. A soft giggle as she shook her head. "How wrong you are, Vahla. I will not be taking your warning. Your brother will never stay away from me. He loves me too." She stepped around the wooden, oval table between us, her eyes icing over even more, causing me to blink from their brightness and the sharp cold stinging my face. "He is addicted to me *and* my storms. There is nothing you can do about it."

The heat in my body rose, and I could feel the swell of fire in my eyes. It would be a cold day in Hell when I allowed her to believe she had more power or influence than I did.

The heat continued to grow as I got closer to the bitch, and I watched closely as water drops started forming and finally flowed down her cheeks. Yeah, she was ice, but I was fire. Literally, I had fire that poured waves of heat into the air.

I laughed back at her. "We'll see about that."

Her own smile fell as she realized I was not afraid of her.

"So, you won't stop the unnecessary storms?"

"Why would I? They will bring him back to me, no matter what you try to do. I'm in love with him. You'll see." She wiped at her face and edged a bit closer to me. "I'll tell Gabriel the same thing when he comes back to see me."

And . . . I lost it. Maybe I was going to trust him, but no way could I control all my anger.

I reached back with my fist fully formed and punched her in her stomach. She doubled over and began heaving. I leaned down, nice and close to her ear. "You will be the one to see,

Essalene. My brother is already fucking someone else. Someone I personally handpicked for him."

I walked toward the exit of the woods. The wind whipped around me and the branches of the trees strained to stay attached. Some began to crack and crash to the ground and gray, angry storm clouds began to swirl overhead. "This isn't the end, Vahla," she said between coughs and clenched teeth.

"Whatever. Bring it on, bitch. Whenever you can actually get back up, that is."

I smiled at her as she threw up on the grass. And wouldn't you know it? She threw up in the colors of the rainbow.

I truly hated that woman.

I STOMPED INTO THE FOREST AND KICKED AT THE GRASS AND debris from the trees. Having a hard time settling my own breathing pattern, I stopped and bent forward, hugging my right hand close to my body. My thumb was *in* my fist instead of *outside* of it when I hit her, and I hoped to Heaven it wasn't broken. I didn't have the time or energy to deal with having to magically freaking repair bones at the moment. I knew how to throw a punch, and I had been so crazed I didn't even make my fist correctly!

Okay, fine, I was pissed that I couldn't control my anger. That was *not* how that meeting was supposed to go! Shit. I negotiated million-dollar deals and ran an entire empire in an underworld full of problematic, unruly, selfish viles and still got the job done. How was it possible that I couldn't get her to understand that her killing people was bad?

Grrrrr.

I needed to go back and explain it again to her. Tell her that Luce could be in trouble if she didn't stop. Maybe that would get through to her.

Even as I thought it, I knew it wouldn't work. The look in her eyes was crazed. Off. Distant. Her rationale nonexistent. She totally believed that she was powerful enough to get away with whatever she wanted. That the rules didn't apply to her.

Kids. Maybe if I just went about this the same way I went about it before, it would work. I told her she was killing innocents, but I never specifically brought kids into the mix.

I had to try.

As I retraced my steps and began to run over my speech with all its bullet points in my head, my feet faltered, and I had to lean on another tree for support.

The sickness and roiling of my stomach returned as I watched Gabriel climb the stairs to Essalene's home. She opened the door and flung herself into his arms for a hug. I couldn't bear to watch what he would do in return. As tears burned my eyes and blurred my vision, I clasped my hands and teleported myself back to the little town I had landed in when I first got to Idaho.

Fucking trust. It sucked hairy balls.

CHAPTER
TWELVE

THERE IT WAS. THE BAR I saw when I first landed here. I needed some drinks and didn't care whether they had top-shelf liquor or not. Desperate times called for desperate measures. The sickness that hit me at seeing Gabe had turned quickly to hot, venomous streaks of red rage, and it wasn't letting up.

I trusted him. What a fucking joke. I took a minute to gather myself. Long, deep inhales and exhales in sets of four. I flipped my hair and applied my lip gloss. I was ready to remind myself that I was just fine. Just. Fine.

The bar itself was set back from the road and surrounded by a few large trees that flanked it on the sides and the back. People were lingering on the outside porch, laughing and drinking and swaying to the music. Flannel. Plaid and flannel. Jeans and boots. A lot of it on both the men and women.

My white T-shirt proudly displayed its homage to The Rolling Stones with the large red lips and tongue. The unlined black bra I wore underneath was suitable with its lift. My dark blue skinny jeans hugged me just right. But these boots? Fuck I loved them. Who knew that my stiletto cowboy boots would come in handy on this trip? I sure as shit didn't. But the black, rhinestone-studded, silver-tipped heeled babies were mission perfect.

My boot clicked on the first step, causing everyone on the porch to still. I was not shocked and surprisingly even less self-conscious than I had ever been. I still struggled with self-esteem issues. I didn't know anyone totally immune to it, human or supernatural, and what I had just witnessed was threatening to crush me into oblivion.

I walked in and went straight to the middle of the large mahogany bar and ordered a scotch, kindly mentioning that the bartender should stay close. Staying close turned into him just bringing the bottle over and placing it next to my glass. I nodded my thanks as I grabbed the bottle, left a hefty wad of cash for him, and headed for the dartboard.

"Next," I called out. Got a few side-eyes, but I didn't fucking care. None of them would remember me, so they could size me up and judge me all they wanted. My sole mission was to drink myself stupid, go home, and pass out.

My turn to play finally came, and I whooped the tall, skinny dude. Then I whooped the short, chubby dude. Then the farm-girl prom-queen thought she'd be cute and try to beat me. She flipped her blonde hair and giggled like the silly little girl she was, which made me want to hit her over the head with my bottle. Since that would have been a huge waste of decent booze, I settled for beating her. At darts, not physically.

Prom queen scrunched her face after the loss and went to go find sympathy. "Anyone else?" I looked around as I flung a dart at the board without looking.

"Woah, girl!"

I shifted my eyes to the sound of the shouter, who ended up being a very big, very good-looking man. Well, large farms did mean large men. This one had to be very popular with the ladies.

His chair thunked hard against the wooden floor as our eyes met. Without any finesse, he stood, not caring that he had abandoned his friends and knocked over almost all of their drinks.

And no. I didn't use some Jedi mind trick to lure him to me. Even this girl liked a reminder every so often that she still had it. Had it all on her own. No magic mojo. No flowy fucking skirts. Just straight-up sex appeal.

The closer he got, the more the floor beneath my boots rumbled. The approach was not smooth, but it wasn't sloppy either.

He came to a stop in front of me and looked down because he was just that much taller than I was. His dark brown hair was sexy messy, and his green eyes sparkled. He sported that lumberjack look with a thick beard, but not too long. Just right.

"You are one damn beautiful woman." His voice was deep, thick with reverberation in his chest. His voice alone made him sound big, strong, and absolutely fuckable. Not my goal tonight, but I sure as shit wasn't going to look a gift-cock in the mouth.

I smiled, enjoying his directness. "Thank you."

"I've never seen you here before."

My smile became a grin.

Yeah. And you won't remember you did after this either.

"First time. Just passing through."

"Got business here?" He inched closer, as if something were physically pulling him to me. Hmmm, he smelled good.

"Does it matter?" I responded. No smile and no grin as I sipped my scotch.

"Nope. You been running that board?"

"Yup."

"Beatin' the little guys."

"You scared, cowboy?"

He snorted. "Let's do this."

Big man went to clear the board. He was writing for an awfully long time. No complaints from me as I watched his wide shoulders and arms move, begging to rip through the solid forest-green, long-sleeve shirt he was wearing. When he turned and came my way, he smiled and nodded toward what he'd written.

Your going to loose.

"Ummm, are you sure that's what you mean?" I wanted to go over and correct it so badly.

"Yup."

Okay, then.

Big man came up to me and shook my hand. "The best man may win."

Oh, for fuck's sake.

I won. Obviously. I let him get close in points so as not to embarrass him. Mostly, I just enjoyed watching his muscles choke the life out of his shirt and his ass fight like a heavyweight champ to get out of his jeans. But it was the bulge I kept going back to. Have mercy. That sucker was not being contained properly by underwear, if he were even wearing any. It dropped so far past the zipper that I found myself staring. So did he.

"Whatcha looking at?"

"Your dick."

"You kiss yo' momma with that mouth?"

That phrase was so dumb.

"No. I suck dicks with this mouth. Please stop talking. You're so much hotter with your mouth shut." And for the love of Guns N' Roses, please brush up on your grammar.

He laughed low and shook his head. Looking from my feet slowly up to my eyes, he leaned in and placed his hands on either side of the stool I was on, caging me in. "Let's go."

I took my scotch-free hand, placed it on his hip, and nodded. I didn't come here for this, but I wasn't going to deny myself either. Why would I? All I kept imagining was Gabe balls deep in someone else. Darkness kept creeping into my vision. I'd been fighting it off with scotch and darts, trying not to drown as anguish crashed over me.

I knew I was better than this, and I knew being pissed that Gabe was probably fucking Essalene made me the worst kind of hypocrite, but I wasn't seeing rational right then. Betrayal swam like sludge in my veins while air was about as easy to fill my lungs with as quicksand would be. Gabriel had kicked me back to square one with a sharp, hot knife lodged in my chest.

I came back to my current situation with the sound of a muffled growl. Big man took hold of my waist, grabbed my scotch with his free hand, and placed it on the bar. Then he grabbed my hand and led me out. The pulse in his wrist was wild. I knew exactly where that blood was headed.

A short ride in his big Ram truck brought us to his house. Although it was dark outside, the rustic red color of the farmhouse was visible with the porch lights glowing brightly through the darkness.

He came around to my side of the truck to offer me his hand, and I took it. I couldn't wait to have them on my naked skin. My body was pulsing with anticipation, and I refused to let any regret in. Instead, I concentrated on his warm, rough palm. Working hands. It made me rub my thighs together in need as we walked up the porch steps. Any feelings of doubt, anger, or sadness were sure to be gone once we got down to business. I was counting on it.

"You don't use locks around here?" I asked, a bit surprised that he hadn't bothered with a key before he opened the door.

"Not needed," Big man lumberjack said as he kicked the door closed behind us.

I would have replied, but why would I bother when I had much more interesting things to focus on—like his ass as he led me up the stairs leading to the second floor. I feared those globes would suffer oxygen deprivation from that tight denim. They needed to come off. Stat.

His room was large and wholly forgettable, but I did note how soft his bed was as he pushed me back onto it before crawling up my body until we were face to face. "Fuck, you're gorgeous," he said.

I placed my hands on his cheeks and caressed the smooth, short layer of hair from his beard. Then I trailed down his neck, over his big, broad shoulders, and down his arms. When they reached the bed, I spread my arms out. "You'll have to be more specific about which parts are gorgeous." I smiled.

He leaned back and started with his hands at my feet, sliding up to the backs of my legs and then pausing to massage my ass. There was a hum of approval that slipped from him as his hands kept active. They shifted and went back down to my knees and up again, tracing the insides of my thighs this time. I closed my eyes and reveled in his touch. His palms were hot against my jeans and my warming skin. When he reached the apex of my thighs, I started to move. I was hot, wet, and so ready to feel him put his muscles to work.

"Yeah. Rub me, sweetheart. Give me a preview."

I sighed and rolled my hips again, growing wetter with each thrust. My heart beat faster, my hands dove under his shirt, and my fingers found the warm skin underneath. This earned me a deep groan from him as he pressed his hips against my thigh. I ran my nails lightly over his skin again and grinned.

Yes, I had definitely chosen well by leaving with him.

"I can't wait to sink my teeth into you." He licked my neck. "And my cock."

Yup, I wanted that. Almost frantically, I pulled on his shirt again, this time pulling it up and over his head so I could see his naked torso.

As the bundle of fabric hit the floor, the door to his

bedroom opened—well, more like splintered to pieces because someone had just barreled through it.

Big man turned and slid from the bed, squaring off against our guest.

Hmmm. A guest to help me lose myself. That could be fun . . .

"Who the fuck are you?" It was all the big man said before his body locked up.

As if in a trance, he moved to the open door that led to a bathroom. I watched in shock as he walked right in and lowered himself into the tub. Leaning his head back with a thud and a sigh, his eyes closed and he began to snore.

My wide eyes tracked from the sleeping man I had been about to fuck to the intruder who had far bigger balls than I remembered if he thought *this* was acceptable fucking behavior. Who gave him the right to invade my space? Wasn't he just busy, oh, I don't know, getting ready to whip it out for Mother Nature? Fuck him.

Anger soaked the air between us. The defiance in our stares more potent than a slap to the face. His chest struggled to rise and fall, almost as if a cinder block of supernatural proportion rested on it. His face, neck, and ears were stained red with fury. My whole body zapped and stung as if it were being attacked by an electrical current. Somewhere between the zaps zinging around in my brain, my mouth caught up with my rage.

"What the fu—"

Before it could even leave my mouth, he was on me. Arms tight, transporting us so disgustingly fast that I felt nauseous. I swear that if I didn't end up on a warm beach after this, I'd hate him even more than I did at that moment.

CHAPTER
THIRTEEN

"**Y**OU ASSHOLE!" I SCREAMED AS I wobbled on shaky legs. When I transported of my own choice, I was always fine. Right then? I was so far from fine I was contemplating vomiting on Gabe. Then I looked around. Nope. Not on a fucking beach. Was that? Yup. Snow. I saw it outside the window of the room I was in. I bobbled around a little more like a drunk and then finally leaned against him to steady myself. I looked to my right and realized we were in a log home. One I was ready to burn to the ground if I could get my bearings.

"It'll pass," his voice said harshly in my ear.

"Fuck you." I lashed out with the strongest voice I could gather.

His laugh was not kind. "I could tell that was your plan with that guy."

Fuck. Him. "Yeah. Obviously." He tightened his arms around me. "Let me go."

"No," he said.

I struggled to free myself. I was in no position to win, and he would always be stronger than I was. He lowered his head to my right ear and whispered, "Show me."

That command became my sole focus. My body tensed as his relaxed, and his hands swept down my back in a soothing glide before cupping my ass and pulling my body tight against his.

"Gabriel." I said his name on a breath. Nothing centered me more than his reminder of our bond—the only thing able to freeze the anger and jealousy coursing through me.

His lips pressed achingly soft to my ear. "Show me, Vahla."

With a deep sigh, I tilted my head to expose more of my neck to him, and he placed a few featherlight kisses over the script inked into the delicate skin on the back of my ear. I couldn't stop the breath it released from me or the roll of shivers that tingled over my flesh.

Most would have said it was a reckless thing to do, to mark ourselves, knowing it would never fade. Saying we were too young and that we defamed our bodies. And we couldn't have disagreed with them more. Our marks were carved into our bodies with a feather from each of our wings. It was the highest form of commitment after we took our vows. Unique in so many ways, including being able to communicate and find each other. Once it was done, our embraces were more powerful, more intimate. I still didn't regret having his name scripted down the back of my right ear. Just as mine was down his left.

"Show me, Gabriel." It was spoken in the same soft tone he had used. Almost a whisper, as if both of us were afraid that speaking too loudly would break the moment, shatter the intimacy he had stolen me away to. My request back to him as automatic as breathing, even after all this time.

He leaned his head down and to the right, pressing his right cheek to my breastbone, and my fingers threaded through his hair. It was just as smooth and full as it had ever been, the blue-black strands like shadows against my skin.

The soft glow of my name looked like the moon reflecting on water. The light rising to create a silver, magical dusting. The warmth from it penetrated my lips as I kissed it.

"Why were you there, Vahla?" he asked, and it was a bullet to the protective bubble surrounding us. Everything from the last few hours came flooding back with supersonic speed. It crashed so hard and so deep into my bones that it threatened to shatter me outright.

Damn him.

I pushed him off me. "As usual, it's none of your business."

"Everything is my business."

I laughed. "Oh, yes. Everything and everyone. All of equal importance."

He reached for my hand. I pulled away. "Not everything is equal for me, and you know it. Tell me what you were doing there."

"What I was doing there? What the fuck were *you* doing there? How did you find me?"

"I told you to trust me. I couldn't sit and do nothing, so I went and met with Essalene. When I arrived, she told me you had just left. You know I can follow our mark anywhere."

I saw red—flashing, bright streaks of it that threatened to spark into an inferno. "Never mind. I know what you were doing there." I needed to get out of there. Too much emotion swirling in me was throwing me into a panic.

"Yeah? Then you know I came for answers." He stood straighter and stared at me harder. "Don't even think about going anywhere. I have my own powers, and you would be wise to remember that. I'm not in a state of mind to be merciful."

I snorted. "I'm not scared of you." Even though I knew his power trumped mine. I'd just be wasting my time trying to escape. "By all means, go back and get those answers from the girl you came to see."

He looked as if he'd sucked on a lemon and reared his head back. "You should never be afraid of me. Never." I should care that I offended him. Right then, I cared about that as much as I cared about the overpopulation of deer in the northeast. Which was to say I didn't care at all. "What are you talking about?"

All I could picture was her and her flowing hair and silky skirts wrapped around him. Both of them smiling with birds flying around their heads and singing some beautiful song. I shut my eyes tightly, trying to picture the birds shitting on them since I couldn't get the thought of them fucking out of my mind. In my red rage, I was also imagining killing those fucking birds.

Focus, damn it! I wanted to get out of there. Call bullshit on his promise that I couldn't. That was what I wanted to do. Run. Teleport. So, I bolted for what looked like a door to distract him from the vibes of my pre-teleport. He blocked me with an outstretched arm and a disapproving glower. "Not happening. I'll ask you again. What are you talking about?"

I changed my mind. I didn't want the answers to my questions anymore. Didn't want to know what they were talking about, how he knew exactly where to find her, why she was so comfortable throwing herself into his arms, and why the fuck he wrapped his arms around her in return. Nope. Didn't want to know. He went to meet with her. He used my love for my brother against me. He and Ms. Nutty Nimbus could have each other. Fuck him and fuck her.

Whatever color came after burning, raging red, it was all around me. "Essalene. I was talking about Essalene. You know, the psychopath you think is beautiful? What was it that you said to her?" I paused long enough to shove down the homicidal tidal wave swelling inside me. "That anyone would be lucky to have her?" My heart was going to explode from my fury. "I saw you. I saw you go up her stairs and hug like long-lost lovers."

He laughed. He fucking laughed.

So I slapped him. Hard.

He smiled and caught my wrist before I could strike another blow.

"She is a beautiful woman. One who needs a compliment every so often."

"Yeah? I guess your *compliment* will be when you finally get to fuck her."

He laughed again.

Asshole!

I struggled in his hold, trying hard to free myself. "Get. Off. Me," I gritted out from between my locked teeth.

He just grabbed my chin and forced me to look at him. "There are so many beautiful people, Vahla. But only one more beautiful than all."

I tried to move his hand. I swore I would have bitten him if I could have. He better hope I didn't get the chance. "Fine. So, she is the most beautiful you've ever seen. Go get her. Let go of me!"

His mouth slammed into mine before the breath of my yell left. He swallowed the air and the anger and the hurt. And, although I knew I shouldn't, I kissed him back. I was such a glutton for punishment. Slowly, so slowly it settled the blood in my veins to his rhythm. He wound the kiss down until he was able to speak through the wing-soft kisses. "You. You stupid, fiery woman."

Then he was claiming my lips again, his tongue dancing with mine before he retreated. "You jealous, beautiful woman."

I did pull away then because even though a part of me registered the sweet smile on his full lips and the way the bonding mark on my ear warmed with affection, another part of me was being obstinate. "Jealous! That's rich. You want to fuck her. You used Lucifer being in trouble as an excuse, and you used me to separate them so you could have her!"

Gabe stood straight and totally still. He didn't blink. He didn't move. I didn't even think he was breathing.

"What did you say?" The pulse in his neck was pounding hard and fast. I wasn't sure his skin could contain it much longer. "I swear to you, Vahla Ray, you will answer me or there will be consequences. What. Did. You. Say?"

Oh. Shit. He used my full name. The last name he gave me in the privacy of our home as we took our vows. I hadn't heard it in so long that the rhythm of it threatened to pull me into another time. I could almost feel the silken scarf sliding and hugging my wrist as I was bound to him for our ceremony.

I wasn't often shaken by discomfort or fear, but right then, I had a healthy mixture of both settling into my gut. "I said you used me. I know you want her," I said, my voice far stronger than the conviction behind the words. I knew it and so did Gabe.

His hand came up to cup the side of my face, and I whimpered. I didn't understand why he was here doing this, making me feel things I didn't want to feel and touching me in ways I'd spent thousands of years dreaming about, when he wanted to be with her. Maybe I had hurt him so deeply that this was the only way he thought he could possibly punish me enough. My comeuppance. I firmly believed everyone was due for theirs at some point. I had liked that thought up until that moment. My thoughts were right there on my expression, and the answering smile he gave me was full of a sad understanding.

My soul, he was beautiful.

Gabe leaned forward and left a small kiss at the corner of my lips, but I didn't respond.

"Stop . . ."

His hand didn't drop, and he didn't back away as he whispered, "No more, Vahla."

My smile became wide right before I bit down on his palm.

"Ow, fuck!" He released me and backed away, but I followed him, wanting to hurt him in the same way he was hurting me.

"Go fuck yourself! I hate you. I hate this!" I pushed him, and he flew back into the wall so hard it caved in. He barely even flinched before he was back in my face.

"Say it again." He snarled the words.

"Go. Fuck. Yourself."

He pressed his forehead to mine too fast and pressed hard. I couldn't stop him from forcing me backward. I banged into the wall behind me, twin to the one currently sporting Gabe's outline.

"Okay, baby. You got it." His words were choppy as he undid his belt and frantically removed his pants. I jumped at the sound of his belt hitting the floor.

What? Got what?

I watched as his eyes rolled and then focused back on me. I heard a wet slap. And then another. I tilted my head down.

Gabriel had his pants undone and his cock out. His hands wrapped around it, stroking harder and harder with each pull. It turned the velvety, smooth skin an angry shade of red. My body betrayed me as I watched his hand move. The venomous anger and jealousy residing within me being pushed aside by sheer lust and pure longing.

"You like what you see?" He groaned. "I'm so fucking hard." He wasn't lying. I doubted I'd ever seen him that hard, and I certainly never saw him so wickedly sexual. "My cock is screaming to get to you."

My breathing was loud, and the whimpers escaping from deep in my throat couldn't be suppressed. I wanted him in me. My mouth, my pussy, my ass—fuck, I'd put him in just my hand if it meant that I could touch him, but the anger I had for him worked like a vice, squeezing my thoughts from every side of my brain.

"You . . . you betrayed me. I trusted you. You . . . you said to trust you!" I cried, fully aware of just how thoroughly all these stones I was tossing were shattering my glass house. "Tell me you want her! Tell me the truth!" I knew his return to me was too good to be true. Life had taught me that the other shoe always dropped. Always.

He released his dick and pinned my hands to the wall above my head.

"I've never betrayed you. Ever! You were right on when you told me to go fuck myself."

I turned my face away, and he used one hand to grip my chin hard and make me face him. Tears poured hot down my face, making this even more excruciating.

"I do fuck myself." He ground himself against me. "I've never, ever touched anyone but you. Ever. You think I don't know what you do with your body? You think I don't know how many hands have touched you? The mouths that have tasted what should have been only mine? How many men have been inside you?" His forehead came back down on mine and made my head press against the wall behind me. "Oh, sweetheart, I know it all."

My body seized and then convulsed so hard my bones shook. I couldn't stop the tears. He hadn't been with anyone? And I stood before him as the whore I was. I dropped my head and began to dry-heave uncontrollably, but he didn't back away or give me space.

Gabe continued to speak as his hips and hand kept me pressed to the wall at my back. His lips covered my cheeks in tiny kisses, soaking up the steady stream of emotions pouring from my eyes. "No matter what you say. No matter what or who you do. You are mine. You just aren't ready. Not yet. But, so help all things holy, I will not stand by and watch you give yourself to another. I'm here to reclaim you. If I must fight even you to do that, then so be it."

I closed my eyes so tightly I had to have broken blood vessels, but the tiniest smile broke over my lips. Then my knees weakened, and Gabe fell with me to the floor, shifting me so I was straddling him and crying into the crook of his neck. After a few minutes, or maybe it was a few hours, my body had calmed, and I finally took the deep breath my lungs were desperate for.

"Enough, Vahla." His voice was soothing. "Tell me why." His soft strokes to my back lulled me into a calmness I hadn't felt in years. The vice grip on my brain loosened, and the world stopped shaking my emotions around like a snow globe.

He was right. It was enough. It was enough emotions. Enough games. Enough fucking hurt. I didn't want to be this person. This crazed, irrational person. As he held me, the cracks and holes deep inside began to close. The pieces of a heart and soul that scattered around deep within me began to seek each other out. They were fighting to be whole again, pulling and tugging and squeezing as warmth radiated through me.

"I . . . don't know."

"You don't know why you were in Idaho?"

I shook my head to clear the fog. Oh, Idaho. Not the bar. "I went to reason with her. To tell her she and Luce were over."

"Did she listen?"

"No." My tears built back up, and again, he kissed them away until his lips found mine.

There was a moment where I thought he wouldn't close that infinitesimal distance.

Where I was scared to breathe or move, too scared to close the distance myself.

This was the moment that I either gave myself back to him

or ran for the rest of eternity. Gabe held me tighter as my body tensed. He didn't miss a thing.

"Don't shut me out, Vahla. Please let me touch you the only way you should be touched," he pleaded.

I closed my eyes and listened to his heartbeat. Focused on the song it created just for me.

I knew my answer the second he asked, but I also needed him to know the truth. My body reacted to the panic, so I waited for my breathing to level out and for the slight dizziness to fade. "I don't regret it. I'm not sorry." I sighed. "I'm not sorry for all the things I've done to survive. To protect my brother."

"I would never expect you to be. I'm not telling you that you *should* be." His sincerity fused some of those pieces of my heart to each other. "I don't want her, Vahla."

Still buried in his neck, I closed my eyes to shield the rage and take in the relief. I remained silent.

"I'm not with her. I'm here." His voice rose slightly as he spoke again.

Love, jealousy, fear, and need were vying for dominance. "You're here even when you aren't," I said, more to the universe than to him.

"Good." His voice softened.

"Good?"

Gabriel lowered his voice but spoke with no less intensity into my ear. "Yes. Good. I want you to be thinking of me. All the time, just as I have thought of you."

"I needed to separate myself. I couldn't . . ." The urge to explain myself made me start tripping over my words.

"I know exactly what you needed, but I want to be the one to give you everything. That includes the same protection you give to others."

I looked into those beautiful, sincere, crystal-clear blue eyes. "You don't need to protect me, Gabriel. I do the protecting."

He closed his eyes tightly. "You do too much of it, and yet, you won't accept that you deserve it."

Oh, how my heart ached at his declaration. "Don't make me out to be something I'm not." I struggled enough with thoughts of Gabriel throughout the years. I found it hard to handle his praise.

"I know exactly who you are." His forehead lifted to press against mine as his thumbs began to caress my hips. The skin below heated instantly, while my inner thighs warmed at his touch. I knew exactly who he was, too. No amount of time could change us, regardless of how hard I had tried.

I barely registered the movement of my own hands until I heard the sound from the tear. I had ripped his shirt open and brought our faces together.

"Tell me to let you leave, and I will." His promise unmistakable as his hands stilled. "I don't want to do anything else unless it is your choice. Unless you mean it."

Then his lips hung parted, and I closed the inch of distance in a tentative kiss. He stared at me while our mouths rested on each other's and held my eyes as I released the slight pressure. My agreement would be the final piece of this puzzle.

"I mean it, Gabriel," I whispered. My heart was pounding, sending my blood pressure through the roof. Even my bones felt liquefied from the intensity of this moment.

I wanted him. I needed him. And if that didn't scare me enough, I loved him too. Fuck, did I love him. My knuckles brushed over his chest as I reached for the hem of my shirt. One swift move and it was off. His strong hands began to shake, and I found a bit of pleasure in the effect I had on him.

My bra came off next, and his body pressed against mine. Our skin so hot to the touch that I was shocked we didn't burst into flames. He pulsed beneath me, and I felt the first flood of wetness pool in my core.

I pushed my body closer, pressing my breasts against his hard chest. "That was your last chance as well."

His head moved just enough to acknowledge that as he smiled and groaned, then I dipped my face so I could lick a slow trail up the side of his neck. Up and up I went until I reached his earlobe, which I tugged gently between my teeth. His body coiled tight with anticipation, and I didn't want to make him wait.

I didn't want to wait.

So, I found the script behind his ear and dusted my lips across it. The man's entire body shivered under my palms as his smile quickly disappeared.

He snapped.

Between one heartbeat and the next, I had moved from straddling him to being trapped under him, his mouth on mine, his tongue demanding against my own. I stripped him of his torn shirt as he kicked his pants the rest of the way off. Frantic and gasping for breath, he yanked at one of my boots and then the other, but then he was out of patience and shredded my jeans.

I didn't care. I needed no more barriers between us.

My core pulsed in various waves, knowing he would be inside me. There would never be a time I wasn't ready for him. Wet for him. Aching in all places for him. My arms and legs shook as he settled himself between my open, waiting thighs, as he seated himself inside me in one swift plunge.

He released a deep, sexy, satisfying moan.

A moan so raw that it matched the one ripped from my own lips as he continued to thrust into me. When he slowed his rhythm, I held his arms and lifted my face to his. I ached for his mouth on mine and stretched to get to him like a flower to the sun.

In all my years, these were the only lips I'd wanted. The

only flesh that would put me into a frenzy. I loved them and tried to hate them. I missed them. I dreamed of them.

But then he pulled away, flipped me onto my stomach, and pushed back into me, and I hissed in pleasure. I lowered my head and pushed back, wanting more. Needing more. I had been starved for this man, and I was taking everything he could give.

As my head hung low, I watched as his cock drove in and out of me. Tears filled my eyes from the erotic scene and the pleasure that overwhelmed me. The sheer strength of his body had his knees cracking the floor below, the wooden panels bending and caving in from his force. As my hands braced and grabbed at the floor, the wood began to splinter around my fingers.

"Do you think those others matter, Vahla?" He hissed the words in my ear.

Nothing but a choked moan erupted from me. He pressed his thumb to my clit, and I was utterly lost to him. His warm wet tongue began to circle my ear before his teeth gently bit down on my lobe. My body tingled, and the familiar pulsating began to roar. I would never get enough of him. Never.

"Do they matter, Vahla?"

"N-no." I gasped. My body arching against him, hips pushing back, urging him to take more.

"Who matters?"

"Y-you." I panted.

"It. Will. Always. Be. Me."

He yanked my hair hard enough to send a new pleasure spiking down my spine and forced me to look at him. "Tell me you're mine."

I didn't answer fast enough, and he punished me with a sharp pinch to my clit before withdrawing. My orgasm was painfully close, and he was merciless as his fingers entered me but kept my climax at bay. Once I met his eyes with my own, he dropped a slow kiss to my shoulder before moving to my lips, whispering, "Tell me."

I chased the sensation of his fingers, panting and whimpering, but then he was gone and I was crying out.

"Still so beautifully defiant."

I stared at him. He stared back. Damn that beautiful face of his.

Fuck, I needed to come. His fingers began to rub my ass, caress the tops of my thighs, and leisurely strum the area around my pussy, teasing me but not entering.

"Tell me."

"I'm yours," I said.

His eyebrows rose.

I rolled my eyes. "Always, Gabriel."

His smile was brief. Then he smacked my ass so hard I yelped from the pain while he flipped me to my back and positioned himself between my legs. One inch at a time, he eased his length back into me, sliding once, twice, three times until he was soaked again from my wetness and I lost the ability to breathe.

"I want it, Vahla. Now." So, I gave it to him. With unrestrained passion, I gave him everything I had. I pumped my hips quicker and pressed my lips to his harder, needing to feel them as I sank my hands into his hair and held him there.

"Vahla, mine." He breathed out on repeat as he thrust into me.

"Ohhhh . . . fuck. So good." Every other one I had was nameless, faceless. Not him. Never this man.

"This is your place. Me in you." His hand cupped my breast. "This body calls to me."

I know. I pumped more furiously.

"These are mine. Feel . . . that?" The pinch of my right nipple and then the left started the orgasm spilling over.

"*Mmmmm . . .* yes!"

He pressed harder into me, and his hands slid to my waist, demanding I relinquish control to him and the punishing rhythm he wanted. "Yes, what? The next words out of your mouth better be that you're mine."

All I could think about was his cock inside me and the way he was forcing my clit to rub against his pelvis.

My eyes flew open, accusation clear on my face. He had forced my stillness with his own. Gabe's jaw was clenched tightly as he stared at me. "Tell me."

"So needy." I challenged with strained breaths. Then he pulsed deep inside me, and I would have told him anything he wanted. "Yours."

As soon I said the word, he thrust so hard that tears spilled from my eyes. For soul's sake, the edge was right there, and I was hurtling toward it.

"Fuck, fuck, *fuuuuck* . . ." He grunted. "You . . ." Thrust. "Are . . ."

I reached for him as my tongue licked each of his lips until he caught it between his teeth. His sudden thrust into me caused my mouth to open and my orgasm to set my body on fire.

"You-yours—" I gasped, as my head tipped back. My body arched, and my core throbbed around him.

"I am only yours," he emphasized right before the roar from his own explosion deep inside me. He had reminded me with every thrust, every kiss, and every whisper that I was his and he was mine.

He kept whispering it as we came down from the pleasure, and when I was finally . . . finally, able to open my eyes again, I found him watching me with eyes that were not his own. They were no longer the brilliant blue I loved. No, they had turned to a mixture of his light blue and my light brown, creating the most stunning hazel in any world.

The ultimate sign of our bonding. Something we would never share with anyone else.

How could I deny loving this man? I couldn't. Not anymore. He knew I used my body for self-serving purposes, whether to manipulate or to drive out my demons.

He knew it and still claimed to be mine. He knew it and gave himself to no one else.

Gabe's eyes narrowed as a rogue tear escaped my eye. He instantly kissed it away and peppered the rest of my face. His hands roamed and rubbed every inch of my skin, and his erection grew. Appreciative hums flowed from his mouth as his tongue took over. Before I knew it, that glorious mouth of his was nestled between my legs. The world could have been burning to the ground, and I would have been too lost to this man to notice.

THAT NIGHT, HE TOOK ME IN EVERY WAY POSSIBLE. MY SKIN gloriously pink from the friction, my back scratched from the floor and the walls. Gabriel's back blazed with red streaks from my nails, and his shoulders, hips, and inner thighs bore my bite marks. My throat was raw and sore from screaming his name and sucking on every part of him. Never, ever, have I knelt before any man but him, and he would always be the only one. On my knees, with him fully seated in my mouth, I came without so much as either one of us touching me. The power and intimacy of that position with him was indescribable.

But I knew too well that all good things came to an end. As I lay curled against Gabe's side with his arms around me and his hand rubbing smooth strokes along my hip, the beautiful calm ended.

He let out a deep breath and asked, "What are you going to do now?"

My huff made him cock his head to the side. I hated slipping away from the peace I was nestled in. "I mean," I said slowly, "she has thrown down an ultimatum that I plan to shove up her polar ass."

Gabe chortled and shook his head. "I should not be laughing right now. But, polar ass?"

"Barometer Bitch, Wacko of the Woods, the Lunar Lunatic. Pick your poison with that one."

His laugh picked up until he sobered again. I enjoyed how the thumping of his chest hit against mine. My nipples rubbing against the spattering of coarse hair, making my core tingle. "Let me help you, my love."

"Just promise me you'll let me deal with her. That's the best way for you to help me."

"Why can't we do this together?"

"My brother. My fight."

"You aren't going to budge at all on this, are you?"

"You know me better than to ask. Yes or no, Gabe. Time is literally ticking for me right now."

He looked to the side and took a few deep breaths as his fingers tapped mindlessly on my upper arms. "Fine. But I'm going to do the one thing you can't."

"Which is?"

"I'm going to see Michael. I want him to know you've kept Lucifer away from Essalene."

"Do you think he'll listen?"

He went quiet for a long moment. "I don't know. Most of them are pretty up in arms about your brother. They don't think Essalene is capable of this magnitude without being influenced by someone. They are all very protective of her after what happened between her and Father Time. They also believe your brother still has his agenda set regarding taking the throne in Heaven."

I nodded.

"So, if I think things are going south with your plan, I'm stepping in."

"You better not." I gave him a hard glare until he relented. Stubborn man.

"Fine. I won't step in unless the others decide to step in."

"Fine." I rolled my eyes. I would be stupid to refuse his help on that one, so I nodded, striking the deal. It was the closest to a compromise as I would get from him.

"Oh, one more thing. Roll your eyes again and see what happens, my darling."

I stuck my tongue out, and before he could react, I was on my feet and ready to travel back to Hell. My farewell gesture? I blew him a kiss and silently promised to see him soon.

CHAPTER
FOURTEEN

Tap, tap, tap, tap.
Tap, tap, tap, tap.
Tap, tap, tap, tap.
Tap, tap, tap, tap.

"SHIT!" I THREW MY BEAUTIFUL Montblanc pen across my office. My brain hurt from thinking.

Gabe was pretty clear that Essalene had the sympathy and backing of the goodie-goodies in the clouds.

Essalene was pretty clear that she thought my brother loved her back. Not true, but trying to reason with crazy was like trying to breathe under water. Not happening.

It left me with the only option I didn't want to be the only option. I couldn't go there yet. I decided to walk and clear my head.

"It isn't like that, Roisin! Fuck!"

I walked the slate road in front of my home and came out of my haze as I heard my brother's roar. I laughed before he saw me because I was loving that this woman had him so crazed and off balance. He even stopped fucking her in public a while ago, which was not like him at all.

"What's up, baby brother?"

He was pulling at his hair with his hands and walking in tight circles. "Women! Fucking women!"

I wasn't successful at suppressing my laugh this time. "What happened?"

"It isn't fucking funny, V! Whorebag Essalene was blowing up my phone. She sent a picture of me naked and then one of her naked and fingering herself. Roisin saw it and got pissed."

"Ouch."

"Ouch? Ouch! We were mid-fuck, and I had her bent over my desk when it popped up on my phone."

"You forgot to block her?"

He looked at me with fury etched on his face. "Obviously."

"Just block her. She'll go away eventually." I hoped.

"She said she was looking forward to our date. To stop denying her because we were happening."

Damn her. My neck stiffened, and I schooled my features so I wouldn't flip out and go topside and do something regrettable. "Just block her. Don't respond."

"That was my plan, but Roisin decided to take the phone and send back a selfie while we were fucking. Now, she's pissed, and well . . ."

So, the tsunamis and sinkholes on the news were Essalene's answers to seeing that. Great.

"What am I going to do?"

He wasn't going to do anything. "I'll handle it."

"But I can—"

"No, Lucifer. No. You need to stay down here because your presence will only make her worse."

"But . . ."

"Go get Roisin. I will take care of Essalene."

He shuffled up to me and kissed the top of my head, sighing with relief. "Thanks, V. You're the best." He took off running after Red. That was some spell D whipped up.

That compliment he gave me was so far from the truth. Would the best sister have swiped his phone from his pocket during that tender brother-sister moment? Nope. But I did.

Asshole answered on the first ring. "My darling, I knew you'd call."

"I just threw up in my mouth. Leave him alone, Essalene."

"Vahla? You stupid bitch. You don't know what you're bringing on yourself."

"Yeah, yeah. Listen, I have to go. I have important shit to do."

"Do you think Lucifer thinks I'm beautiful?"

Where the fuck did that even come from?

Dealing with crazy is hard. "No."

She gasped. "You say that because you're jealous. Your brother thinks I'm beautiful. Gabriel thinks I'm beautiful." She paused. "Who thinks you're beautiful, Vahla?"

Gabriel does, you stupid asswipe of a woman.

She laughed. "A little birdy tells me Silas does."

My knees took the brunt of that statement about as well as they'd take a hit from a baseball bat.

"What the fuck did you just say?"

"Hmmm . . . I know something you don't know . . ." She sang the words in true lunatic fashion.

"Really? Because I find it hard to believe you and reality have any kind of relationship."

She sighed. "I *do* know something you don't. Aren't you curious at all about what it might be?" Her voice lowered. "I'll give you a hint. I am going to help him get what he came for."

My body stilled at her words. "Who and what exactly would that be?"

"Well, you, my dear." She whistled. "Sucks being on the losing end of this battle, doesn't it? Some queen you are."

Fuck her.

I reclaimed my bearings and then tsked her. "You know who would be super happy to hear you've taken up with Silas? My brother. They loathe each other—have for years." It was my turn to laugh. "Oh, you didn't know that? Poor, poor, Essalene. Lied to by yet another man. I would think by now you would know better."

"You wouldn't." The woman screamed and must have stomped or something because I could have sworn I felt the vibration of it down in my underworld. It must have traveled across the entire world above.

"I would. Did you really think that shit would work with me? Come on, you know better. The only thing I care about is keeping my brother free and clear of the shitshow of mayhem you put on every time you throw a tantrum or get off. Do you think that nonsense goes unnoticed? Do you think *they* haven't realized that the balance is being screwed with, and not in the good way?"

"If you say one word to Luce, I will go straight to Michael."

Desperation made people threaten to do things they never would.

"You aren't listening to me. Silas will never get close to me, and Michael wouldn't side with you over me."

"Oh my gosh! You're so stupid! You left. You didn't choose Michael or his side. You chose the fucked-up one to follow. *My* fucked-up one."

I wish I was close enough to hit her, but it would solve nothing.

"Don't forget to bring my man back to me. You have forty-eight hours. Don't be a minute later."

Forty-eight hours. She could kiss my perfectly shaped ass. "Or else what?"

"For a self-proclaimed smart woman, you really should look up sometimes." She hummed. "The skies are ready to open, all I need to do is give the word."

I was in Hell, so there was no way to look out a window and look up.

"Ah, by your silence I can tell you haven't paid attention. I'm the only one who can save him. Give him to me or watch your world burned to ashes."

Well, she was wrong there too. It wasn't my anything. It was His world.

Michael and I had never had a problem with each other because I chose to fall. I was kind of told to watch my brother, so in a roundabout way, I was here because Father wanted me to be here. But he was also Silas's brother. I knew what I was willing to do for mine, so I needed to assume Michael would do the same for his.

"Don't contact my brother again."

"You can't—"

"Blah, blah, blah." And I hung up on her. I had no idea what revelations would have come out of her mouth if I had continued to listen. All I knew was that I couldn't take anymore. If the angels were on her side, if Silas was helping her in exchange for what he wanted? That would be very, very bad for Luce and me.

CHAPTER
FIFTEEN

When in doubt and feeling like the entire universe was against you? Go see your best friend. I probably should have called first, but if she wasn't home, I'd track her down wherever she was. Plus, the fresh air was doing me good. Well, good for a clearer recap of the circus that was my life. The meeting with Aldorex went to shit, and then the one with Essalene went to shit even faster. My awesome, spur-of-the-moment plan to get drunk, which almost resulted in having the rage screwed out of me by that big, burly farm man got diverted and I ended up almost being fucked blind by Gabriel. Blindness by orgasm with Gabe would have been so worth it. That I couldn't deny.

I still had the soreness between my legs and the scratches from his teeth on my neck. My ass still had his handprints, and it was still sort of hard to fully sit. But I loved it. Every ounce of every single thing he did to and left on my body. I was more relieved by his touch than I'd been by the fact that he did not have sex with Essalene or want that fruitcake in any way.

My heels clicked louder as they hit the blood red bricks that made up their walkway. I stared ahead at the enormous stone house. The large earthy colors were warm and welcoming. I approached the huge, mahogany double doors that I'd seen a hundred times and still looked at them in awe. Intricately hand-carved wood displayed the many symbols that represented the witches: their family crest and the five elements. Those are what captured my attention the most.

Earth and air took up one of the two doors, and I could almost feel the breeze that the artist created. The left side was occupied by fire and water. They waved and licked at each other. Some may have seen the battle between the two, but I saw the dance, the beautiful, harmonic dance. It was my favorite side. And the fifth element was carved from one door to the next in a fluid design. The spirit element wasn't something that could be replicated. It was a sense, a feeling . . . the force that unites all things. The symbolism was created from sketches each of the sisters gave to the artist. It was surreal and completely spectacular.

With all the designs there were to enjoy, I'd always really loved the large doorknockers. The black iron, so intricately designed and heavy, created the perfect knock each time. I didn't get to even use one as the door flung open as soon as I hit the porch.

"Ugh. To what do we owe the pleasure?"

"Well, hello to you too, Petra."

Her hand rested on her cocked hip as she stood and stared at me. No fucking manners at all. I used to think she was so beautiful. Tall and thin, with shiny light-brown hair that bordered on blonde and had a natural beach wave, and mesmerizing spring-green eyes. Then she opened her mouth, and she was so fucking ugly.

She never had one damn nice thing to say to anyone. Petra hated her sisters' choices in clothing, décor, and men, and she didn't mince her words about any and all topics. But once I heard her tell her youngest sister, Sissa, that she was short, fat, ugly, and stupid. She ended up with sharp words from me and my fingerprints staining her neck. Sissa was the kindest, sweetest witch I knew. I didn't know how she remained so unjaded. Her thick curves were beautiful and her blonde hair looked like rays of the sun. She had freckles that were freaking adorable, and deep, amethyst-colored eyes. I never wanted her mixed up in my shit, but I certainly would beat the fuck out of Petra if she was cruel to Sissa while I was around. Her spells be damned, I'd take on this bitch any day of the week.

"Whatever, Vahla,." She snorted as she remained in the doorway.

"Can you move? And maybe cover yourself up? It's kind of chilly out. Not really a nipple-showing kind of night. Unless, I missed the memo?"

"Jealous much?"

"Nope. Got my own. And they're pretty spectacular."

"As if, you cow."

"How old are you? Fifteen?"

"Go to hell, Vahla."

"I own Hell, sweetheart. Can I come in now?" I asked so sweetly my teeth hurt. I hated that I needed permission to enter their house. With six of them, when their spells were unified, they were extremely powerful. They took security very seriously, so no one was getting in without an invite.

She looked me up and down, not caring about nipple-gate at all, and scrunched her nose with the obvious disdain she had for me. But then I saw it. Something behind her gaze that made my skin prickle with awareness. Petra had a smugness tonight, a confidence that surpassed her typical bitchiness. Characteristics not indicative of who she was. Not in that amount oozing off her, anyway. The grin that followed on her lips sent a chill through my spine and a familiar ache through my bones as she smiled. "Yes, home sweet Hell, how lovely for you. I'm sick of looking at you anyway. I have something better to rest my eyes on." She waved her hand and I entered. Delayna was a stronger witch than she was, so Petra knew better than to fuck with me.

The large door creaked and closed gently on its own. The grand staircase before me was impressive, and I headed for it, loving the way my heels clicked on the highly polished steps. When I hit the top, I cut right and headed toward Delayna's private section of the house.

The paintings of the witches' ancestors made me feel as if I were being watched, so I kept my eyes straight ahead until they segued into beautiful portraits of nature. Each of the sisters had their own space, but Delayna's was the farthest back, and her suite boasted of the largest and most windows because nature was her jam.

Ironic that nature was the reason I was here.

I walked a little quicker down the carpeted hallway, the dark green-and-white giving way to a lighter green with bronze swirls. The closer I got, the more I was able to smell the freshness that was unique to her side of the house. The scent of lilies mixed with the subtle smell of the ocean was just strong enough to be almost elusive, pleasant.

Until I opened her door and gagged. My eyes watered and my nose wrinkled at the assault of a hostile odor. My feet actually stumbled from the foul attack on my senses. "Uh, hey, D." Her room was a mess. Like, a disaster of a mess. For a girl who had some OCD issues herself and was a neat freak, this was alarming. Her boots were all over the place, stockings hung from the dresser, empty bottles littered her nightstand and the floor around her bed. There was a large ceramic bowl with some kind of crusty crap all over the inside. I leaned in to look closer and barely suppressed a retch.

Delayna was lying on her comfy chaise on the very far right side of her room in the corner. It was situated in front of where the large windows met, and it was her absolute favorite place to sit. She turned her head lazily in my direction and gave me a small, sad smile. "Hey, my fave friend," she managed to slowly roll the words from her mouth.

I put my arm out in a waving motion. "What the hell happened here?"

"You said hell." She slurred the words with a giggle as her eyes looked over her room. "Nothing." The accompanying shrug dislodged a large chunk of her hair that had been stuck under her. The shiny black cascading down to its freedom, almost touching the floor below. Such a beautiful contrast to the white of her lounger.

"Um, something sure as shit did. And what the fuck is that smell?"

She grumbled loudly and rolled herself off the chaise. She made it to her feet and rocked a bit before she caught her balance.

"Are you drunk?"

"Huh? No, but I wish I was."

Okaayyyyy.

"Do you want to get drunk?"

"Shit, Vahla. It isn't that simple."

I went to her, not concerned about the chaos around us, and took her hands in mine. "What's wrong? Tell me what I can do to help you."

She bit her lip and squeezed my hands. "I wish . . ." She looked away. "I wish there were something you could do because I would totally ask you. Or force you. Or bribe you." She looked back to me, trying desperately to make her smile work. "Or have Gabriel bribe you." She winked with unshed tears flooding her stunning hazel eyes.

I rolled my eyes. "In the words of Petra, 'as if.'" I started to laugh and immediately stopped. Delayna's face froze, and the seriousness that followed shocked me.

"Stay away from her as much as you can for now. There's something up with her. I feel a type of dark, dark force around her. Until I know what it is, everyone should be wary."

I dragged her over to her bed and cleared off all the clothes, throwing them carelessly to the floor. I sat her back against the headboard and plopped myself right next to her. Still holding hands and facing her, I asked again, "What's wrong, D? I hate to see you upset. You never keep things from me. You're scaring me."

She laid her hand on my cheek. "No one scares you, Vahla. You are the queen of Hell, the empress of your empire."

"Don't make jokes. My bones can feel it. Something is wrong."

She removed her hand and took a deep breath. "It's nothing that can be solved in a day, so let's get to why you are here. I can feel things too, you know. And I've heard the whispers. You know all the girls who have fucked your brother are gossip whores. Since Petra was one of them, she hears it all and can't keep her mouth shut."

"Not enough bleach for my eyes to rid myself of that image."

"But I'm right, aren't I?"

"Yes. You are."

"Helping you is exactly what I need to get my attention off . . . other crap."

I didn't like being held out on. I was a need-to-know-immediately type of personality. "D?"

"After this. We will talk after we take care of you." She stared at me with such a sense of urgency I itched to dig into her mind. "I need this right now. I need to work on your problem."

"Okay." I didn't want to give in. I really didn't. But I wasn't about to invade her privacy, so I dropped it.

She nodded her approval and let go of my hand. "Okay, but first, I need something from you."

Oh, good! Maybe she would tell me after all. "Anything. Name it."

"War."

Well, shit. She went straight to the big one. "Really? I thought we were gonna wait and take care of me first?"

"Oh, V. This way we can strategize while we strategize."

"Damn it." I groaned. "But can we please open a window first?"

An hour later and four full decks of cards combined, our game of war was still going. Card games were her go-to. They focused her, calmed her, and gave her enjoyment while distracting her from the problems in her life. We were such opposites: she played cards, and I fucked like a crazed wilde-beest, but we worked. There was an understanding, a respect we had for each other and a complete judgment-free outlook regarding each other's choices.

That wasn't to say we didn't fight or disagree. She even tried to stage an intervention because my sex rages were getting a little out of control at one point. She tried by taking me to the Bodies Exhibit in New York City to show me the shit that can happen to a person's body when abused. It took me some time to admit to her that I was thoroughly grossed out and super thankful I couldn't get that shit, but she'd made her point, and I loved her for it.

"Tell me what you will need to do so I can pull together the spells."

I flicked my card and won her king with my ace. "How do you know I even need spells?"

"Oh, silly, silly girl. You are going to tangle with Mother Nature, yes?"

"Yes."

"She holds the Weather Zenith. You know she can make

any weather a hundred times more powerful with that, right? Bullets got nothing on her hail. Even though she will suffer consequences from your . . . well, from the highest powers if she uses them against another."

"Okay, so what do you have that will counter the Weather Zenith?"

She was quiet for a minute as we flipped a few more hands. "I know it isn't my business. But when will you let him deal with his own consequences? I mean, at some point he's—"

"I know, I know," I cut her off. "It isn't that point yet." I put my cards down. "Does that mean you won't help me?"

"Shut the fuck up with that talk, V. You know better. I may worship the elements, but I don't like her abusing them like she does. If it weren't your brother, it would be someone else. He needs to grow up sometime, though, and eventually, someone is going to call you an enabler and you're going to blow up a continent." I raised an eyebrow, and she clapped her hands together.

"Really? A continent?"

"Oh, don't pretend like you couldn't. Now, talk your needs so I can talk my spells."

I filled her in on my meeting with Essalene. She growled at the information I gave her from my meeting with Aldorex. She dated Father Time for a little while and said even infinite time and space couldn't hold his insanely large ego and then laughed saying that was the only large thing about him.

Then I filled her in about Gabriel. She stared at me with over-the-top googly, lovey-dovey eyes. She was so ridiculous.

"You think Gabe might interfere?"

I huffed. "I'm not sure. He promised he wouldn't, but if it were me?"

"Yeah, you'd make sure you weaseled your way to him at a time that didn't clearly break your promise."

"Right." She knew me so well.

"And you're, what? Worried he wouldn't be able to handle himself? He's a full-on angel, I would think he trumped that crazy bitch in power."

"He does, but this is on me, and I think she has some powerful angels in her corner."

She looked at me as if she wanted to ask for names but then just shook her head. "I can give you stones for protection and power amplification, and an elixir for healing. But there are some things I can't mess with."

Looking down, I shuffled my cards. Over and over I watched as they bent under the pressure of my hands and listened as they slapped into each other. "I know."

"You have so many powers, though. Thermokinesis, terrakinesis, and pyrokinesis are great and will help you. Your neurokinesis can confuse her, and if you have to teleport, I'm sure you'll be able to power through her winds."

"Yup, I got kinesis-es coming out my ass. My being able to manipulate heat, dirt, and rocks will be minimal to hers. I guess manipulating her mind could give me an advantage, but that's only if I can get in to it. Especially before she decides to use the Weather Zenith."

"Look, it won't be easy, but at least you aren't taking a knife to a gunfight. You have some comparable powers and some exclusive ones. They will all serve their purpose." She chewed at her lip and looked anywhere other than at me. I knew she wanted to say more.

"What?"

I could clearly hear the grandfather clock ticking outside of her bedroom door. Her silence was painful for me as I sat still and waited for her to speak. Even the sky outside grew darker and the room's temperature dropped a bit as I waited.

"The crystal dusting to amplify your powers will take me some time. I want to get the mixture right. You'll have to coat yourself with them before you fight her. Each one serves a purpose, and the most I can combine is four. And, trust me, four is incredibly potent."

"Is that really what you wanted to say?"

"Ugh, no." Her face fell, and I knew what she had to say couldn't be good.

"Then what?" I pressed her.

"Shit, Vahla. You'll have to cut yourself and offer your blood so the spell works. I could try to find another way but—"

"No. We probably wouldn't have time for another way. I'll be fine."

I'll be fine.

"You'll need a deep cut, Vahla. A shallow one to your chest, right in front of your heart and one to your . . . to your right wrist. It has to be in an X, and it has to be deep." She placed her hand on my leg. "I'm so sorry. I don't want you to have to do this."

I swallowed over the nerves that bundled in my throat and gripped my chest. "I'll be fine. I got this."

"When was the last time you . . ."

"A long time ago. Don't worry, I'm fine."

"Are you still having the dream?"

"You mean the nightmare of waking up to Lucifer pumping my chest to revive me? The four crushing pushes that broke my ribs yet saved me?"

Her voice lowered. "Oh, Vahla."

"It's one of the remaining pains I can't get rid of."

"Except for when Gabriel is near?"

I gave her a small nod.

"And what about your brother?"

Just like that, I went from uncomfortable with the conversation to grinning at her. "Ha! He'll be, um, busy with his new redhead." I laughed. "Thanks for that, by the way."

"He's so easy." She laughed. "Okay, then, let's get started. I need to review the spell with you. I'm not sure how you will keep that alpha angel hottie of yours away, though."

"It's this thing he likes to call trust." I gave a mocking shiver. "Should we get hammered while we spell?" We always did.

Delayna's look turned sad as her smile became half its size. "No, I just . . . I think I need to concentrate extra on this."

I could have called bullshit because her red wine that soaked ages in the whiskey barrels in her basement were a staple for her. When she spelled, she would sip and her magic would flow. Never abusive or overindulgent while she worked, but focused and relaxed as she created.

I watched as she concentrated on her spell. The large, brown leather book filled with ages' worth of knowledge was a sight to behold. So much history, so much dedication. As she worked, she explained that the stones needed to sit together for a certain amount of time once mixed, and we agreed that she would bring it to the Scarlet and leave it with Abhitha if I wasn't there.

I stayed a little longer and picked up some of the scattered clothes and garbage in her room. Before I left, I hugged her a bit longer and reminded her that I was there for her. Her appreciative smile couldn't hide the current of sadness I felt coming from her.

I would be back soon enough to ask her about it.

On my way out, I passed Petra, who never could leave well enough alone. "Way to overstay your welcome, Vahla."

At least I didn't need her permission to get out. "Don't be jelly. Isn't that how you little people say it?"

I laughed and headed for the door. Before I left, she shocked the shit out of me and gave me a hug. She patted and rubbed my back. I never lifted my arms to reciprocate, so it was rather awkward. She rubbed a spot on my back so hard, I left feeling like I had rug burn.

And like I needed a shower.

THE NIGHT AIR WAS BEAUTIFUL, AND I DECIDED TO WALK BEFORE teleporting back to Hell. With a nice breeze and a beautiful sky, I called to check in with Abhitha.

"Hey, it's me."

"Hello, my Commander in Chief. How are you?"

"I'm good. Just left from a visit with Delayna."

"Seeing your friends is good for the soul."

I snorted. "I don't think I have a soul."

"I call bullshit. You have a great one."

She was like the champion of my self-esteem.

"All the orders have been fulfilled on time. We're actually ahead of schedule. Lucifer called me to tell me he thinks he discovered a new stone. Said he was looking at some new part of a bridge, got distracted, and his leg caught in a hole. When he was digging himself out, he found it. I didn't ask for details, but he said he would bring me a sample, which means you'll need to bring it since he's under house arrest."

"Ha. Ha. Ha. You're hilarious."

"Thank you, thank you. Please, hold your applause until the end." Her laughing at her own jokes was contagious, and I tilted my head back, looking up at the sky as I let my own peal of laughter out.

Then I stopped.

It was dark, but I could see what others couldn't. Clouds puckered in areas that resembled formations. That was what Essalene had been talking about.

I continued to gaze up, lost in my thoughts and worry.

"Vahla? Will you be back soon?"

"Um, yeah I just . . . ah! Ouch!"

"Vahla? Vahla!"

"Ab-Ab—I'm . . . help me." My neck stung from whatever hit me. The burn was so intense and flowed fast and furious through me that it had my phone tumbling from my hands as I dropped to my knees. I tried to teleport and nothing happened. I tried to fight the hand that gripped my hair and yanked me backward, but I was weak. Too weak. Something wasn't right.

"Fight all you want, princess. Your powers are gone. You're mine."

Abhitha's voice as she screamed my name turned distorted as my vision waved.

"Help me," I whispered as Silas crushed my phone with his shoe and dragged me away.

CHAPTER
SIXTEEN

Crack!

THE PAIN STREAKING ACROSS MY inner thigh was sharp and hot, jolting me awake. My body automatically tried to protect itself, but it was no use. My wrists and ankles were bound by coarse rope that bit into my skin every time I tried to move.

"Nice to see you finally waking up. Losing your powers makes you so weak and vulnerable. I don't like how quickly your body gives out. No worries, though." His fingers wrapped around my chin with such aggression. "We have quite some time before that spell wears off."

I was in such pain. Sharp stings wracked my body, and my heart beat too hard in my chest. I bit back any sound that was trying to escape. I didn't want to give the son of a bitch any more satisfaction.

"Hmmm." He hummed as he swung his whip around him, causing a muffled scratching sound against the floor. Each swish of the leather caused bumps to rise across every inch of my skin while my stomach revolted. I was briefly relieved that I had my whip stored on my body as a tattoo and not a bracelet. Bastard would have all too gladly taken it. Then the leather of his whip hit my nipples with such force that they immediately stiffened from the torturous pinch. I had no doubt that, with another lash like that, they would bleed.

"Cry out. There's no one to hear you. Just me and these walls." He came to face me again. "I thought whips were your thing? I brought this just for you." He raised the handle and dangled it in front of my face.

He stepped back, allowing me a better look at him. The black shirt he wore was rolled to his elbows and stretched over his tightly corded muscles. He was bigger than the last time I saw him. Dark brown hair was slicked back from his face, accentuating the yellow highlights, which were the exact color of the sun. Gleaming white teeth were showcased by the huge smile spread across his face. His eyes, one blue one green, held steady on mine.

He shook his head, keeping his smile firmly intact. "I wasn't ready to come after you yet, but then your brother had to go and stir the pot as usual. Just a tiny push, and everyone will be after him. All eyes on you means none on me."

What did he mean by that? Silas walked toward me like a predator to his prey. "But you can still rile up my buddy, Gabe. I figured he'd be over you by now. He has so many better options constantly begging for the chance. I mean, look at you? All tied up like the trashy whore you are."

He sighed, taking his free hand and twirling the long strands of my hair. "What a waste. You're an exquisite woman. Such beauty it's almost painful to look at you." The anger in his voice rising with every word. "Painful beauty that causes even more painful erections." He crushed his body to mine so I could feel how hard he was. Slowly, he drew the lock of hair twisted around his fingers to his nose before inhaling deeply. "Yet, no one compares to you still."

With another tug of my hair, he forced a wince and a tiny squeak from my throat. "Let's see how good you still smell when I'm done with you. We always get what we deserve, Vahla. *Always*."

I moved my head side to side as violently as I could to dislodge his hand from me. I was caught in a nightmare. Terror gripped me, and my very marrow was screaming at me to do something.

"I will never give myself to you. Never! It will be nothing more than you taking what I will never freely give you." I gathered whatever saliva I had in my mouth, and spit in his face.

He wiped it away with a grin. "Still mad about that?"

"About you attacking me the day I left Heaven? About the fact that you were his best friend? I thought you were trying to help me. You'll never be the man Gabriel is."

His nostrils flared and spit flew from his mouth as he spoke. "Help you? You never even *saw* me. Not even when I was right in front of you. You teased everyone around you and my friend Gabe fell for it. He isn't better than me. I always wondered what you saw in him. Why you never looked at me."

"It's only ever been Gabe. And it only ever will be him." My truth came out with a force and strength I didn't think I had in me. Even if I never saw or touched Gabriel again, I wouldn't ever deny my love for him. I would, instead, die proclaiming it.

Silas grabbed my face, causing it to be more of a hard slap, and pressed his mouth to mine, trying to viciously thrust his tongue between my lips.

I shook my head side to side. "No. Damn it, no!" I mumbled.

It was happening again, but this time, there was no way to escape. I had run from Gabriel when Lucifer fell through the clouds. I had needed to cut my ties back then. I was blindingly dizzy as my heart and head warred. Rational thoughts didn't exist within me then because I knew I had to leave. I ran away and when Silas caught me, I thought for sure he was going to bring me back to Gabriel.

When he had caught up with me all those years ago, I expected him to let me go, to step away from me and let me run, but he hadn't. He'd leaned closer with an unsettling smile on his lips. A glint in his green and blue mismatched eyes. "Why are you here, then?" I had asked him.

"For this." Then he crashed his lips onto mine. Momentarily stunned, I hadn't been able to move. Once I registered what was happening, I tore myself from his grip and, in doing so, he ended up ripping one sleeve of my dress, making it fall on one side almost low enough to expose my breast, which was exactly where his eyes had landed.

I put my hands up to cover myself and backed away. "Leave me alone, Silas."

He stalked forward with a sly grin. "Or what?"

"Or . . . or I will tell Gabriel," I had said with a shaky voice.

He laughed. "Nice try." Then he'd lunged at me, trying to take another kiss, and squeezed my body to the point of pain. "I've wanted you for far too long, Vahla. Without Gabe, you will be mine."

Silas had been insane back then, and that hadn't gotten any better. Unraveling right in front of me. How my sleeping with him would rectify any perceived wrong to his sister was beyond me. The crazed look in his eyes told me I shouldn't bother trying.

No more Gabe? I was *bonded* to Gabe, which made his statement an implausibility. Even if the angel who held my very heart were not at my side, that fact wouldn't change. Last time Silas tried, I had lifted my knee as fast and hard as I could, and hit him between his legs. He grunted and fell forward, giving me an opportunity to get away. Moments after I struck him back then, I fell from Heaven.

"Why are you smiling, Vahla? Has the loss of your power caused insanity to set in?" he mocked.

"No, Silas. I was just thinking about the last time you tried to kiss me. I'm pretty sure your balls ended up in your throat."

He punched me in the stomach, making the bile rise and fly from my mouth. Then he ripped my shirt off.

"Look at this pretty lace covering my prize. Too bad it's about to get destroyed. Like the rest of your body. Don't worry, though. We'll get you a decent wheelchair, maybe it will match Ziza's."

That did me in. The mention of the wheelchair caused the damn to break and my sobs to come out.

"You're not allowed to cry! You're the one who snuck my sister out. You're the one that started the chain of events!" he punched me quickly in my side.

"Ziza was my best friend. My brother loved her, and she loved him." I cried harder.

"Yeah, and how'd that work out?" Another blow, this time to my face.

"It . . . it didn't. Luce never meant to hurt her. You must know that. Somewhere in your heart, you have to know." I had to spit the blood out that pooled in my mouth. The sharp tip of my tooth told me he had chipped one. I was sure it wouldn't be the last.

Silas decided to abandon his fists and began to strike me with the whip instead. "What I know is you and your brother think only for yourselves. What I know is that it is his fault she will never walk again. What I know is that you two deserved far, far worse than being banished!"

The stinging pain across my back was too much. Blackness began to wave through my eyesight. Every word spoken sounded as though it were being said underwater. The lulling of it making me want to fall under. Just succumb to the pain to make it stop. "Si . . . las. She was only trying to . . . to stop you two from fighting." My lips cracked and bled as I continued. I had to get it out. "It was an accident, Silas. Lucifer drew his sword to protect himself from yours. That's . . . that's all."

"Shut up. Shut up!"

"He . . . loved her so much."

As my body began to succumb to the pain, images of Luce and Ziza danced around my head. They were a beautiful, happy couple. Sweet and attentive. He was ferocious in protecting her, and she was consumed with showering him with her love. I could hear their laughter, even in my memories.

My pants being ripped from my body brought me back to the nightmare of my reality. The water thrown in my face to wake me up, burned every open crack in my flesh, making each lump and every bruise on me scream.

"It's too late to plead your case. Your pathetic attempt to change my mind is a waste. I know what you are. What your brother is. And now I will take what I want from you and then take the only thing left that your brother loves." He stood behind me and bit hard on my shoulder before he continued. "You'll be able to watch from the wheelchair. You know, once I break you inside, there is no healing. I'm reminded of that fact every day. And I've asked for her to be granted that healing. The answer is always no. He always. Says. No!" His anger could have fueled ten armies. "It's time to get you to the bed."

This was it. I couldn't fight, and there was no escape. I'd rather die than beg. Rather be tortured than give in to his disgusting touch. When Silas released one of my hands from the bindings, I used every ounce of strength I had to reach up and rub my finger on the mark behind my ear. "I will love you always," I whispered as the tears fell down my face.

Instantly, the ground began to shake, and a distinct and disturbing growl permeated through the walls.

"No! Fuck!" Silas yelled. "How the fuck did anyone find us?" He put his hand around my neck. "We're not done here. Not by a long shot." He bit into my lip. "It's only a matter of time until I break the secret to your portal. I will get to Hell. I will get to both of you no matter where you are."

The room was silent for a brief moment before the door flew off the hinges and crashed into splinters.

The roar that sounded both scared and soothed me. My whimpers were no longer able to stay put, and the relief I felt made my body sag under its force, which wasn't good since I had one arm still bound and responsible for holding my body up. My muscles had begun to stretch, pinch, and then pull. The pain so intense that I knew they were going to be ripped to shreds.

"I'm here, Vahla. Hang on. I have you, beautiful."

Once the ropes that bound my arm and legs were off, I collapsed into his arms. I looked up, already knowing whom I would find. My eyes not roaming, just seeking his.

Gabe. Magnificent. Stunning. Saving me.

My lips cracked as I tried to speak. I tasted the blood. "How." The word, which was barely audible, fell from my lips.

He swept the hair from my face. "Abhitha and our mark." My eyes fluttered closed as his lips brushed against my forehead.

My sob was the most desperate human sound I'd ever made, and with an excruciatingly painful turn of my head, I buried my face against his chest.

"Look at me." He gently moved my face from his chest. "Look at me, my love. You are safe, and we are leaving."

He rose to his full height with me in his arms, the soft jostling igniting more bone-crushing aches and causing a whimper to slip from between my lips. "Shhh. I have you."

The cool air as we exited the house tingled across my skin, and he hugged me a bit closer. My eyelids slowly lifted open, and I glanced up at Gabe. His face unreadable as he looked forward. It reminded me of when he was on a mission. Extreme focus was always his way of doing things. Determination. Dominance. I felt his anger and fear pour off him just as strongly as standing under a powerful waterfall.

"I'm going to teleport. There was a force inside that stopped me from being able to do it. It may hurt, but I need to get you home. Okay?"

The best I could do was nod my agreement.

CHAPTER
SEVENTEEN

I BREATHED THROUGH THE PAIN of the transport, even though my skin felt like it was tearing away from my muscles. The next sensation to hit me was Gabe lowering himself into the tub in the master bathroom of my suite in the Scarlet, sinking slowly with me still in his arms. I whispered a low, pain-filled sound as the warm water hit each open cut on my body. Only once I was mostly submerged, did he softly pull my back to his chest. My body sank against his, and the tension in my shoulders released.

"Gabriel," Abhitha said in a hushed voice.

"Not another ounce of discomfort for her, Abhitha," he responded in a tone so serious it made me wonder how battered my body actually was. I moved the slightest bit and felt the pinch of the buttons on his water-soaked shirt graze my tender skin. I whimpered at the discomfort.

Gabriel's arms came around me under my shoulders and supported me as I tried to move. "What can I do to ease your pain?"

With his help, I carefully turned my body to the side and pressed my cheek to his chest to avoid the buttons. "No shirt," I whispered. I needed his skin on mine. I would heal faster that way.

Gabe gestured with his hand, and the next sound was the whooshing from his shirt coming off his body. "I'm sorry if my moving hurt you." He kissed the top of my head and let his lips linger for just a moment. I nodded so he knew I heard him.

"I'm going to lift under your shoulders a little, baby. Just a second because you slid down too far."

I nodded again. When my cheek came back down, I was skin to skin with him, and I couldn't contain my shiver. "Vahla? What is it?"

I began to creep my hand from his strong thigh, up to his hip, and finally to his side, where I paused for just a second. He, too, shivered as my fingers lightly traced their path. The move surprisingly kind to the rope burns on my wrist, and it gave me encouragement to continue. Once I landed on his chest, I began to rub circles. When the pad of my thumb brushed across his nipple, he sucked in a breath, and it was the first time my lips lifted in a smile.

Everything about this man gives me strength.

The thought made my weak body bolder as I took his nipple between my fingers and pinched. His low grumble at my touch stirred the fire in my belly that only he could ignite. When I pinched him harder, his hips rocked up to press his length into me. Then his hand landed on mine. "No, Vahla."

The rejection stung, even though the rational side of me knew I was in no shape to pursue anything. I went to drop my hand from his skin, but he grabbed it gently and laced our fingers together.

"Shhh. There is plenty of time for that." I tried to pull my hand away again out of my own shame, but he just gripped it a bit harder. "Stay there. I love when you touch me," he whispered.

Well, as inappropriate as it may have been for our current situation, my belly had a full-on fire in it and my core throbbed at his words. I wanted to fall into his skin so far that we had no beginning or end. Drown out the agony in my body with the pleasure I knew he could give me.

Light footsteps echoed in the room, and Gabe shifted. I forced my eyes to open and found Abhitha standing at the side of the tub, handing a cloth and a few bottles to Gabriel. She touched the top of my head, and I smiled at the affection and comfort in her eyes. To my surprise, she did the same to Gabe. Another type of warmth spread from the center of my chest outward through my body. A moment passed between two people I would die to protect. They worked together to find and save me. Having them taking care of me was overwhelming, and my mind was telling me I was undeserving. I squeezed my eyes shut, and my breathing came in short, hard bursts, which wreaked havoc on my injured ribs.

"Don't cry, baby. I'll take care of you." He mistook my tears for sadness and pain. "I'm going to wash you now. Cleanse you. I'm sorry for any discomfort this will cause."

I knew it would hurt. My wounds and my human body would feel even the gentlest of touches. My head was a cement block as I tried to lift it.

"Stay still. As still as you can."

"Gabriel?" I whispered.

His hands stilled as our eyes met. "Yes?" His eyes were so blue, so loving. But also shadowed with worry and fear.

"Kiss me first." I blinked as my tears of need and anticipation of the coming pain fell.

"Anything for you, my love."

Love.

His lips met mine, soft and warm. A cautious and loving kiss was wonderful, but I leaned closer, urging him to deepen it, which he did. The twitching of his hand on my hip told me that he was fighting his own body's reaction. Unwilling to use his hands to take more, he used his lips instead. A slow, seductive pace was set as he consumed my mouth. My moans could not be mistaken for anything other than pleasure, and each sweep of his tongue and groan that vibrated in his chest made my body release the tension in waves. The tingles in my spine and the pumping of the blood racing through my body left no room for pain.

"More." I breathed into his mouth. He was big, so thick and long as he pressed against me, that my mind could think of nothing else. He listened to my demand, and continued the restrained assault on my mouth. Gabe's hands began to move as he washed away the blood and horror of the night. By the time he pulled back from our kiss, I had been thoroughly washed and hadn't felt an ounce of the pain I was sure would accompany.

Abhitha returned with my favorite big, fluffy, white towels, and I was more alert than the last time I saw her. My little smile of delight wasn't lost on her.

"Ah, you see what I have?" she said as my smile grew larger. "Let's get you two out of there and dried off."

Gabriel moved me forward so he could stand and then gently lifted me to my feet, making sure he braced me enough so I didn't have to hold any of my own weight. Once we were both fully out of the bathtub, he reached for the towels, and Abhitha pulled her hands back. I knew she felt helpless, and I saw her eyes narrow to him, but then they softened when she looked into mine. I mouthed *thank you* to her, and she nodded with the grin that told me she knew my talk of plans to avoid Gabe when he showed back up was clear and utter bullshit.

He sat me on the large edge of the tub and dried me off, wrapping my hair in one towel and then my body in another. I was able to lean on the sidewall for balance when he took his hands off me. He stepped back just a fraction so he could remove his pants.

At that moment, I was happy that his belt and pants hadn't bothered me while we were in the tub, because watching him undress the lower half of his body was an incredible sight. His eyes were glued to mine, watching me as I was watching him. It was such an amazingly hot scene to get lost in.

The snap and release of his belt mesmerized me. The slow pull of the leather through the belt loops had my body deliciously tense with anticipation. The leather danced around his solid, toned waist, coming full circle to the front of his pants, which held back a larger bulge than they had a few seconds ago. Gabe's hand flexed and pulled the belt the rest of the way out before dropping it to the floor. Once it was gone, his pants fell, showing the V his muscles created.

I think I might spontaneously orgasm.

That was not a joke either. My fucking pussy was pulsing in time with my furious pulse. Fuck, I was so turned on, and he wasn't even trying. I swallowed hard and tried not to blink at all. I didn't want to miss one second of this.

A quiet pop and the slow tic of the zipper making its descent made my mouth go dry. Gabe's fingers hooked into the sides of his pants, and he slowly pushed the material down.

Fuuuck. Nothing under them.

I rubbed my knees together because, yeah, I was ready to come. I had just been beaten, and I wanted the man in front of me to take me in any way he wanted. How fucked up was that?

His pants dropped to the floor, and his cock jumped out. It was so hard and glistening at its tip. I wanted to lick it. I wanted to sink to my knees in front of him and taste him so badly my mouth flooded with a rush of saliva. I wanted to fill my mouth with him more than breathe.

The thought of sucking on that cock until he couldn't take it another second was overwhelming. My whimper came flying out of my mouth, causing Gabe to grab a towel and wrap it around his waist, quickly kneeling in front of me.

His hands gently pressed on my knees. "What is it, baby? What hurts?"

My vagina hurts because I need you buried inside me before I combust. "Nothing."

"It isn't nothing. Tell me," he insisted.

The concern etched on his face wrecked me. No way I was going to lie to him. "I want you, Gabriel. So badly it hurts. Not the hurt from tonight. Hurt from my need for you. I'm . . . I'm sorry." I sounded like a depraved whore and I knew it. I lowered my head in shame.

His hand cupped my chin, and he lifted my head. "Look at me, Vahla."

I sniffled and closed my eyes. "I can't."

"Then I will tell you with your eyes closed." He took a deep breath. "I want you. So badly it hurts. I want to kill the one who did this to you. I want promises from you that you are not ready to give me. But I do not look at you and want to judge you. Quite the opposite. I want to love you."

My eyes sprung open. "You do?" I whispered in shock.

"I do," he said as he helped me up from the ledge and pulled the towel around me. Gabe easily lifted me into my arms and started walking into my bedroom. His strength of body and soul turned me on so deeply, so thoroughly that it hit the very essence of my spirit.

"You're shaking, Vahla. Hold on to me. We're almost there." His lips met my head again, and he gave soft kisses to my hair. I held on tighter while I relaxed closer to his body. Truth be told, I couldn't get close enough.

As he laid me onto my bed, Gabriel's sweet hum broke through my attempt to hold him tighter. His face was once again buried in my hair. "Honeysuckle and lemon," he whispered more to himself than to me. A reverence in his voice solely for me.

I closed my eyes for just a bit so I could bask in his words as they wrapped around me like a warm blanket. When I opened them again, it was so quiet in the room that I found myself turning onto my back to see if he'd left. He wasn't at my side where he had been, and the punch to my chest at that took the rest of my breath away. Then a small movement at the end of my bed caught my eye. Gabriel was there, still in his towel, just staring at me. His black hair, which was still wet from the bath, was almost lost to the shadows of my room. A shaggy mess that I knew would feel like silk if I were to run my fingers over it or brush back the chunk that skimmed his dark eyebrows.

He is so beautiful.

Gabriel's blue, blue eyes stayed on me as he reached around and undid his towel. I heard the thump of the wet, plush cotton hit the rug. His body was on full display. The slight dark hair on his chest, the darker line of hair that traveled down his abdomen. His muscles that rippled with each breath and seemed to dance as he moved to the side of the bed opposite of where I laid.

I could only watch him move so far, my muscles still aching from the torture I endured.

The bed dipped low, and the heat from his body reached me even before his skin did. Once my back was flush to his chest, he covered us with the blanket and held me firmly yet gently. I sighed, feeling content.

Gabriel placed a breath of a kiss on my neck and then rested his soft lips near my ear. "The heart will tear or fill at the sight. The throbbing crash, ahead of anticipation. A cloud-filled space, parted by the sun's rays. At first sight of the eyes that hold me captive, I shudder at their power. A glimpse of the lips that part with the breath my spirit seeks, they pull me closer. My body bows to his. A denial would crush. A welcome would set my soul on fire."

My smile was immediate. "You remembered."

"I remember everything, Vahla. I remember how shy you were to share your poetry with me. I will always remember the first time I kissed you. The day when you finally told me you wrote that poem for me." His nose rubbed against my hair. "Do you remember?"

"I do. I remember how you teased me that day. You snuck up and startled me." I playfully disputed his recollection.

He chuckled. "I didn't sneak. You just had your nose in that book of yours and didn't see me."

"I always saw you. I just hadn't realized you ever noticed me."

His arm held me a tad tighter. "From the time we were young, I've thought you were the most beautiful girl I would ever see. Then, I saw you alone that day and I knew it was my chance."

"Your chance to tease me?"

"My opportunity to see if I had a chance with you."

Of all the angels, he had his pick of any. "Are you still happy you took that chance?"

"Absolutely. Don't ever doubt that. I've dreamed of that kiss, when we laid in that field and you looked up at me like you had been waiting for me the same way I had been waiting for you."

"I was never getting rid of you after that, huh?" I giggled.

His smile against my shoulder melted me. "I would always come for you, Vahla. I planned on working for all of eternity to get to this moment with you. To get back to us."

"Mmmmm." I was the definition of swooning.

"Are you with me, Vahla? Are you truly with me?"

I moved my body just enough so that turning my head allowed me to look into his eyes. "Yes, Gabriel. You are the only one who sets my soul on fire."

BEING LIKE THAT, IN HIS ARMS AS MY BRUISED AND BATTERED body fell asleep, was incredibly intimate. The safety and the calm lulled me into sleep.

But as much as I would have loved a good night's sleep in his arms, my body had other ideas. It was completely unrealistic for me to think I would get off free and clear of the pains of regaining my powers. I hoped for it, but I knew it was inevitable.

It started with the sharp pains running through my torso, up my neck, and right through to my head. Nothing relieved the pressure or stabbing pain, and I was shocked that my skull didn't crack wide open.

My back had to have been breaking. It was the only way to describe it. At any moment, my spine was going to snap right in half. Stretching, turning, attempting to crawl into a fetal position changed nothing. I slowly and awkwardly rolled out of bed, crashed to the floor, and groaned as another wave of pain washed over me.

The rustling and eventual tearing of the sheets was so agonizingly loud to my senses. "Vahla! What can I do? Tell me what to do." Gabe's voice was desperate, and he was clearly frantic to do something to ease my pain.

But he couldn't do anything. No one could. I knew this pain from the previous times I chose to be human. The rare occasions when Delayna and I played with spells and I was stupid enough (or drunk enough) to be the test pilot, was how I knew this had to run its course.

"N-noth-nothing." My teeth chattered as the fever, mixed with the freezing chills, wracked my body.

Then the seizures started. Gabriel was like a whirlwind around me, getting blankets and pillows to cushion me. The curse of the whole process of my powers coming back was that

I never blacked out, and even in the most excruciating throws of it, I still knew and felt everything happening to me.

Good times.

I knew I had hit the midway point of the spell when I was able to slide my almost paralyzed body closer to where Gabe sat. Not too close but not too far. When he saw I was headed to him, he automatically lunged to get to me, the desperation to help me so clear in his eyes and in the deep lining of confusion and concern on his face. He looked like he had aged eighty years.

With the smallest shake of my head, he stayed put, but he didn't like it. When I finally reached him, I rested my head in his lap and managed to say, "Hands . . . on."

A second later, he had one hand on my head, the other on my side.

The light was peeking through the blinds on my window, and angel or not, I knew Gabe was struggling to stay awake. Fear for someone else, and for such a lengthy amount of time, wreaks havoc on everyone, human or super. His breathing was even, so I assumed he had finally succumbed to the sleep that had been pulling at him for a while.

The first brave thing I tried, to test the state of my body, was to take a deep breath. A few tiny cracks sounded, but I was okay. Next, I decided to twist onto my back. A few pulls from my muscles that elicited not nearly the amount of pain I had been suffering, and I knew I was ready. I needed to get to my feet to rid myself of the last of it.

Rolling off Gabriel, I positioned myself on all fours and began the slow task of rising. When I pushed upward, that was when the pops ran through my body like firecrackers. Or maybe like bubble wrap being popped at some insanely fast speed. To some, it probably sounded like bones breaking, but I knew it was my body renewing itself. I closed my eyes and enjoyed the sensations as they flowed through me.

I opened my eyes to find Gabriel standing in front of me, his mouth parted just slightly. "You're glowing." Awe apparent in both his voice and stare.

"Yes." I knew the final stages well.

"It's beautiful."

"It doesn't last long. But it's all my energy and powers pushing through that spell." It was so much easier to speak, and I would answer any questions he had. For anyone who has never seen this before, it was definitely a sight to behold.

"Spell?"

"Yes. A spell can strip me of my powers. Essentially, making me human." I cracked my neck and loved the relief of the stiffness that tried to hang on to my limbs. I started rubbing where I had been stuck and rolled my neck from side to side. "Ugh, Silas caught me by surprise," I grumbled.

Gabe's expression melted to one of frozen rage. "What did you say?" Whispers were supposed to be soothing. This whisper gave me goosebumps of a non-soothing variety.

Oh, shit.

I looked down and backed up, only to have him follow me until my shoulders pressed gently against the wall. His hands were flat behind me on each side of my head, successfully closing me in. He tried to take a deep breath, but his shaking wouldn't allow it. "Listen to me, Vahla. What did you say?"

After swallowing hard, I repeated myself. "I said Silas caught me by surprise."

He continued to shake involuntarily. "Where was he?"

Gabriel's eyes closed as his shoulders tensed and the veins in his face and neck pushed against his skin. The red and blue-ish purple looked like the precursor to an explosion. The sudden crunching sounds echoed in my ears. Gabriel was closer to me, almost nose to nose, not because his feet moved but because his hands had pushed through the wall behind us up to his elbows. Paint and plaster crumbled into clumps on the floor. The dust floating through the air made me think of magic sprinkled in the air.

This wasn't how I planned to tell him. My voice was quiet but sounded as loud as a fighter jet engine in the stillness of the room.

"He attacked me when I was walking from Delayna's house. I . . . I didn't see him. I was on the phone with Abhitha."

The shaking in his shoulders flowed in a wave and took over his entire frame. I waited for the inevitable explosion. "No. No. No. No!" The last no was a roar more powerful than I'd ever heard. It shook my bedroom and cracked the floor so savagely that it continued its break up the walls and to the ceiling. Then a powerful wind blew through, shattering the windows and piercing my ears with its blaring whoosh.

If he was in awe of my glow a brief time ago, I was in a whole other realm of awe at that moment. Gabriel stood before me, his enormous wings blindingly white. His torso showing his tensed muscles, cut so severely they cast shadows all over his body. His outstretched arms, dwarfed by the size of his wings.

I stared in wonder and amazement at how glorious he was. How beautiful those wings were even though they were missing a single feather. The one used to script his name on me. My back throbbed in remembrance of and reverence to what it no longer could summon. A heartbeat resounded from where my wings had once been, a phantom rhythm from the despair of not having them anymore. The tightness in my chest pierced me with sadness and envy. A longing I couldn't suppress.

When Gabriel's hands came down and fisted to rest in front of him, it broke my mournful reverie. The muscles from shoulder to fingertips pulsating and shimmering with a sheen of sweat. His chin sunk low, and he looked to me through his long, obsidian lashes. The way his chest was heaving breaths in and out as he stewed in his rage, could put the fear of the highest power in anyone.

I walked to him then, my beautiful angel consumed by so much pain. It radiated off him enough to take my breath away. I walked in slow steps until my body pressed against his. I stepped closer after I gently pulled then pushed his arms to his sides. It allowed my next step to put us skin to skin. Heart to heart. His eyes followed my every move, yet his body remained still.

"I'm okay, Gabriel." I touched his cheek, which burned hot with his fury. "I'm fine."

"He hurt you." His voice gravelly and deep.

Yes, he did.

"Everything he hurt is healable."

Gabriel's exhales reminded me of a bull ready to charge. Hot and heavy breaths soaked the air. I had to gulp in the air to be able to fill my lungs enough. He finally reached up and grabbed my wrist. "Has he touched you before?"

Fuck.

"Yes." I swallowed hard. My arm began to vibrate in response to his shaking.

"When? And do not leave anything out."

No such thing as taking a fortifying breath or being ready for this conversation. No more hiding.

"The day I left Heaven. He followed me and . . . and grabbed me. Tried to force himself on me. I fought him, and then I . . . I left." I looked him over and wondered which of his veins would be the first to pop. His head, neck, and arms looked like they were losing the battle of containment.

"There is more. I see it in your eyes. I feel it in your pulse."

He had always been able to see right through me. I felt him go beyond my eyes and reach into the depths of my soul. Of course, he saw. His mesmerizing blue eyes so intent on seeing me. Feeling me. Knowing me. I shook at the power pouring from them. "He was the one that beat me at the meeting. He was more powerful than I remembered. I should have tele-ported. By the time I tried, it was too late."

"I'm going to kill him." The gust picked up as Gabriel's wings began to move, lifting him from the ground.

"Stop! Please, Gabriel. Wait." I struggled to tether him to me. "He's working with Essalene. Silas has promised her my brother and has used that to encourage her storms. If I don't deliver him, I don't know what will happen." I placed both hands on his face, securing him to me. "It will do no good to go after him right now. He will have the upper hand. He will be believed. Over any of us, Gabriel. He was sent to check this out, you said so yourself. The one I will need to shut this down is Essalene. It will be her word that has the best chance to free my brother from accusation or blame. I will become distracted if you go after Silas. Lucifer first. Please, Gabriel. My brother's name cleared first."

I knew this man. This angel. My husband. He would never deny me this.

His anger still poured from his body, but he heard me. He knew what I needed. "Then I must take this up with Michael. You've done your part. Lucifer is away from her."

"Yes, but it isn't enough. She has to choose to walk away from my brother or none of this will work. She has to convince them. Don't you see? I know you do, Gabriel."

"I will go to her, then."

"No. I need you to go to Michael and tell him what happened. Tell him what Silas has been doing. Let me deal with Essalene."

His mind warred with logic, his warrior's instinct to fight and his love and devotion to protect me. "Then I will stay and help you."

"I know you want to, but if I can't get her to change her mind, I will need Michael on my side. I have no influence anymore. You know this, my love."

At the catch of his breath from my words, his lips were on mine, and my arms were around him. He kissed me so thoroughly, so intensely, I almost missed that I was enveloped in the center of his wings as we floated in the air, a few feet off the floor. I released one arm from around his neck so my hand could touch the downy white feathers. At that moment, I could have died a happy woman. The silky perfection of each feather, like a blanket absorbing my stress. The smell of the fresh, clean air that naturally emanated from them. The reflex of Gabe's muscles as I softly stroked every inch of the white perfection engulfing us.

When the kiss ended, Gabriel was gone. I hadn't even opened my eyes until I heard the crash against my wall.

Abhitha flew through my door, and I realized he had left. "What the—"

My eyes still glazed over as I briefly caught the state of my bedroom. "I think we need to call someone to fix this up." I smiled.

"Uh, ya' think?" She rolled her eyes.

"I gotta go."

"No worries. I know where your credit card is."

For a hot second, I thought the rumbling shaking my room was Gabriel returning. I ran to the window and looked out and up in hopes of seeing the flash of blinding white as he flew back for another kiss. When I saw the sky was clear, I looked down below. People on the streets were bobbing around like drunks, trying to find their balance. Leaning against cars, buildings, and each other. The rumbling grew louder and more violent. The earth cracked open right in front of my building.

I was pretty positive that bitch set off an earthquake in my city.

CHAPTER
EIGHTEEN

I LEFT ABHITHA TO THE repairs and returned to Hell, knowing it was time to make another, harsher move on Essalene. Abhitha assured me no lives were lost in that earthquake, but I knew that Climate Cunt was sending me a message.

I sat in my thinking chair, which was an oversized Queen Anne chair that I stole from a queen because . . . fuck her and her asshole ways back in the day when I crossed her path. I wore my favorite hoodie pajamas that had lightning bolts all over them and was wrapped in my most comfortable furry blanket. A fantastic cabernet was dripping over the rim of my wine glass. I wanted, albeit selfishly, a few hours to rest my body. Then I would use the spell Delayna had given me and go topside to confront Essalene.

"What gives, V?"

I closed my eyes as I heard my brother enter my room and answered him. "Hey."

"Every time I hear 'Comfortably Numb,' I know something is up."

"I just need to wind down, Luce."

"This a big wind down?" He chuckled and lifted his chin in the direction of my glass and the open bottle on the table next to me.

I swung my body up so I could sit and face him. "Not really. I just haven't done Floyd in a while. No need to fret, little brother."

He sat on the floor and smiled at the endearment. "You sure, V? You know I can help, right?"

"I know, Luce. Thanks. But everything's good. How's the little red goddess doing? You finally catch up with her?"

A huge smile formed on his face. "I did. It was not a pretty conversation."

"I'm sure it wasn't, but you're all good?"

"We're good. She's good. Really, really good." He winked.

I was sure she was since you could hear them fucking from miles away a short time after he started chasing her. He hasn't tired of her yet, but no spell lasts forever.

"So I've heard." We both laughed. "She gonna stick around a while?"

He looked to my ceiling. "Yeah. I think for a little."

Good. The relief from that knowledge washed over me. I knew it was the calm before the storm, but the relief that at least part of my plan worked was welcome.

"That's good, Luce. Really good." He wouldn't meet my eyes. "What's wrong?"

"Man, V. I saw Essalene today."

I stomped my feet to the ground. "I told you not to go topside! What the fuck?"

"She almost caught me fucking Roisin. We were done, but she still got a look at her. Her face went all twisted and she kept saying that tomorrow was our big day. That we would come back to each other. Then she kept repeating 'there's always hope.' Whatever that means."

It meant that she still thought my brother would give her all the things Aldorex didn't. "Did you not understand me when I said you couldn't go up there? I thought you understood. Damn it!"

That was definitely where the earthquake came from. Her anger and a warning. The chaos filling my mind was like it was the scratching post a cat was having a field day with.

He jumped forward and stood in front of me. "If something's going on, tell me. Is she threatening you?"

"Can't you just listen? For once in your life, just listen to me!"

"You know what? You didn't fucking listen, either. You and Gabriel and your bullshit you pulled. You did whatever you wanted with him and now you're judging me?"

My eyebrows drew together with confusion and anger. "Is that a joke? Me committing to Gabriel is very different from you putting yourself in the path of a complete psychopath!"

He raked his hands through his hair and paced the room before stopping and looking at me. "I know. I'm sorry, but I'm sick of being stuck down here."

"It's temporary. Let me take care of it."

"Take care of what?"

"Of her! Essalene has lost her screws, and you going topside is only making it worse. I just need you to stay down here for a little while longer, okay?"

It looked like he was going to argue, and I ground my teeth, waiting.

"Fine." Okay, not what I was expecting, but I'd take it. "I'll stay down here, but only because I can't deal with crazy women."

"Thank fuck." I huffed as he stomped away. Wait. Crazy

women? Was he talking about me or her? Or both of us? That little shit.

Give me strength.

A FEW SONGS FROM PINK FLOYD, DESTINY'S CHILD, AND SELENA Gomez (shut the fuck up) along with finishing my bottle of wine, and I was ready. I was procrastinating and drinking and stewing in the bullshit my brother spewed at me and my semi-plan to get Mother Nature to give up on him.

I needed to oil my whips and sharpen my knives. No way I was going up without being fully armed. I had no idea what to expect, and I never underestimated something or someone else's power. Like the time I underestimated tequila's power. It was U-G-L-Y. What little I remember, I'll be taking to my grave.

I tried to refocus on my tasks but was pretty wobbly from drinking. I never truly enjoyed the feeling of having drunk too much wine. It reminded me of sitting in a tiny fishing boat and rocking back and forth. I either leisurely drank or got wasted. This in-between shit sucked.

I closed my eyes, which flung me into overthinking the unpredictability of this plan. Another glamorous effect of the middle ground of drinking. Unpredictability made me stress out. Essalene had a crazy streak a mile long. She was impulsive and emotional. She was hostile and then calm. She needed some serious therapy. Her life had been turned upside down and she had yet to heal, even in a small measure that stuck. Being emotionally unstable because of a broken heart only got you so many excuses. At some point, you had to pull yourself back together and move the fuck on.

But I couldn't let her have my brother or make him pay for her abuse of power. Neither option was a viable one. Yet, someone always had to pay for destruction and unbalance like this, and I refused to let it be him. She was absolutely expecting him tomorrow. Unfortunately for her, she would be getting me. My knees weakened at what the repercussions would be if I killed Mother Nature.

Then my thoughts wandered to Gabriel. The closeness we just shared scared and excited me in equal measure. With those feelings came so many others. The uncertainty of my decision to leave Heaven still lingering. My worthiness of him. My need to believe his declarations of love, and the time and energy I spent running from it. Debasing myself because of it. What I learned? The truth does not allow you to turn it off. It allows you to create chaos around yourself, temporary distractions because real truth never abandons its home.

And Gabriel is my home.

My curse.

My truth.

I shook my head hard. Tapped my forehead.

Fuck, I was regretting that wine.

CHAPTER
NINETEEN

"Stay with me, Vahla."

"You know I can't."

"Actually, I don't know that."

"You belong in the light, Gabriel."

"Don't you see, you stubborn, beautiful creature? I belong wherever you are."

I shook my head. *No. No, you don't.*

I lay on the floor, and he rose to his knees, lifting his body from mine.

Come back.

The cold sweep of air that brushed between us was like sharp tacks rubbing across my skin.

"We can be in the twilight. My light is you. Then. Now. Always."

Melting.

I was going to turn to liquid along with my resolve and melt into the ground below. "I'm no good for you."

"What you are is my reason."

"Reason?"

"The reason I love. The reason I would die for. I would die for you."

I closed my eyes as the thought of him dying seized my lungs, making air impossible to consume. Immediately, throbbing in my temples and powerful heart palpitations took over.

One . . . two . . . three . . . four . . . breathe.

Again . . . again . . . again. Stop the tears. Again . . . again.

"Never. No! You will not die. I will protect you."

The grip on my chin became tighter, the feel of it shifting from familiar to foreign. "Tsk, tsk, Vahla. Making promises you can't keep."

It was harder. Colder. Viciously digging into my skin. No doubt leaving bruises to form. My eyes flashed open. A strangled sound like a wounded animal gargled its way up my throat.

He laughed low and cynical. "Oh, how fun this will be. I'll get to you by going through him or I'll get to him by going through you. Win-win for me."

Fear. White-hot fear pulsed through me. He began to laugh again . . .

I gasped and sat up.

I was alone.

It was a nightmare.

A way, way too real nightmare.

More of an omen.

A promise from a madman.

My chest was heavy and the pressure of how real that was made it hard to breathe. The air I could take in wasn't enough to fill my lungs, and I had to fight to shake off the feeling of his weight on me.

I shook my legs and flailed to free myself of the residual sensation of my nightmare. But the sharp pinches continued to assault me. As I wiped at my face, chest, and neck, the nicks of pain intensified. I opened my eyes to see that a thick, gritty layer of something coated my entire body. Panicked, I sat up and tried to shake off whatever it was. Specks rained down and onto the black silk pooling around my body. I couldn't tell what it was as I pushed it away in a frenzy. Was it dirt? Pebbles? *Crystals.*

At that moment, the violent tremors registered, moving my body across the sheets. I looked up and was met by another sprinkling of my crystal-encased ceiling. In all my years down here, there had never once been a damn earthquake.

And then I heard it. My name within the lingering vibrations. "Vahla!" Another wave of quakes rocked my home. "You bitch!"

The glass chandeliers rattled. "You will learn!" The shriek came again.

It was clear that Essalene was crazed, a usual state for her psyche. I dragged my body to the edge of the bed, letting the silk do most of the work. I was slow, sluggish, and still fuzzy from my nightmare. The amount of wine last night was certainly not helping me either. My feet hit the floor just as another vibration hit, and I lost my balance. "What the fuck!"

I stomped over to my dresser, caught a glimpse of myself in the mirror, and groaned. I looked like a freaking train wreck.

I went to the bathroom to pee and plugged in my flat iron. Miss Dippy Dew Point could wait until I was damn good and ready to go see what the stick up her ass was about. I glanced at the clock to see it was still well before midnight. I had until tomorrow to fake-deliver my brother, so I had no idea what her assholery was for. I finished fixing my hair and froze.

"Such pretty, pretty red hair she has," reverberated through my room.

I hauled ass to Luce's room. My bones told me something was up.

"Luce?" Shit. "Where are you?" I dug my phone out of my pajama pocket and heard the Beastie Boys ringtone he set for me start blaring in his room. I dug through the shit on his bed and then the stuff on the floor, called it back so I could follow the ring, and finally found it tucked under the dresser. I fumbled with his code, and once I got it, his texts popped up.

> **Luce:** if you are threatening my sister, you won't like what I do to you.

> **Mother Nut Job:** I like everything you do to me.

Yuck.

> **Luce:** Back off.

> **Mother Nut Job:** Too late, baby. Others are coming if you don't come back to me.

> **Luce:** That sounds like a threat.

> **Mother Nut Job:** Easy to do when higher powers have your back.

> **Luce:** Music to my ears, bitch.

Cold, sharp tingles ran through the entirety of my body. Her shooting icicles into my veins at point-blank range and at the speed of light would have been less severe.

Lucifer had gone to her because he thought it would be his chance to confront the angels.

Fuck that.

As I left his suite, I questioned how I missed it. Out the window of his great room, as far as the eye could see, were viles. Not just any viles. Soldiers. Fuck. I recoiled at the sight of them. I shook from my nerves. My skin became damp with sweat. I never factored in Luce going off all half-cocked. Then one of the angels who had always sided with him in Heaven looked up. The wink and smirk that graced his face told me he was waiting for his signal. Something told me he knew he could get out with that army and get topside.

So much for best-laid plans . . .

CHAPTER
TWENTY

I RAN TO MY SUITE, stripped off my pajamas, grabbed the black and red candles from my nightstand, and sat on the floor. "Fuck!"

I couldn't go anywhere without performing this ritual.

I was *au naturel*—exactly the way my friend told me to be. To bond with the elements, I had to humble myself in front of them, revere them, and respect the power within them. Come as I was with no pretense, and I would be rewarded. Hence, I was naked. I wasn't one to fuck around with power. I was a bad, bad bitch, but balance was my jam. I had no illusions about my invincibility. It didn't exist.

My hands shook as I took the matches from the bag that also held the crystals. They trembled as I lit the red candle, the one that would signal Delayna that the time had come. I was crawling out of my skin as I waited for it to extinguish. Once it did, I would begin the chant, as she would begin hers from wherever she was.

I opened the velvet bag, giving it praise and appreciation as

I coated my skin with the dust. "Thank you agate, black tourmaline, selenite, and aventurine. I honor your presence in my journey to restore balance and protect those I love."

I continued my chant, centering myself and drowning out the earthquakes still happening around me.

There was another disturbance as my concentration peaked. My anger gave way to a fire in my belly. Mother Nature was going down. Fuck her and her destructive weather, her eighty degrees one day and thirty the next. I would be doing the entire universe a favor when I knocked her down a notch . . . or ten.

As I continued the ritual, the painful stretching crashed into my body. Each muscle pulled and extended in unnatural degrees. Binding this amplification spell was no shits and giggles. My body trembled like crazy as the power exchange occurred, making me feel like I was a rubber band being stretched to its max. And that was only the first half of the spell.

I needed to give blood for it to work. Unfortunately, the blood cascading slowly from my ears would not suffice. Oh no, of course, it wouldn't. I had to cut myself with the labradorite stone.

Do not pass out, Vahla. Do. Not.

Having to cut myself would normally bother me, but as my eyes started rolling to the back of my head, I figured I'd skip the dramatics. When the magic snapped into place, pain like needles hit me all at once, making me cry out. I shook hard—bone-rattling hard—and inhaled air that was like icicles being shot into my body. My nails on my hands and toes felt as if they were being pried from my body.

Kneeling and sitting back on my calves was a difficult pose to maintain. The rocking back and forth took over on its own. I was possessed.

My trembling hands reached to my side, sliding around the floor until I found the labradorite stone. I grabbed it and dropped it twice before my grip on it was steady enough to cut a long, shallow cut in my chest, right over my heart. My blood pooled lightly to the surface. My reaction in the past was always an adrenaline rush. A desire to watch it emerge in a bright red fire and then savor the following coolness as it became darker.

At one time, I'd longed for it, but as I sliced the stone across my right wrist, I realized it terrified me. The stone tumbled to the floor and I collapsed onto my side, stretching my arm to the middle of the circle and closer to the candle.

Once the blood hit its mark, my body began to convulse. "Ah!" My bones rattled under my skin, popping and pulling. "Fuck!" Huge bright white flashes filled my room, striking like lightning bolts of massive proportions. Just as quickly as they had come, they were gone.

Sticky from my blood and sweaty from the mental and physical stress of what I had just done, I crawled to my bed to brace myself as I pulled myself up. The rumble underneath me prompted me to get my ass moving. "Alexa. Turn the chandelier on low."

Her mechanical voice came back. "Say please."

Fucking, Luce!

If we didn't die, I was going to beat the shit out of him.

"Please." *Bitch.* On came my chandelier. I rolled onto my hands and knees and placed my hands on top of my bed. I had no more time to waste. I had no idea what Essalene was doing, nor did I know if she'd already summoned the angels.

I slowly moved over to my clothes, not wanting to use an ounce of power to dress in case I needed it later. I would even drive to my teleport spot. It was a pick-your-poison choice. Waste time or waste energy. Time wouldn't change the cluster-fuck, but losing more energy could.

I stood on wobbly legs, and my room slowly came into focus as I moved the last few steps forward to get my clothes. A wave of nausea rolled through me as I struggled to clear my blurry vision, but I swallowed it back and forced myself to step into my pants.

"Ugggh." Deep breaths. "Alexa, play 'Run This Town' by Rhianna . . . please."

The sharp beats started, and I stood as straight as my body would allow.

Well, this should be a fun encounter with that crazy bitch.

With my black-and-silver, titanium-threaded battle armor finally on, I felt stronger. I swiped my Kat Von D Everlasting Glimmer Veil Liquid Lipstick in Dazzle across my lips and stuck it into my pocket. Then I headed out to my precious mini tank and chose the song for my ride— "Let The Bodies Hit The Floor" by Drowning Pool—and turned it up all the way. My ears already bled once today, so I didn't give a fuck if it happened again.

CHAPTER
TWENTY-ONE

I T WAS AS CLEAR OF a day topside as I had ever seen. Not a cloud in the sky, just a blanket of beautiful blue stretching from horizon to horizon. Did that mean the Heavens wouldn't open up and rain down heavily armed, super soldier angels?

The air was still, but I knew it was a deception. The delicate silence sat more like a heavy fog and was quickly broken as the next rumble of the ground shook the entire field where I stood. Her scream shattered the air in a gust of wind that blew me back so hard I needed to dig my heels deeply into the ground, but I was still dragged back a few feet. I grounded my body as best as I could and waited until it calmed down a bit.

"I'm here!" I yelled as soon as I was able.

"Come see the destruction you caused!" Essalene cried back. Her voice sounded like she had rocks lodged in her throat. It was a crying grunt, and I didn't like the sound of it one bit.

I walked through the field, digging hard into the earth in case the winds flared again. A familiar scent caught my nose a split second before I came face to face with Essalene. A fierce, very pissed Essalene.

A white skirt of thickly cut sections floated around at her knees. It rolled in soft waves and gave off a blinding white light as it sank and lifted and swirled around her. The light throwing iridescent shock waves that reflected harshly on the land and trees around us.

I should have brought my Oakleys.

Her skin had a shine to it that I had never seen before, but it was her eyes that worried me. Crazed. Without balance. Without fear. And neon green.

It probably would have been less unnerving had she not been floating a foot off the ground. My eyes followed her as she started to move, and that was when my heart skipped. The last thump of it causing my shoulders to slouch forward, rendering me unable to stand straight. In all my planning, I never expected this.

Tied up between two massive oaks was my brother. Ironic that this was how I found her when I had caught them together. I could see the distorted flesh of his body as it swelled and choked around the vines that bound him by his wrists, upper arms, ankles, and thighs. He was completely stretched as far as his limbs would go. His head hung low, the weight of it causing his chin to rest on his chest.

"Lucifer!" I yelled, and his head lolled from side to side. "You fucking bitch!" I screamed and started to run toward him.

A heavy blow struck my chest as I approached him. The flashing of a light that rivaled the ones in Heaven blinded me. The bolt that hit me lifted me off the ground and spun me until I slammed back down. I could smell the burning leather, but it was the smell of my burned flesh that made my stomach roll with nausea.

As I pushed myself to my hands and knees, I caught sight of Roisin. She lay at my brother's feet in the fetal position, her bloody hand outstretched as if reaching for my brother. I had to concentrate to see if she was still alive. Her shallow breaths told me just barely.

He wasn't supposed to come up here. I'd told him to stay put. Leave it to my brother to go on his own and disregard my order.

My ability to keep my fear for him at bay was weaker than I imagined. It wrapped around me, stealing my breath and flooding my veins with adrenaline. Black spots danced around my vision and mixed with the gold shimmering dust that swirled around the vines holding my brother.

If this didn't work out, I'd probably lose my life. I took solace in knowing that if that happened, at least I wouldn't have to feel guilty for not being able to save him.

I stood and I tried a calm yet stern voice. "Let him go, Essalene."

She shook with rage as if she were a volcano readying to erupt. The vibrations made the grass below her move and billowed a constant cloud of dirt above the tops of each blade. Her hands fisted, and her neon-green psycho eyes landed on mine. "You will pay, as will your brother!"

"You don't want to do this. Think about this and think wisely." I leveled a determined stare on her. Once I felt the heat explode in my eyes, I knew they had changed. The brown had given way to the red. Could it be a deterrent? Worth a try. "Look at me," I said between teeth, which were locked together. "Look very, very closely."

Her voice rang out and echoed. "You do not scare me. You do not deserve the ground under your feet. And him?" She looked to my brother. "He deserves to suffer and have his precious, evil waste of a sister watch."

No. She. Fucking. Did. Not. Just call me a waste.

My laughter came out of nowhere and, in turn, flipped her ballistic-meter. Her grin was sinister, and her finger rose, bringing a host of fire ants with it. A small flick had them shooting in my direction, and thousands of the tiny red insects landed on me. Biting, nipping, pinching, and pulling at my skin. It took me a moment to refocus from the pain and release a fiery heat from my skin to burn them off. Those little fuckers got their pound of flesh.

"Let my brother go. This is between us."

"I told you that he and I were meant to be together! You kept us apart! And he brought that whore with him to throw in my face!"

"You were destroying the earth. Killing and creating an imbalance! And you wouldn't take a fucking hint!"

"You don't understand our love!"

I wanted to kill her. "I don't need to because he doesn't love you! For fuck's sake, have some damn self-respect. He was here fucking someone else. Does that scream love to you? It doesn't to me. Walk away, and that can be the end of it."

She stepped forward, screaming, "I will kill you all for this!"

My answer? I unfurled my whips, allowing them to pool to the ground at each of my sides. "Don't say I didn't give you a chance out of this."

I barely saw her smirk before the leaves of the trees came at me with such speed I couldn't shield myself. They cut and sliced and shredded at each part of my exposed skin. The leather and titanium of my clothes began to thin as the needles of the far away pines made their attack wave. My breathing faltered, the air coming out sounding more like I was getting punched in the gut.

"Fuck! Shit!" That hurt like a motherfucker. I made quick circles of the whip to my right and created the gusts of wind to ward off the needles and leaves. In a swift flick, I cracked my whip and captured Mother Nature by her ankle, dragging her floating form and making her crash to the ground. She roared and reared back, sending her vines to wrap around my body, squeezing the air from me and causing numbness to settle into my legs. I splayed my hands around my waist and stomach and slowly, painfully snaked my fingers to the O ring at my belly button. If I could just . . . release . . . the metal . . .

Once my fingers hit the cool titanium, the tiny knives embedded within it discharged with a sharp zing. I looped my fingers around the metal and cut at the vines with a crazy, chaotic effort until they began to break apart.

Essalene clutched her wrist, crying out as I severed vine after vine. The next thrashing to the vines caused her to wince. I sliced again, and she flinched. A deeper cut, and she screeched in pain.

I cut with more vigor, as much as my body could spare. I saw the pain reflected in her eyes. The wrinkles around them and her mouth. The continued gasps, slight whimpers, and cringes as each vine burst open from the impact of my blades. The overall grimacing she emitted in time with my movements.

Once freed, I launched the blades directly at her, hoping at least one would strike and slow her down. She lifted her joined palms to the sky and spread them wide, allowing the sun to streak down. Essalene's eyes glowed with a renewed madness as she looked to the sun. My blades melted when they reached within inches of her body as the sun hit them.

"You can't defeat me, Vahla. You've let my sweetness fool you." The possessed growl in her voice was creepy.

I stood straighter and wiped the last of the vines from my body. "Oh, yeah. You're super sweet. Sweetest murderer in town."

"You . . . you made me do this!" she screamed.

I electrified the whips at my sides, spinning them until the fire lit each strand in a liquid red and gold. "Bullshit! That's bullshit! You have a choice every single day. *You* did this, you stupid bitch. *You!*" Well, maybe I had her for a minute with stating the fact that she had a choice. But the "stupid bitch" part just hurled her back into crazy town.

Snarling her answer back while snow squalls spun around us, "You didn't care about my feelings. You just wanted to get your way."

"Again, I call bullshit." The snow was turning to ice and burning me as it hit my skin. I was horribly reminded of how much I hate the fucking cold. "Do you like killing innocent people when you get off? I did consider your feelings. I considered you to be the person who didn't want to do harm! I came to you. I talked to you. I showed you more respect than most. And now you want to abuse your power even more?"

"But . . . but . . ."

"But what? What the fuck, Essalene?" Thankfully, the snow and ice finally slowed. My lips were numb, and my speech was so slurred I didn't even recognize the words coming out.

"You made him leave me!"

"You aren't the first, and you won't be the last!" I screamed. She gasped as if horrified of that truth.

"That can't be . . ."

"Oh, would you shut the fuck up already? You have a job to do. Do your fucking job!"

And . . . she lost it. Crying, screaming, thrashing, moving the ground in waves like those awful bouncy houses kids jump in. She sent bark flying into my brother's back, and he cried out in agony.

Essalene was going nuclear-psycho, but her focus was on my brother. He was still conscious enough to feel the pain, and I couldn't tell if she was enjoying it or feeling remorse as he continued to moan. The glistening gold haze that hung around him must be what she used to keep him in a weakened state. My gaze shifted to a movement in the grass below him. A snake started moving toward the curve of Roisin's ankle, slinking up between her thighs, and I lost it. Rage. Pure fucking rage rocketed through me at the thought of where it was headed.

No way . . . no fucking way.

My hair stood on end as all my energy pulsed through my body. I couldn't hear the sounds around me because the thumping in my ears drowned it all out. My body ignited from the inside like a stirring volcano. The insane burn in my chest spread like wildfire through my entire body. As soon as I felt the scalding intensity burst through my eyes, I crashed down to one knee. I slammed one hand to my chest where an accumulation of the dust from my spell had clumped together and pounded my other hand to the ground. I summoned all the power I could and amplified it with the dust. I hoped to hell it was enough.

Even though my eyes grew heavy with the weight of what I was doing, I saw the distraction in her eyes a split second before Xavier came hurtling through the earth and landed at my feet. He lifted his body like he was doing a pushup and our eyes connected.

Trust me, I mouthed to him. With no pause and not an ounce of reservation to be seen across his beautiful face, he nodded and remained still. He was a warrior through and through. I reached for him and clasped his forearm in my hand. He grabbed mine in return. With a nod, I breathed in hard, pulled out my whip, and wrapped it around Essalene's neck.

"No!" she yelled so forcefully that it sent out a blast of tornado-force winds, which tore off branches of trees. I leaned my body over Xavier's to protect him from the shards and planks of wood falling. He tried to flip us, to get me beneath him to shield me. Fuck, this man was good to the core. And strong. No match of strength for the real devil, though. But dayummn . . .

She reached for the whip and held on to it with both hands. I knew the second her mind connected with Xavier's. Her hands fell to her sides. She stilled and stared at him as tears filled her eyes and she began to cry. I looked to him, and I was punched in the chest at his equal concentration on her. Unfortunately, I was flooded with both of their stories, reliving their pain, and my body was failing me.

I had no idea that was what a miscarriage felt like. I sucked in air that was nothing but pure pain as I felt how she had to deliver that baby boy and then bury him. Without Aldorex. Without anyone. A baby being the only thing she truly ever wanted and prayed for.

My power oozed from each pore of my body like a dam breaking, but I stood taller and hoped no one noticed my wobbling. I convinced myself the turn of events made me more powerful. Well, hoped it did. "Let my brother go. Now." I commanded my whip back to me.

The panic in her eyes told me this could go either way. The neon green faded enough that I knew her rage was calming. She looked back and forth to my brother and then me. Then to Xavier. I swore she was going to have whiplash. Maybe I'd luck out and she'd snap her own neck.

I needed her answer, and I wanted it right then. I stood back and looked at Xavier. I hoped that he saw the silent word fall from my lips. *Sorry.* For what I did and what was possibly to come. It was all ad lib at that point. Making this up as I went. Remorse and a bit of nausea churned within me as I tightened my grasp and sent my whip to engulf Xavier's neck. Then I pulled hard. The sweat of my palm almost making the handle slip from my grasp.

"I'll give you until the count of four. Then they both die." I nodded to my brother and then Xavier. Tears pooled in my eyes. My heart tore at me, telling me to fuck off at those words. "And I will slaughter you after you watch them die." My brain had short-circuited. I could never kill my brother, but it rolled off my tongue like I would.

Could I actually overpower her? Would she call my bluff, knowing I would never harm Luce?

"One." I waited a few beats. "Two . . ."

"Okay, okay! Just don't. Please don't do it." Essalene yelped.

In that instant, my brother fell to the ground and wrapped his body around Roisin. Neon green flashed in Essalene's eyes, pissed off by his show of protectiveness. With my hands to the ground again, I breathed in deeply and screamed out as I released more energy to transport them both back home.

"You took him away from me again!" She sobbed as her body lifted off the ground again, but she didn't scream at me to bring my brother back. I was not her therapist, and I refused to listen to any more of her bullshit.

"You listen to me now, Essalene. And listen well." She looked up, and the sadness in her eyes hit like a hammer to my chest as I released Xavier. "You will never, *ever* contact my brother again. If you cross paths, it's just that. You cross. Say hello, but you do not touch each other. Ever. And you never, *ever* lash out with intense weather because of him. Got me?"

And there went her tears. The grandest waterfalls had nothing on her. "I thought he loved me." She sniffed and turned her attention to Xavier.

"Damn it, Essalene! Do you love my brother or do you just not want to be alone?" Fuck, I was having a hard time getting up.

"Everyone leaves!"

"Did he promise you anything?"

She shook her head, and I finally made it to my feet.

"I just . . . I just . . ." She was starting to hyperventilate.

I barely had my footing back when Xavier passed me and came to a stop in front of Essalene. "What the fuck?" I murmured.

I saw how they looked at each other. No words were spoken, just gazes of thoughtfulness and concern. Her eyes turned back to the golden shimmer they normally were, and her feet settled to the ground softly. No more elevated psychopath.

The crack of my whip and grunt from Xavier tore them from their reverie. I pulled him back slowly and watched as she stumbled forward to him. As soon as she was within reach of him, I yanked back so hard that he landed on his knees at my feet, facing her. I had brought him here as a threat to use against her, but this was becoming far more interesting.

"No, Vahla. No, please . . ."

"Please what?"

"Please don't hurt him."

"I haven't decided what I'll do to him. That will depend on you." She stared like a frightened deer in headlights. I took a quick opportunity to place my hand on Xavier's back. The slightest move from him created a curve and forced a heavier touch from my hand. From that shift, I knew he understood.

It was then or never to have her meet my demands. "Never again. You will never contact or touch my brother again." She nodded, and it wasn't even close to enough. "Essalene."

She looked to me, defeat clear in her swollen eyes and slumped shoulders. "Yes. Yes, I agree." Xavier lifted his head and kept his focus solely on her.

"You will not play Silas's games. He is bad news. Very bad news. You will never share another detail about my family or me again. Understand?"

"But Silas said . . ." She flinched at whatever her thought about him was.

I grabbed Xavier by the hair and commanded my whip to tighten. Xavier recoiled, she saw, and just like that, I knew I had her. "I don't give a fuck what he said! You will give him nothing about my brother or me. There is no compromise with anything I am telling you!"

She looked to Xavier and nodded.

"Swear it. As an oath."

She swore it on a sacred oath that she could never break. "And Essalene?"

"I can't take . . . any . . . more." She held her hand up to stop me from speaking and stumbled back a step.

"Look at me," I said softly.

She looked up. Her body had drained of its energy and her color had paled. "If he wants to stay, will you keep him safe?"

"Huh?" She exhaled. "Wh-what are you saying?"

I released the whip from around his throat and nodded down at Xavier. "Would you have him if he wants to stay?" I repeated my question.

"Why would you give up a vile, Vahla?"

Because he didn't belong to me and deserved better. Though, I wasn't entirely sure she was better than Hell, but I wasn't going to start splitting hairs. He was always Xavier, and I would make sure he remained so. I could see the anticipation in his body as he drew in a deep breath, his spine relaxed, and his head drooped. "You know why, Essalene." We both knew that when their minds connected, it was powerful and emotional for both of them. I tilted my head to him and leveled her with my stare. "I won't ask again."

She moved quickly over to where he was on his knees and she knelt down in front of him. I took a few steps to the side. "Will you stay with me, Xavier?"

At the sound of his name, his head snapped up, and he looked her in the eyes.

She repeated, "Will you stay here with me. Please?"

He turned my way. I nodded. "You are free at this moment to choose. So choose wisely." I winked at him. The only other person that could read me like this was Gabe.

He stood and put his hand out as they both rose. "I would be honored to stay with you. Whomever you fear, I will protect you from them."

Well, fuck me. She alluded to something about Silas, and he was perceptive enough to pick up on it.

"Wait," I said before they could leave.

"No, Vahla! I promised . . ."

Xavier stopped like the good soldier he was trained to be, and I approached them until I stood in front of him, reaching up to put my hands on his shoulders. "I will give you the power to remain in the beautiful form that you are." Because he definitely was a beautiful specimen of a man. "I will give you strength to protect her. But I warn you, don't cross me."

"I won't, my Queen." He smiled.

I put my hands to his temples and let out a low laugh. "She is your queen now. You need to protect her from the fuckers who are out there and from the poison her mind has been in for far too long."

"I will protect her with my life. Until my dying breath."

Essalene sucked in a breath and whimpered from the words he spoke. "Good." I lowered my voice, "You are a good man. You never truly belonged with me."

"May I say something?"

There was a short pause before I nodded.

"You don't belong there, either."

I couldn't respond. Shock rang through me because that was not something I expected. And I did belong in Hell, he just hadn't spent enough time with me to know it to be a fact.

I caressed his temples with my thumbs and rubbed softly with the rest of my fingers that settled into the hair behind his ears. "This is gonna hurt like a motherfucker." I winked again, and he smiled bigger.

Xavier absorbed everything I gave him and never even came close to collapsing. Essalene was getting a champion. I bet he rocked in bed, and I so hoped one day he would kick Aldorex's ass.

He raised his hand and softly touched my right cheek, his

thumb sliding over my chin before he turned on his heel and put his hand out for her. She took it slowly and smiled so brightly and blindingly that it was like the sun came out and sat on the very ground in front of me. Then they disappeared. Or just walked away. I had no fucking clue because one, I couldn't see, and two, I was exhausted and my focus was shot.

CHAPTER
TWENTY-TWO

I TURNED TO LEAVE, BUT the second I hit the tree line, I knew he was there, felt the breeze of his teleport. "Why are you here?" I asked without needing to look in that direction as he jogged toward me. The Baywatch beach run had nothing on my man.

"Hello to you, too. How was your day, dear?"

I stopped and waited, looking straight ahead as he made it closer to me. He was grinning at me with that perfect mouth of his. "Wise ass. You know what I mean. Did you find him? Did you speak with Michael?" I folded my arms over my chest. "And didn't I tell you not to try to help me?"

He laughed. "I didn't try to help you, I just got here and I only heard a muffled version of the last part of the confrontation at the tail end of my teleport. I never got to see Michael, and no one has seen Silas. The army was told to stand down, so I decided to come back." He came to stand an eyelash's length from my body. I could feel his heat and smell the fresh musk that was all him. He was so close that I had to lift my head to look at him. My body responded to him in ways I had repressed for years, and I basked in it. The warmth, the quakes, the anticipation of his touch. "But I would not have stayed back if I arrived and you were in any danger."

I rolled my eyes at him. "Puh-leez! I was fine. And I don't need your help."

He laughed and raised a brow as he eyed my clothing. Burned patches, slices to the material, and a few leaves and bark still stuck to it. "Okay, tough girl, but you'd get it if I deemed it necessary." Cue another eye roll from me.

I was so wiped out that I couldn't stop my head from hitting his chest. He wrapped his arms around me and spoke so softly I almost didn't hear him. "Tell me why you did it, Vahla."

"To protect my brother," I slurred into his shirt.

"I know that part, beautiful. Why did you let him stay with her? How did you know it would work?"

I took a deep breath and closed my eyes. As he rocked me back and forth, the story just rolled from my tongue. "He didn't belong with me. His past, it just didn't . . . fit." I paused, and he waited without interruption. "He had a one-night stand and knocked the girl up. They were never going to be a couple, but he wanted the baby. I could *feel* it when I touched him. He wanted the baby more than he wanted his next breath. He checked on this woman every day and took her to all her appointments. She was planning on giving the baby to him, giving up her rights. I could see it in his memories."

"Wow. That's never easy to give up one of your own." I knew his mind went to the man he had considered a best friend but who he would hunt for eternity if that was what it took.

Such true words that we both knew all too well. "It isn't. Anyway, when he was stationed in Texas, he was investigating some drug ring on the base. Military families had kids who were buying the drugs, and it was a mess. Of course, those guys got kicked out and had sentences to serve. What he didn't realize was that they were part of something bigger. So, one night, he shows up to check on the woman and his unborn baby . . ."

"No," Gabriel said, completely horrified as he realized where this story was going.

"Yes. He walked in and found masked men there. They stabbed her repeatedly and in her stomach. They knocked him out, and I know he would rather they had just killed him. Since they didn't, he sought them out. It took him eight months to learn who they all were, and then he went after them. One by one. He killed them and made each of them suffer."

"Oh, V. That's terrible. But I cannot blame him."

"Yeah. Me either." I sighed. Shit, my body was sore. "I knew Essalene could relate once I linked their minds and she saw what I had seen. I guess I played my hand well."

"Hmmm. What if that didn't work?"

"I threatened to kill my brother and Xavier," I said so low that I hoped he didn't hear me.

"I'm glad she didn't call your bluff."

Yeah, me too.

"Don't even think about it. Your plan worked, and you saved your brother."

"This time."

I felt his nod on top of my head. He understood that every situation with Lucifer was a ticking time bomb. Who knew when it would explode in my face and take me down? "I have to go." I was so tired.

"I know. But I'm taking you."

"Okay." I had no strength to put up a fight.

"Well, that was easy."

I snorted into his chest as he lifted me into his arms.

"Oh, my sweet girl. You are definitely going to need your rest."

"Yeah, to keep my brother out of trouble."

He leaned down to kiss my ear. "No, my love. Because you rolled your eyes at me. Twice."

My body shivered at the promise behind his words. I held on to him even tighter.

And just like that, he was stepping through a portal he'd just opened up to my bedroom in the Scarlet.

CHAPTER TWENTY-THREE

I WOKE TO THE BEST kind of soreness and in the best position imaginable—wrapped in Gabriel's arms. Yes, I had some lingering aches and pains from my fight with Mother Nature, but the sore I was smiling about all belonged to Gabe.

The construction in my bedroom wasn't complete, so we went to the eighty-third floor to sleep. That floor held my playroom and all the sexy toys I'd accumulated over the years. It seemed Gabe was more well-versed than I expected. When my skepticism of him knowing what half the stuff on floor eighty-three did, he might as well have screamed challenge accepted. I smiled inside when he would only use what had never been used before in that room. And he made me a promise that he and I would be redoing that room because it was *ours* and no one else's. I melted. And shivered. And orgasmed without permission. Then I wondered where my bad-ass she-devil was.

Gabriel left the following afternoon. He had a group of angels looking for Silas and he wanted to check on their progress. The trail was cold, of course, but Gabe wouldn't rest until his mission to find him was complete. I worried about what finding him could look like, but I respected his need to do it all the same. I was doing that whole trust thing Gabe liked so much. He had kissed me long and slow before he left and, although I begged, I knew we couldn't stay locked away forever.

I had gotten out of the shower and had begun to brush my wet hair when the circle mark on my hand ignited. That circle in my palm was the connection to all the others I had given a matching one to. My cooling skin turned clammy as my nerves tore with panic at my chest.

"Valencia," I whispered. I clapped my hands and flicked my wrist to immediately dress my body. I swear I left a trail of fire behind me from the force and speed of my teleport.

I landed in her driveway and hauled ass to the house and through the front door. I didn't splinter or disintegrate it because I didn't want to scare the children. But I was seriously on the verge of hyperventilating if I didn't get to her quickly.

The soft sobs coming from the inside of the house had my panic jump and amplify to a level I had never known. I jogged forward and came to a stop in the family room at the back of the house. Children played quietly on the floor while Alazia sat on the couch, her arms wrapped lovingly around a younger woman, whom I assumed to be her daughter and Aldorex's wife. A baby lay nestled between them, sleeping like an angel.

"Vahla?" Alazia's voice was quiet with wonder.

The younger woman looked my way, and that was when I saw the bruising on her eye and both cheeks. Tears poured down her face, leaving red streaks from her anguish.

"Is this the first time?" I asked through gritted teeth. My gut already knowing the answer as she shook her head no. "What the . . . where is Valencia?" I tried to keep the ferocity of my words at a minimum. It was hard. Really. Fucking. Hard.

Jizzy cried harder and wiped at her face. "She's . . . she

won't . . . come out from under her bed. She . . . oh . . . I couldn't—"

Fuck.

"It'll be okay. I'll be back."

I ran up the stairs, not knowing where or in what state I would find her. I pressed my palm with the ignited circle to my temple and let it guide me. When I came to the closed door with sparkles all over it, I knew I had found the right room.

I turned the doorknob slowly, not wanting to startle her. "Valencia?"

I heard sniffling, and my heart started to crack, cutting me from inside my chest. This little girl's pain was crushing me.

"Where are you, sweetheart?"

"I right ova heeya." Her tiny hand crept out from under the bed.

"Will you come out and see me?"

"No. I yook ugwy."

I took a step closer to her bed. "No. You're beautiful no matter what."

"Vahla? Will you hold my hand?"

With my heart barely hanging on by a thread, I agreed. "Of course."

I lay on my stomach on the floor and took her hand in mine. The wet spots that touched my skin told me that she was still crying hard. The bed skirt denied me any chance to get a glimpse of her.

"Valencia? What's wrong, honey?"

A shaky breath, then, "You pwomised you would come, and you did."

My chest felt a blast of warm fuzzies. "I will always come when you need me."

"Does that make you my best fwend?"

"Sure does. If you want me to be."

"I do. I do want you to be."

"Then we are. Will you come out? Please?"

"'Kay."

I held her tiny hand and helped her shimmy out from under the canopy bed. I moved back and rested on my knees and watched as she pulled herself fully out.

Then she turned to face me.

I didn't think my jealous rage for Gabriel compared to what I felt when she looked at me. I was screaming in my head, and I heard at least one tooth break in my mouth under the pressure of my clenching.

I swallowed over the massive rage lump in my throat, as I gently held her arms. She stood in front of me with giant tears marring her beautiful face.

"Oh, Valencia. Who did this to you?"

Her left eye was swollen shut and her cheeks were a mixture of angry red and blue-ish purple. It was hard to see anything else through the inferno that overwhelmed me.

"I'm okay."

"I know you are very strong, but please tell me."

She looked down to her feet and back up at me. Her lip quivered so furiously. "My daddy." She sobbed. "I must have been bad."

Oh. Fuck. No!

I drew her to me and hugged her. I was gentle as I pulled her as close as I could. "You did nothing wrong. Nothing. You are good and perfect and beautiful."

When she held me tighter and her cries became softer, I couldn't stop my own tears from falling. The drops poured out the relief and devastation of finding her . . . and rage . . . so, so much rage for what her father had done. It took a while before she let go, and I certainly wasn't going to be the first one to break the hug. When she was ready, we walked downstairs together and into the family room.

Valencia was holding my hand tightly when we entered the

room. Alazia and her daughter sucked in breaths and were unable to hold back their whimpers. When Valencia looked up at me, I nodded, and she went to the couch and into the arms of the women.

"Should I take the children somewhere?" Jizzy's eyes darted around, surely paranoid that her husband could be near. "I can have our family doctor meet us somewhere else if you think it's safer."

"You'll be fine in your home with your children. I promise. Let the doctor come here and check each of you." Alazia looked at me. With a slight nod, I knew she understood. I also knew she would shield her daughter and grandchildren from that shared understanding. I had no doubt she knew my intentions.

"Take care of your family. I'll be back when I can."

I turned to leave when the little voice reached my ears. "I wuv you, Vahla."

"I love you too, little V."

When I tell you that shit was on?

It was fucking on.

⁓

I HATED THE COLD. I DIDN'T GIVE A GRAND SHIT THAT I WAS perpetually warm, I still loathed it. But I loved New York City and would suffer through the seemingly never-ending winter because of her.

I went directly to the Scarlet after seeing Valencia. Once I completed my sexy wardrobe change for the night, I took off.

Using my magical charms and my barely covered curves, I passed straight through security and into an elevator that would bring me up to the top floor of the hotel.

After dropping dumb and dumber guarding the outside door, I walked right into the suite that boasted floor-to-ceiling windows and a million-dollar view of Times Square. If they hadn't been staring at my tits, they could have put up a decent fight. I headed for the moaning. Hearing it and smelling the sex in the air led me right to him. The shine from the ball right outside the window was almost blinding. Huh, this suite had the right to boast about the view.

When I rounded the couch, I was blasted with a mini porno playing out. Aldorex lay on the couch while a blonde sat on his face and a brunette was at the other end blowing him. He might be a super, but his dick was not impressive. He was getting off while his family needed to cover their faces in ice packs.

My body was humming with rage I was barely keeping in check. They didn't notice me until I spoke up. I raised my palm toward them, evoking my power to control their minds.

To the brunette I said, "Bite hard, but only take the tip."

"What the—Argh! Fuck!" Aldorex's words were muffled by, well, a muff. He screamed and flung blondie off his face while kicking the brunette away from him. She sat back, looking at me for approval, which I happily gave. She smiled back with the tip of his dick still stuck in her teeth, and blood dripping from her mouth.

Father Time rolled off the couch, grabbed his shirt off the floor and pressed it to his crotch. When he looked at me, I saw the pure hatred and fury burning in his gaze.

"You fucking bitch!"

I smiled. "First of all, I take that as a compliment. And secondly, a missing penis tip is the least of your worries."

"Guards!" he barked. I thought the smirk on his face was also for my benefit.

I huffed a breath onto my fingernails and rubbed it off on the little bit of material that made up my skirt. He was staring at me, and I didn't care. I gave him my carry-on face.

"What the fuck? Guards!" he shouted louder, calling to

them from over his shoulder. Yeah, 'cause that was going to work.

I met his confused stare. "Yeah, about them." I couldn't contain my smile. "They aren't coming."

"What did you do?"

"It's disappointing that you care more about those strangers outside that door than you do your own family." The movement to my side reminded me that the girls were still there. "Okay, my sweets. Get your clothes on and go home. And you, make sure you clean up before you go. Leave that little, tiny, minuscule penis tip on the coffee table." They smiled pretty smiles and did as they were told.

"Shit." He realized with more concern that his shirt was soaked through with blood, than the fact that I was there to confront him about his abuse. "A little hypocritical, Vahla? You didn't give a shit about your family. And they're better off without you."

"Ugh, thank the universe you're at least a little pretty because you aren't very smart."

His brilliant response was to give me the finger. "I am smarter than you."

"It wasn't very smart of you to put your hands on your wife." The fire in me that had lessened to a simmer, started gaining back some ground.

His jaw tightened. "Mind your fucking business."

"Um? No. Because you also put your hands on that perfect little girl."

He stepped closer to me, and my anger swelled. My fists opened and closed of their own volition.

"My family. My property. I suggest you leave. You're already going to suffer consequences for this."

"What part of me screams *I give a shit about consequences*? That would be none. No part."

"Wait until I go home. You just made this worse." He grunted. "And I'll punish my kids as I see fit."

Valencia's face flashed in my mind. I saw her bruises and the smile she gave me even though she was in pain. The trust she gave me because of whatever she saw in me. And she called me her best friend.

"You're a monster. Undeserving of all you've been given."

"It's discipline they've earned. They heal after a short while anyway." He shrugged.

Black-out rage was a thing. It had to be because I didn't know I had released my whip that I had worn coiled around the entire length of my right arm. It was firmly wrapped around Aldorex's neck, constricting his airway and making his breathing sound painful. The red on his face almost matched what he had done to his wife and daughter. Almost.

The whole thing was so quick and satisfying, that a sensation similar to an orgasm worked its way through me. It only intensified as his hands desperately tugged at the whip, trying to loosen the powerful grip it had. Then our eyes met and his hands froze. His widened mouth hung open and his exhale stilled.

"What. . . the—" His voice cracked. His stare was beyond his fear from a moment ago.

The roar of the crowd outside alerted me to the beginning of the countdown to the new year. I turned to the window and gasped. I realized why he was more than afraid.

The red of my eyes glowed more brightly than they ever had, and there were brilliant white streaks cutting through the glow. That was new. They shot out and shimmered through the long, dark lashes that couldn't dull the color that burned brighter than a roaring flame. My dark hair was surrounded in gold dust from the top to the tips, as it floated just off my shoulders and head. The handle of the whip I had tightly secured in my hand cast white light like a never-ending burst of lightning.

The white streaks swam through the tightly woven material, flowing through each braided piece.

My powers had never morphed like this before, but I welcomed it. Nothing about it felt unnatural. I reached down to the zipper of my tall boots and released the chains hidden meticulously within them. I sent them careening toward Father Time, and they immediately bound his arms and feet to the ceiling and floor. Every clink and jingle of the chains made him flinch while it made me pulse with excitement. Considering the noise from the crowd outside and the ball scratching its way down the metal, this suite was eerily quiet.

Once he was tied up, I reined in my whip.

"My family needs me, Vahla." His pompousness turned frantic. Begging was not attractive.

"There will be repercussions," he continued.

Still don't care.

"You'll prove everyone right." He tugged against the chains. "They'll all come after you."

Still not caring.

"You're right."

His shoulders relaxed and his knees unlocked. "I knew you'd come to your senses."

He definitely mistook my sigh and sympathetic look for agreement with him. "Oh, my dear. You're confused." I stepped right up into his space. Our breath mingled between us. "You were right when you said a family can be better off without someone."

Aldorex's terror soaked the air. He honestly thought he was getting out of this unscathed.

"Valencia will never forgive you. Never." I smelled his desperation.

At her sweet name falling from his abusive lips, my body heat flew past anything measurable. Blisters started to form on his face. I knew what my eyes and skin felt like, so I couldn't believe his face hadn't melted off Indiana-Jones style. My hair lifted again in a breeze that seemed to only surround me.

"When you love someone, they come before you. Sacrificing for another is the only way."

I let out the roar that had been filling my chest and let my fists fly. The cracking of his cheekbones and jaw were invigorating. His ribs were stronger and demanded I put more effort in. I punched him until he was on the brink of blacking out, then I lifted his jaw and my nails dug into his skin. He shrieked from the contact. "Open your eye." I left him one to see from, like he had done to my tiny best friend. When he complied, I continued, "Enjoy your last moments. Everyone is replaceable. Another Father Time rises once you're dead. I'm sure someone told you that."

I listened to the countdown and watched him as he watched the ball drop.

"Happy New Year!" rang out from all directions.

And then I slit his throat.

By the time I had cleaned myself up in the bathroom, he had bled out. Eyes open as he watched his last New Year usher in.

Champagne sat chilled on the island. I grabbed the bottle, popped the cork, and took it for my commute home.

I woke his guards on my way out, manipulated their minds and directed them to clean up the mess. A bit of magic would cover it up nicely. I took one last look and a deep, cleansing breath before heading toward the elevator.

Then I tipped the expensive bottle of bubbly and drank half before coming up for air.

CHAPTER
TWENTY-
FOUR

I WAVED TO THE MEN in the lobby as I left. They smiled big, not realizing they wouldn't remember me once my feet hit the sidewalk.

It was late, but the city was still buzzing with celebration. My car waited for me a few blocks away, as instructed. I wanted some fresh air and some time to myself. Walking these streets was calming and invigorating all at once. With this bottle of Dom, it was even better.

There wasn't one single shred of remorse for what I had just done, for any of the torture I'd inflicted. No one got to do the shit he did to his family. I had my confirmation that hadn't been the first time Aldorex had been violent with them, and I was quite certain it wouldn't have been the last.

I continued my slow walk, watching as the traffic lights changed color. The red, yellow, or green reflected off the glass of the windows of the surrounding buildings. Partiers of all ages stumbled around, some stopping to kiss each other like their lives depended on it, while others held hands. And some were so alone that I could feel their pain and misery waft off them as I passed.

My ears perked up at a tiny, almost indiscernible whine. I looked to my right, down the alley between the buildings. I listened hard but heard nothing more. The number of people on the streets started to thin out and I was on a stretch where the only sounds I heard were the lights ticking as they changed. I continued to walk, but then stopped abruptly when I heard it again. There was an urgency to it, one I could not ignore. I walked slower, going back and forth to each end of the sidewalk as I moved ahead. Finally, a slight movement grabbed my attention.

On the corner of the street, right on the edge of the sidewalk and the next alley, was a duffle bag. I walked closer, keeping my steps slow and cautious. When the bag made a jerking move, I jumped, not expecting it. Then I heard the whimpers turn to soft whines.

I dropped my own bag to the ground and bent down, frantically pulling at the bag's zipper. "What the . . ." As soon as the top fully opened, four little heads turned to look at me in unison. "Oh, where did you guys come from?"

I lifted the first puppy because he was practically tumbling out of the bag. He licked my cheek and buried himself in my neck. I couldn't help but snuggle him. "You poor thing." I continued to pet him. "You must be so scared."

I picked him up higher to take a better look. He was mostly brown with spots of white. I fully understood the phrase puppy-dog eyes as I took in his sweet little face. Without warning, they all flew out of the bag and tackled me. I went into a fit of giggles as they knocked me over and all started licking me. "Okay . . . okay, okay, okay." I laughed more. "Up, little guys. C'mon, let's get up."

They calmed just enough for me to sit up. The first one that jumped out at me stayed on my lap as the others huddled closer to my side. It was then I saw their collars and the small glint of light off the metal from their tags.

"What's your name, little guy?" I turned the tag to read it. "Hound." *Hound?* I reached down to check the others. "Hound. Well, I guess you're all hounds, huh?" Then it hit me. "Who the fuck left you puppies here like this? You could have been killed!"

I grabbed the bag and took a good whiff of the handles. Each human had a distinct smell. If I could decipher it, I could track it. My head snapped up and honed in on a car two blocks up, idling in front of a drugstore.

I put the puppies back into the bag, hoisted it over my shoulder, and started to walk. I was only a few feet from the car when some dude came out, carrying a case of beer. He looked at me. Oh yeah, did he take a good look. Then he saw the duffle bag and bolted for the driver's side of the car. Obviously, I beat him there.

"Why in such a rush, my dear?"

He swallowed hard. "No rush. Just need to get home."

"Did you get everything you needed?" My voice was way calmer than my attitude toward him was.

He lifted the case and glanced at his beer. "Yup."

"You sure?" I cocked my head to the side.

His eyes narrowed at me. "What're you getting at, woman?"

"Don't you need, oh, I don't know . . . dog food maybe?"

"Nope. All good."

"Hmmm. I think you left these precious pups on the sidewalk. I'm very confident you are the one that dumped them."

He snorted. "Prove it, bitch." Ah . . . guilty and defensive.

Well, okay then. I smiled as I put the bag gently on the ground at my feet and grabbed his head really fucking hard. I was flooded with his memories of dumping them. Then I stared into his eyes and filled his brain with rules when it comes to pets, kids, and old people who were good to others throughout their lives. I threw in respect for the military because, Xavier. "Never, ever disregard or harm an animal again. Understand?"

"Yes." His voice was strained.

"Good. Go home. And be a better person, for fuck's sake."

I released his head, and he opened the door, leaning in to place the beer in the passenger seat. He took more care with his beer than with these precious little babies. When he leaned back and stood straight, getting ready to climb into the driver's seat, I looked to the puppies that were watching me. "Close your eyes, babies." I turned the bag around. Then I reared back and punched the puppy-dumper right in his face. I put him in his car and clicked his seatbelt closed. He'd be all ready to go and have a new lease on life when he came to. I didn't kill him, even though it was tempting.

He was granted a new lease on life all because of the puppies he meant to throw away. How ironic. I bent and grabbed the bag of puppies, giving each a small scratch on the head before I moved to my waiting car.

"I will take care of you, my little hellhounds." I smiled as they curled together in a fluffy heap of cute and fell asleep.

I CARRIED THE PUPPIES INTO MY ROOM AT THE SCARLET AND took the big, fluffy blanket off my bed. I arranged it on the floor and took out each pup, placing them gently on it. Only the puppy that had been the first one to tackle me on the sidewalk opened his eyes. I pet his head as he stared at me. I swore I could see appreciation in his eyes. I pet his head slowly and watched as they closed and he fell back to sleep. I left the door open halfway in case they woke up. At least there would be a little light for them to walk around without getting hurt. I smiled, imagining Valencia's face when I brought one to her. I didn't think her mom would mind.

Entering my living room, I stretched my arms above me and rolled my head and shoulders, loving the pops and pulls as they brought relief to my aches. I was always filled with tension, but tonight was extra brutal for me. It wasn't easy to confront the man who took advantage of his position—a man who abused his family, a father and husband with a divine gift who was so undeserving of either. It was exhausting.

I needed a drink, and I needed to make a list of supplies I would need for my new puppies.

I walked slowly over the rug, dragging my feet, squeezing my toes and pretty much making orgasmic sounds as I went. Before my feet hit the tile to my kitchen, there was a pounding on my door. "Ugh. Who the fuck would be here now?" I grunted. Whoever it was, was getting their ass kicked out of my building ASAP.

I swung the door open harshly to set the tone for this encounter. But I was definitely not expecting the face on the other side. "Really?" I asked in a huff. All I got in return was a smirk. "Why the fuck are you here?" I was so not in the mood. I always turned into some version of an annoyed teenager every time I saw this face.

"Nice to see you too," she said and pushed past me to enter my home. Uninvited.

"Nice to see you too," I mocked in a quiet, high-pitched voice. I got a side-eye in response. "Come onnnn! I'm tired. I just got home, and I'm not in the mood for any bullshit."

"Well, well, well. Wouldn't that be great if you actually had that choice based on your moods?"

"I left, asshole. I do have a choice. You aren't the boss of me."

Laughter. Nothing but laughter came from my older sister's mouth as she laid her coat over the island stool and grabbed my most expensive bottle of champagne. Expensive and unoffered champagne.

"Sure you do," she mocked me in return with her head tilted to the side as if she were talking to a child. "What is a free-to-choose badass such as yourself doing with pink bubbly stuff anyway? Thought you'd be all bourbon, whiskey, piss, and vinegar."

I liked pink bubbly stuff. And sparkly stuff. And leather and whips. I was the poster child for a balanced life.

"Whatever." I huffed and slammed my front door.

"So mature, Vahla."

"Fuck off, Azrael." More laughter from her, and I stuck out my tongue in quick response. She was so annoying and had the uncanny ability to catapult me into a juvenile, whiny state.

"Oh, man, this stuff is good," she said as she licked her lips and continued to sip my champagne.

"It should be for what I pay for it." I put my hand out. "Pour me some." From out of the blue, Alexa piped up, "Say please." My sister laughed, and I cringed. I was going to kill my brother.

"I know you didn't train that thing to keep your manners in check," she said as she brought the whole bottle to the island with an extra glass for me. I guess we were drinking.

I gave her the stink eye.

"I'm assuming our little brother pulled this prank on you."

I gave her a death stare and pointed at her. "Fuck you. You don't get to talk about him. You did nothing to help him."

Azrael took a deep breath. "He was too far gone. I tried."

"Bullshit!"

"I'm not here to fight with you about our brother. When you calm down, you'll remember that there was nothing more I could do."

As true as her words were, I still didn't want to hear them. We continued to look at each other. A good old-fashioned stare down.

"Sit," she said, breaking the silence.

"I prefer to stand."

"Suit yourself." She poured a full glass for each of us. No dainty pours or delicate manners in how we drank together. Az held her glass up, and I hesitated a beat before we clinked them and drank. The lump in my throat slowly growing bigger by the second.

"You gonna tell me why you're here?"

"Yup." She poured more into her glass and drank it.

"Any fucking day now, Az."

She put her empty glass down and pushed the tall, sparkling bottle my way, while she leveled me with a stare. "The witches."

I held my flinch as best I could. "What about them?"

"They're back at it, Vahla."

She rounded the island and grabbed her coat as she walked toward the door. I stared intently at her back, feeling my nerves jump like live wires. As she buttoned up, she turned and dropped the bomb. "Reel them in, or I'm going to kill them. Every. Single. One."

Fuck!

"Understood?"

I gritted my teeth. "Fully."

"Good. I'm doing you a solid by giving you this chance. I know you're friends with them and they took care of some sticky situations before." She sighed and moved to the door.

"Oh, geez, thank you so much, all-powerful Angel of War."

"Really, Vahla? You can't appreciate that I didn't just chop their heads off already?"

"If it were really bad enough to do that, you would have. You wouldn't be here pretending to do me a solid." I air quoted that last word.

She took a deep breath. "Listen, V, I know not all of them are bad. Not all of them do crazy, destructive shit. But even the ones I like, especially the ones you are closest to, they protect their own. You've seen it. You've lived it. They won't stop each other until it's almost too late. I'm giving you time to find them before I start on my own mission." Another step closer. "Some of them are killing innocents, so it'll be guilt by association. And if any of them step in to defend the others? I can't promise they'll live through the judgment."

I knew she was right. The witches protected their family, even to the point of their own destruction.

"You know I'm right," she said.

I was not giving her the satisfaction of agreeing with her.

"V, it's almost too late."

My nerves were working their magic of getting me closer to a panic attack.

So, I huffed to cover it up.

She smiled. Even after all this time, we knew each other well.

After putting her coat back on, she turned to face me, rearranging the knives I knew were hidden below each inch of her clothing. "Remember that I still love you, sister."

Boom. My knees weakened. As if her statement weren't dramatically wonderful and awful in equal measures, she had to step it up yet another notch before she finally left.

"Oh, and, V?"

"Yes?" I sighed from sheer exhaustion of the last few days and this conversation.

"I heard you kicked ass." The corner of my mouth lifted with pride at her statement and fell just as quickly with her next words. "Silas hasn't been seen for a while. Would you happen to know anything about that?"

"Why would I know anything about Silas?"

She tilted her head and studied me. "I'm not sure about the why. Yet."

I lifted my chin. "I don't care what he does or where he goes. He isn't my problem."

My sister walked closer to me and stood just a few feet away.

"I don't like that Silas has been able to avoid me. I want to have a conversation with him."

My heart hammered in my chest. First, Essalene had a run-in with Silas and threatened me. Then Gabriel found out more than I intended to tell him and was hell-bent on finding him. I still didn't know what Silas's game was, and I didn't know what to think about anything anymore.

"Nope. No idea where he is, and I don't care. But I will go and see the witches. I'll take care of it."

She was skeptical, trying to read me. She had mad skills that way, but I was blocking her. Not many people could. Family gift, I suppose. "Hmmm. Okay then. See you soon, sister."

"Hopefully not, sister," I said.

The door clicked, and she was gone. "Fuck!"

My sister, the baddest, best warrior of them all had my friends in her crosshairs. She never missed her targets. Never. Maybe I wasn't close to all of the witches, but there were some who were truly friends to me. Not that it started off that way for us, but whatever. We had become friends. I had to figure out how to fix this situation and keep my friends safe, which meant I had to figure out what the damn problem was.

"Ugh!" I groaned and looked to the ceiling as if it would have the answer. Then I grabbed the bottle, leaving the empty glass on the counter, and headed for my bedroom. "I'll worry about that shitstorm tomorrow."

EPILOGUE

Okay, so I will never claim to be a great writer. Or storyteller. Or strategist. Or sister. Or wife. Or fill in the blank. You get the drift. But I hadn't realized how chaotic that situation was until I put pen to paper in my journal.

I got annoyed at myself looking at the situation on these pages. Like, the fucking lightning bolt was coming, Vahla! Duck, stupid! It should have been simpler. Break them up and my brother was in the clear, right? When dealing with supers, there's no such thing as simple. Egos, egos, and more egos muddy the water. This happened to be the situation that brought the good, not so good, and the very bad back into my life.

Ziza wasn't so easy to forget. I had a hole in my heart that she used to fill. But Silas left me wondering about a bunch of things. I gotta be honest, as much as I didn't want to write it, say it, or even think it, Silas rattled me. I had forgotten about him for the most part. Why didn't he just keep stalking Luce and wait for an opportunity to fight him? Or kill him? Not that my brother isn't extremely powerful, so maybe Silas wasn't sure if he could take him?

He seemed more sinister with his intentions. Like he was polishing his strategy for his own end game. That gave me a creepy feeling and had my bones aching when I thought too hard about him. And then there was the comment about the portal. It was still fuzzy, but I think he said something about trying to get into Hell. That's enough to give me nightmares.

I'm nervous that Gabe is going after him, which is a new feeling for me. For so long, maybe forever, I believed Gabe to be infallible. I never doubted he could hold his own. But what I saw in Silas that day? The fury and blind drive of hate that burned in him? It made me anxious.

I don't know what Gabe will do if he finds Silas.

I don't know what Silas will do if he remains unfound.

Are you all thinking, *why'd you fight getting back with Gabe? Why didn't you get back together years ago? Why'd you get all crazy over Mother Nature?* Yeah, yeah, yeah. It's hard to explain my reasons. Part of that was due to the straight-up, stone-cold fury that was jealousy, but another part was self-doubt.

I struggled. Like, hard-core struggled when I left Heaven. I thought I had to cut everything and everyone off. Had to concentrate on changing. You have been enlightened as to some of my fabulously healthy coping mechanisms. My road to transforming to the new me. My evolution. The pretty obvious train wreck. And once I went down that road? I was tainted. Gabriel deserves perfection because that's what he is. Who knew he still thought I was perfect for him? Go figure.

My soul, I love that man . . .

It'll take me a beat to reconcile all the different parts of my life now that Gabriel has reentered it. It would behoove me to make a list of pros and cons. But I won't. My decision to be with him is made. There's an irresistible force between us, constantly pulling us closer to each other. There are only a few things I'll need to get over.

He's good. I'm bad.

He saves. I kill.

I can't go up to Heaven. He can't come down to Hell.

Welp, the Scarlet it is. Honestly, I'd be with him anywhere.

Anyway, enough of my rambling. I have other shit to take care of.

Oh, wait! Are you wondering if Roisin's spell wore off?

Yeah, I am too. She and Luce are still healing from the Mother Nature woodland fiasco. They've hidden themselves away in an undisclosed location until he is one hundred percent again. My brother won't show the viles any weakness, nor will he come out in public with so much as a scratch on his perfect face.

I can't worry about him right now. It's the first fucking day of the new year. I couldn't sleep in, even with all that yummy champagne in my belly. I didn't get to kiss Gabriel to ring this year in. But when he gets back, he's got some making up to do. Some naked, kissing, licking, sucking, thrusting kind of making up to do.

As much as I would like to focus on that, I have this other issue to deal with. My nerves are a shitshow because of my sister. She is a legit badass and I don't doubt she will follow through on her threats.

I knew something was up with the witches. I just knew it. If Delayna is in trouble or being threatened? You can bet my perky ass I'll be there for her. No one screws with my friends.

Not sure how I got crowned the Supernatural Police Chief —it was never part of the deal—but here I am, having to clean up the messes in the middle.

First thing's first. I have a puppy to deliver to a certain little girl who stole my heart.

Excuse me while I grab my cape and badge from the front closet and get on with it.

ACKNOWLEDGMENTS

Not one single step of getting this book to this point has been easy. I was incredibly naïve and quite foolish in how I thought it would go.

What it has been is exciting, disappointing, invigorating and humbling. I felt so good one day, and filled with disappointment the next.

But you know what happened?

This. Book. Happened.

How the hell did this book happen?

Wine.

Just kidding.

Mostly. . .

My dad is a man of few words. He told me when I was little, he thought I was a really good at writing. He called it a gift, and so did my mom. It meant more than I could express at the time. But I've carried it with me my whole life. I love you guys.

Fast forward. . .

Life moves on.

Elementary school ends. I love to write.

High school ends. I want to write.

College ends. I want to write.

Graduate school ends. I want to write.

Marriage and career happen. I want to write.

Son One comes. I want to write.

Son Two comes. I want to write.

Son Three comes. I need to write.

I finally sat my ass down and wrote with less time than I'd ever had in my life. Because my husband loves me so, so well, he would make time for me to write. I'm quite sure he knows I'm grateful, but I'll say it again. Thank you, baby, for making me and everything I love a priority. You've shown our boys that hard work, dreams and their mother matter.

To my boys; you are the greatest loves of my life. Thank you for your love, patience and encouragement and for constantly telling me there's nothing I can't do.

To Jenn and Stacy, the very first ones to read the mess of words I put together in each draft I finished. Thank you for your time, energy, encouragement and love. Jenn – you took the brunt of my emotional ups and downs. Your honesty and ability to refocus me was my saving grace at times. And your passion for each story on paper, or that I talked about as it floated in my head, has meant everything to me.

For the squad behind me cheering me on; Barb & Frank, Christy & Tim, Darren & Adene and my friends who knew my secret life of writing, I love you fiercely.

Tom D. – our talks kept me going at times. Thanks, pal.

Chris S. – thanks for tolerating the 1.5 million questions I had and having complete faith in me that I could do this.

This entire writing community has been amazingly kind and supportive. It was so much more than I could have imagined. Thank you, Kimberly Kincaid, for giving me some of your time, even though you didn't have it to spare.

Thank you, Janice and Erica, for your hard work, but more so for your guidance and kindness. I am so, so fortunate to work with you.

Tiffany! Your patience and all the information and time you gave me was such a gift. You are a beautiful person who does amazing work. I am so glad to have worked with you on this book.

And Ashley. Dear, sweet, Ashley. . .

I'm still baffled as to why you took me on as an author. Whether you were sleep deprived, felt like doing a good deed, loopy from moving or in a happy-scone place. Whatever it was? I'll take it because I felt like I won the lottery.

But then I discovered a few things. I never knew I could hate the word 'okay' until I met you. I had no idea I had been spelling it wrong my entire life, either. I never knew the utter pain of cutting 10,000 words or cutting a character that I thought was fantastic. *He didn't move the story along. . . it's just gratuitous violence. . .* blah, blah, blah.

But you were right.

And then you loved a character. Praised (most) rewrites. Talked to me on the phone. Taught me so much along the way that I was happily bursting with information. It was good-bursting, like the way I get filled up with Double Stuf Oreos.

So, don't break up with me ever, even though you will not be pleased with the style in which I wrote the next draft I send you. My goal is to make you cry or throw my draft across the room.

You kicked my ass while hugging me. You're the Russ to my Clark. You made the messes make sense and made me figure out how to make the lights come on to create the best story I could.

More than anything, you are my friend. (Even though I totally dig flashbacks and you don't.)

Thank you to everyone who has shown me kindness along the way.

To my readers, all I can say is thank you for taking a chance on me. xoxoxo

ABOUT THE AUTHOR

Stacie Santoro lives with her family in New York, in the town where she was born and raised. She is the mom to three amazing boys and wife to a great man (who swept her off her feet with his basketball skills). When she's not running with her family, you can find her enjoying a glass of wine or cup of tea, reading a book or daydreaming about a million things; like stories to write, putting her toes in the sand or owning every lip gloss created. Or maybe having one created just for her.

She's also smiling big from the release of her debut novel, The Real Devil; Journal One, and a firm believer that it's never too late to make your dreams come true.

facebook.com/stacie.santoro11

twitter.com/stacie_santoro

instagram.com/staciesantoro_author

Made in the USA
Middletown, DE
07 November 2019